DAISY'S CHAIN

A Story of Love, Intrigue and the Underworld on the Costa del Sol

by

Owen Jones

COPYRIGHT

Copyright © Owen Jones 2025
Bangkok, and Fuengirola, Spain

Cover by GetCovers

DEDICATION

This edition is dedicated to my wife, Pranom Jones, for making my life
as easy as she can - she does a great job of it.
Thanks also to Wes Waring for his advice on snipers' rifles.
Karma will repay everyone in just kind.

INSPIRATIONAL QUOTES

Believe not in anything simply because you have heard it,

Believe not in anything simply because it was spoken and rumoured by many,

Believe not in anything simply because it was found written in your religious texts,

Believe not in anything merely on the authority of teachers and elders,

Believe not in traditions because they have been handed down for generations,

But after observation and analysis, if anything agrees with reason and is conducive to the good and benefit of one and all, accept it and live up to it.

Gautama Buddha

Great Spirit, whose voice is on the wind, hear me. Let me grow in strength and knowledge.

Make me ever behold the red and purple sunset. May my hands respect the things you have given me.

Teach me the secrets hidden under every leaf and stone, as you have taught people for ages past.

Let me use my strength, not to be greater than my brother, but to fight my greatest enemy – myself.

Let me always come before you with clean hands and an open heart, that as my Earthly span fades like the sunset, my Spirit shall return to you without shame.

(Based on a traditional **Sioux** prayer)

"I do not seek to walk in the footsteps of the Wise People of old; I seek what they sought".
Matsuo Basho

"Have I not commanded you? Be strong and courageous. Do not be afraid; do not be discouraged, for the LORD your God will be with you wherever you go".
Joshua 1:9

"Whatever misfortune befalls you [people], it is because of what your own hands have done- God forgives much-"
Quran 42:30

Myself when young did eagerly frequent
Doctor and Saint, and heard great Argument
About it and about; but oft-times
Came out, by the same Door as in I went.
Omar Khayyam
The Rubaiyat XXIX.

CONTENTS

1 LA VILLA BLANCA, MARBELLA, 1995

Teresa was lying on her back on the bed breathing deeply with a wide grin on her face next to her boss, John, who, at sixty-five had taken far too much punishment in life to be able to take an active rôle in making passionate love himself. He liked her to swear as she pleasured them both, but it did not come naturally to her, so she usually forgot to in the heat of the moment. Teresa was forty-two and proud to have John as her lover. In fact, she had loved him for years despite the large age gap. She had first been attracted to the distinguished Englishman when he had used to come to buy things from her in Fuengirola market, and had fallen in love with him since almost the first day he had taken her on as his cook and housekeeper. Little did she know at the time that his frequent visits to the market had been excuses to see her.

"That was great, Teri, girl... Oh, yes... You're enough to make a grown man cry".

Teresa rolled over towards her lover onto his waiting right arm. She put her right arm across his chest as they kissed.

"You are the best", he said to her.

"It is easy for me to make you happy, Johnny, because I love you. You are my hero and my saviour", she replied, as she frequently did.

An explosion sounded as a muffled crump from outside. The phone rang as John was reaching out for it. It was the person he had been about to call just as he knew that it would be.

"What was that, Tony?" he asked without a trace of anxiety in his voice.

"I'm not sure yet, boss, but we haven't been hit…" He was interrupted by a second explosion similar to the first and then a third of a different kind. "It's coming from down the road some way off. I think it's the O'Leary's place judging by the plumes of smoke. I'm going outside now to get a better look". Tony was a big man, the shape of a door with a bald head on it. He was John's chief of security and had been with him for ten years.

John could hear him running over the phone, not breathing heavily at all, and then stop. "I'm about two hundred yards from their front gate now. It looks like the house has been hit, and the front gate… and there are bits of motorcycle everywhere… Two men are down… on fire… Oh! I think they have just been offed with a single baseball bat strike to the back of their necks. Looks like a drive-by with RPG's to me. I'm coming back in. I don't want to be nabbed as a witness to this".

"No, of course not. Come back and play dumb, but see what you can find out on the QT. Appraise me later". He rang off.

Five minutes later, John had fallen asleep, as he frequently did, and Teresa quietly got up, dressed and went back to work - it was time to arrange her employer's dinner.

During the meal, Tony gave John his verbal report of the bombing.

"This is not official, boss, but I got it from one of O'Leary's lads, so I reckon that it's as near the truth as we are ever going to get. It was a drive-by and they did use rocket-propelled grenades. Apparently, they fired the first one as they passed by. It went through the railings of the gate and hit the house. The gatekeeper, who was probably counting his lucky stars that he wasn't blown up got a few shots off.

"The riders then came back past the gate and fired again, but the tail-fire from the RPG must have ignited fuel leaking from a bullet hole in the petrol tank and it blew up. The second grenade did strike the gate, as the first one was probably meant to, and blew it in. When the bike exploded and the riders came back to Earth on fire. O'Leary's men broke their necks with baseball bats so there would be no loose ends".

"Who was responsible, do they reckon, Tony?"

"He said they don't know, but when I suggested that it was a rival Irish gang from back home, he didn't say that it wasn't".

"Anyone else besides the riders hurt, was there?"

"The gatekeeper is in a bad way. He's got shrapnel wounds and those big wrought iron gates gave him quite a whack when they blew in, but he'll probably live. A cleaner got some splinters of glass in her arris, but she's all right. The O'Leary's were around the back near the pool, so they are all OK too.

"Did the police get there? I heard some sirens, I think, but I was asleep by then and could have been dreaming".

"No, they got there all right... and the fire brigade and the ambulance, after it was all over. The O'Leary's had even put the gatekeeper and the cleaner in the Range Rover and taken them both to hospital by then. The ambulance took away the riders' bodies; the fire brigade sprayed the smoking wreckage then checked the house for structural damage and the police cordoned off the area. There's still a load of them out there now trying to look concerned and busy.

"They asked me if I'd seen anything and I said only the smoke. They don't really give a monkey's as long as there are no Spanish involved".

"No, you're right. Well, thanks for that, Tony. Well done, as always. Do you think that we're in any danger?"

"No, boss, it was just the Micks, er, sorry, boss, the Irish, having a turf war. Nothing to do with us. I've brought a couple of extra hands in though, just to be sure".

"Good. Have you eaten yet?" he asked motioning to a chair.

"No, but there'll be something waiting for me in the office when I get back. Thanks".

"If you're sure, Tony. You're always welcome, you know that. OK, up to you, don't let me keep you from your grub. I'll see you later on my rounds". John liked to walk around the gardens near the house twice before going to bed as part of his exercise regimen.

∞

John Baltimore had first moved to Marbella twenty years before when he was forty-five, but it was only on a part-time basis, although his periods of stay gradually lengthened. He hadn't fled there as many had before him, but he had made and inherited enough money to make him think that it was probably a good idea to get out of the UK before people, meaning the police, the Inland Revenue and the press started asking questions. If enough stones were overturned, something would eventually lead to him, so he had emigrated, although both he and his father before him had had property in Andalucía for decades.

The press had dubbed the coast of the province of Malaga, the Costa del Crime, but there was more truth to that than most people, meaning the general British public, knew. It was quite an apt description as far as concerned a sizeable British minority in the area. Many of the British Mafia had moved to the Costa del Sol with the intention of giving up their old life of crime, but became bored and went back to it. Some simply ran their old operations in Britain remotely, and others tried to muscle in on the local community, which the Spanish and others resisted. It often led to violence; sometimes the Brits won, and sometimes they didn't.

John had given up everything in Britain, but had a string of profitable businesses in Spain, which he was gradually losing interest in, although, being a workaholic and not having an heir or even a wife any longer, he had to just keep going. He had been married three times and had had many affairs. Some of his lovers had claimed to be bearing his child, but he had never accepted responsibility, because he had expected to have a legitimate heir one day. However, that day had never come and, at his age, he had given up hope that it ever would long ago.

He had plans to make Teresa comfortable for life, as he had his 'real' wives, and he was toying with the idea of leaving the rest to a charity for women who had fallen on hard times. He and his father had had a hand in putting many women in that predicament, so it only seemed fair.

John's father, after whom he had been named, although his father had originally been called Sean, had been sent by his mother to London from Dublin to prevent him from becoming involved in an uprising proposed by the Irish Republican Brotherhood, rumours about which had started to spread amongst people in the know from late 1914. They planned to take advantage of Britain's heavy involvement in the First World War, and Germany had offered them weapons if they could organise some sort of a revolt. She had become frightened for his safety after a friend told her that John was becoming serious about joining 'The Cause' – to reunite Ireland and rid it of Westminster's influence.

He had been a petty criminal in London's East End in the first year of the First World War, but had lived in a room in a house where female Belgian refugees had been billeted. There were hundreds of thousands of Belgian refugees in the UK, most of whom were women and children. He had noticed that many of them had to go on the game to support themselves, so he had shrewdly borrowed enough money from a loan shark to rent a house, which he had used as a brothel. He had ten young Belgian women and girls living and working there around the clock within a week, and had a dozen such 'businesses' within a year. Within five years, he had owned the houses outright.

The first thing that he had done when he started to make money was call his younger brothers over to help him run his new, increasingly complicated affairs.

He was a millionaire before he was thirty, which he was particularly proud of, since he had arrived in London in 1914 with less than a pound to his name.

John junior was the product of one of the many liaisons with one of the working girls, but not one with the man he had called father, his adoptive father, because his own parents had been killed by his own family in two separate gun fights. John senior had adopted John junior, because he was ashamed of what his brother had done, and of how his offspring had wreaked their revenge. It was also rumoured that a low sperm count ran in the family and John junior had always thought that he followed in the tradition of his male antecedents.

∞

Two months later, after another session of lovemaking, but before John drifted off to sleep, Teresa whispered in her boss's ear:

"Johnny, my darling hero, you are going to become a father..."

"Eh? What are you talking about, Teri? I can't have children... I've never had any and I'm certainly too old now! Anyway, you told me that you had passed through the menopause, so you can't have any either".

"That is what I thought, so this baby is a gift from God for us, Johnny..."

"A bloody miracle, if it's true. Have you been to see a doctor yet?"

"No, not yet, but a woman knows these things; she doesn't need a doctor to tell her".

"Maybe not, but a man does, so you go and find out for sure tomorrow, my girl".

"But what if it is true, Johnny, what will you say then?"

"It simply can't be true. I cannot, and you cannot have a baby!"

"But, what if it is true?"

"Rubbish, it can't be. You've got wind... or you're putting on weight. That's what it is, you've put on weight".

"No, Johnny, our baby is only the size of a peanut! I am not bigger because of that. In fact, I am the same weight as always: fifty-two kilos, but I am with child. Impossible as it may seem, I am pregnant. I remember the feeling from before, but I will check with the doctor tomorrow".

"Good! You do that and you will see that I am right".

Seconds later, he was asleep and Teresa was going about the business of ensuring her beloved's comfort.

∞

When John heard the news that he was to be the father of a child before the year was out, he didn't know how to react. It all seemed to be happening so fast, but he was secretly overjoyed, although the hard man in him won over, so he insisted on a DNA test. When the amniocentesis test at ten weeks proved him to be a parent, he offered to marry Teresa, but was disappointed when she seemed reluctant.

"I thought you would have liked to marry me, Teri", he said.

"I would have," she admitted dolefully "but not just because I'm carrying your baby. I would have liked you to ask me to marry you because you love me".

"But I do love you, Teri, you know that. I'm just not very good at saying things like that, but I thought you knew it".

"A woman likes to hear it as well, Johnny..."

"I suppose a man does as well, my dear, I will admit to you that I do, 'though if you ever tell anyone I said it, I'll deny it".

"You silly macho men", she mocked him gently as she lay in the crook of his arm. "You want to hear it, but you don't want to give the same pleasure to the people you love. That is selfish, is it not?"

He didn't answer for several minutes, but Teresa was willing to wait.

"Yes, I suppose it is", he finally admitted. "I am so sorry that I have not told you before that I love you. I have never said it to anyone in my whole life, except perhaps to my mother. I don't remember. Have I ever told you about her?

"Her name was Fleur and she came from Belgium, but we won't talk about her any more for now. Will you, please, marry me, Teri? It will make me the happiest man in the world, and I know that that sounds corny, but I am a man of action, not words... I think you know that already too".

"It does not sound corny, Johnny, they are beautiful words…" Her eyes filled with tears. "I will marry you, Johnny. I have always loved you, but I want you to promise me that you will look after our child. I don't care about myself, but our baby must be taken care of, or it would be better if I left now".

"My dearest Teresa, if you will only marry me, our baby, boy or girl, will inherit everything that I own".

"In that case, Johnny, I accept. I will marry you".

∞

John wanted the marriage ceremony to take place within a week, but Teresa insisted on planning and doing everything properly, except that she did not ask John to convert to Catholicism and she didn't ask that the baby be brought up a Catholic either.

At fourteen weeks, after the huge wedding, Teresa told John that they were expecting a girl. She was worried that John might be disappointed, but she couldn't detect any sign of it.

John, for his part, thought that he should have been disappointed, but was surprised to find that he wasn't.

"What name should we give her?" asked Teresa one morning in bed.

"Could we call her Daisy?" he asked.

"Of course", she mused. "Daisy... Margarita in Spanish... a pearl... a hidden gem. It is the perfect name for our daughter, our gift from God, who should never have been".

2 DAISY'S EARLY LIFE

Teresa's pregnancy, her third, though the others had terminated prematurely, was straight forward, although she was naturally anxious because of her past. John was aware of this and provided a private nurse for her and a second car, so that the gardener could take her to hospital, if he or Tony were not at home. However, all went well, and Daisy was born at home on December 14th, a sunny afternoon, with the assistance of a midwife who was provided by the family's insurance company. It was a trouble-free birth and John gleamed with pride at the sight of his beautiful wife holding their beautiful baby.

John had never been one for photographs, but within a week he had hundreds of them. He showed them to his friends and acquaintances, and when they said that she had his nose or eyes, he was as proud as punch, although he couldn't see it himself. To him, she was the spitting image of his darling Teresa, and he would not have wanted it any other way. He never took her outside the gates, but he liked to stroll around the garden with her in her pram, describing the flowers and the birds to her, when he was certain that nobody could hear him. He had melted Teresa's heart one morning when she was popping in to see Daisy and saw John singing 'Ba, Ba, Black Sheep' to her. He had flushed red with embarrassment when he saw her listening, and she had never seen him do it again.

The garden walks had stopped taking place shortly afterwards, and that had an effect on Teresa as well, because John was not used to socialising without a partner and so wanted his wife to accompany him, which meant that they needed a nanny. Although, it was not what Teresa wanted, she felt that she had to comply, because John had been so kind to her.

The periods of time that baby Daisy was left with her nanny, Lisa, grew longer and more frequent, until the baby showed more affection towards Lisa than her mother. It broke Teresa's heart, but there was nothing she could do about it. Around about this time, Tony, noticed that little Daisy was often alone in her playpen in the garden, so he began to stop by to amuse her. He didn't have a problem with anyone seeing him or thinking him a fool and liked children, always having regretted not having any of his own. Daisy took to him too and they became firm friends.

John was absent from home ever more often, although his office was there, but not knowing any different, it didn't bother him. It was how he had been brought up.

As a toddler, she proved to be a quick on the uptake, learning Spanish and English at roughly the same speed. Teresa used this opportunity to improve her own command of English, which until then had been reasonably average for the area and her background. It was to stand her in good stead in later years and improved her relationship with her daughter.

Despite that, however, Daisy grew up more or less alone, or, more accurately, with the servants. She lived in the same villa as her parents, but John was used to being single and was too long in the tooth to change. He liked to go out for drinks and meals in the evening and he expected his wife to accompany him as his friends' wives accompanied them, despite the fact that this usually resulted in the women sitting at one end of the table and the men at the other after the meal was over.

By the time they got home, more often than not, little Daisy had already been tucked up in bed by her nanny and gone to sleep while being read a story. To be fair, Daisy's nanny could not have loved her more if she were her own, and Daisy's mother did her best to make up for her regular absences because she never stopped feeling guilty about them, but she was now confident that Daisy's future was secure and that was what she cared about more than anything.

Daisy would never have to do what she had had to do to secure a future for herself and her children when she had them one day.

Daisy followed the path of many children of wealthy parents. In her early years, it ranged from being spoiled by guilty parents to being neglected by them again the same day; then, when she reached five years of age, she was put in pre-school, where teachers attempted to replace the children's parents and nannies. Everyone was well-meaning, but it only resulted in more confusion, isolation and loneliness for the children concerned, including Daisy.

She was growing up a little cold-hearted; a loner who didn't look for friendship or company. That didn't stop other children trying to befriend her, but none of them got close to her. She had no idea what a best friend was.

School was just more of the same, although Daisy did seem to excel at it. If the truth were known, it was because she was trying to get her father's approbation. She was more certain of her mother's, who did spend some amount of time with her when she didn't have to fulfil her 'duties' to John's social life.

It was at this stage in her life, in junior school, that she first started to hear about her father's exploits and reputation as a 'hard man'. Some even went so far as to describe him as 'merciless' or a 'cold-blooded killer'. However, these descriptions of her father did not make her question his character, they only served to enhance his hero status in her young mind. After all, didn't her mother consider, and frequently call, him 'her hero'?

She never spoke of her feelings on the frequent occasions when people spoke badly of her father, but neither did she respond when people spoke of him in awe, although inwardly, she was glowing with pride for the person she was learning more about from others than she was firsthand from him.

She was taught in English and Spanish at the same school and was completely fluent in both. She mixed just as easily with the rich and poor Spanish kids as she did with rich Brits. She never met any poor British people, so, until she went to boarding school in Britain at sixteen to do her 'A' Levels, she had no idea that they existed. In that respect, she was like a lot of Spanish children.

Her parents took her to London to start boarding school, but when they left her there, her mother in tears, she found that it was the man she called Uncle Tony, the head of security for her father that she missed the most. The nannies had come and gone, just as her teachers at school, but Tony had always been there, which was more than she could say for her parents. He had taught her to ride a bicycle with support wheels, and it was he who took them off and caught her when she toppled over. He had also taught her to swim, climb trees, kick and throw a ball and even the rudiments of boxing and karate. She had fond memories of watching rugby with him on the television and enjoyed seeing him get excited when England scored points or played especially well.

Several times, she almost shed a tear for those happy days, which she knew were probably gone forever.

It was in boarding school and university, where she studied Business and Economics at the London School of Economics, that she developed the thick skin of a rhino and the cunning of a fox. She had always had the uncanny ability to remember every word that anyone had ever said about her, her family, and especially her father. She was also in the habit of writing it all down in diaries, and had been doing so for a decade, but it was only a way of committing it to memory. She had discovered in her childhood, that once she had written something down longhand, she never forgot it.

For something to do outside of school, and then university, she took lessons in mixed martial arts. She was adept at full contact Kyokushinkai Karate and had studied Aikido and boxing by the time she had left school.

John and Teresa felt like the proudest parents on the planet when they went to London to watch their daughter receive her first-class honours degree. They celebrated at the Ritz directly afterwards with friends and then at friends' of Daisy's in the evening. It was a perfect day, and perhaps the only one for ten or fifteen years when Daisy had felt of worth to both her parents at the same time.

John and Teresa offered her a round-the-world, first-class flight ticket as a reward for her achievement, and had a brand new Porche 911 Carrera S Cabriolet in the garage in Spain as a surprise, but to their amazement, Daisy declined the ticket.

"I'd rather just fly back to Malaga with you, if it's all the same", she said. "I want to contribute something to the family business. There will be plenty of time for flying around the world later. I want to work in the family firm with you, Dad".

Dad, at eighty-six, wasn't sure what to make of that, but felt a warm glow in his heart. He put his arm around his daughter and squeezed her. It was a rare moment of togetherness for both of them.

As an alternative to the round-the-world flight, Daisy's parents treated her to a £5,000 shopping spree in the heart of London. John made his normal excuse of a bad back for not accompanying his wife and daughter, but they knew that he didn't like shopping anyway and went alone. They had a whale of a time and paraded their new outfits in front of him on their return. He feigned interest, but again, they both knew him too well to expect any enthusiasm about fashion from him.

Worried about the British press, John decided that it would be safer for him to head back to Spain the following day and his small family were all too pleased to go with him. He had been away so long that Britain, and not even London, felt like home any longer. Teresa liked London, but only for the shopping and Daisy was keen to begin her new life. She felt older, more responsible, and more able to get to know her parents on a higher level than was possible when she had been a child.

"Don't you have a boyfriend or someone special that you would like to say 'Goodbye' to?" asked her mother.

"No", she replied rather shyly, but she wasn't being coy because she did have a boyfriend, it was just that she was acutely aware that people expected a beautiful young woman like her to have one, but she did not. Teresa didn't believe her, but let it drop. The fact was there had been scores of boys and men after her in the five years that she had been away, but she had not been able to get emotionally close to any of them.

She had tried in the first year, really tried, but she did not enjoy kissing, especially French style, and she didn't like being groped or being expected to please boys. She had made love three times with two different partners, but she hadn't enjoyed the experiences. After that she had given up, and used the excuse of a fictitious fiancé in Spain to keep her pride. She hadn't even had girlfriends who were close enough to have noticed that they had never met her fiancé, whom she called Dick, because it made her laugh.

She had come to the conclusion that she was asexual, but knew deep down that that was not true either. She did fancy boys, not girls, but she didn't like them, or at least none of the ones she had met so far and she had to admit that that was quite a few in university.

However, in order to throw her mother off the scent, she went out on her own for a few hours that night, but it was only to see a film and have a burger.

The three of them, especially Daisy, were happy to fly back home to Spain the following afternoon.

3 THE APPRENTICESHIP

On the Sunday afternoon after their return, Daisy said to her father after lunch, "Dad, I am ready to help you in any way you want to use me. I want to be your right-hand man, girl, or, er, woman, whichever you care to think of me as. I think that our affairs are best kept within the family, so, if you like, I will take over Tony's job as your deputy from tomorrow".

She had expected, or at least hoped for another hug from her hero for that declaration of loyalty, but she was disappointed again, not that she had let such things show on her pretty face for many years.

"Tony has been with me for thirty-odd years… You can't just step into his shoes like that, my dear… and anyway, what on Earth would your mother say? Tony has a dangerous job. I can't put you in his position…"

She was heartbroken, but only she knew it.

"I just want to help, Dad. I want to play my part in the organisation you have set up and that has paid for our lifestyles… mine and Mum's".

"That is very sweet of you, Daisy, but I don't see how you can… I'll tell you what I'll do. Give me a couple of days to think about it and I will get back to you with a position in our family business. Is that OK?"

"Promise?"

"I promise, chicken, by the end of the week".

She loved it when he called her 'chicken', and kissed him on the cheek.

"You run along now and let me think about it", he said

∞

John was proud of his daughter and the way that she hero-worshipped him, but he was worried that the hero-worshipping would not stand up to much scrutiny, if he allowed Daisy to know too much about his business interests. So, he tried to keep her at arm's length by giving her a job, which only had connections with the legal face of his financial affairs.

"Daisy, I have found the perfect job for you", he said to her one day. "We are going to convert your study into a proper, prestigious office and you can keep tabs on the finances. You will be the firm's bookkeeper... or accountant, when you are completely up to speed with the financial laws in this country. I know that you've studied all that with regard to the UK, but Spain is slightly different, so you are going to have to get your head around that now". He was hoping that by piling this extra load onto her, she would not have the time to study his affairs.

"You want me to be a clerk? After spending all that time studying - sixteen years or more - I will become an apprentice bookkeeper?"

It was clear that he had offended and disappointed her, and that sidelining her was not going to be as easy as he had hoped. It was a problem that he had not foreseen.

"You have to start somewhere, chicken, and that cannot be at the top. Everyone has to earn his or her place in an organisation by starting near the bottom... And you won't be right at the bottom. Every firm needs good accountants, or the government and some employees will skin you alive.

"Your job will be to stop our firm from leaking money". He was thinking on his feet now, which he was good at. "You will have to analyse each aspect of our business and match it to its financial results. Then you will be able to suggest improvements to how we do things. You know, I am getting old, and I can no longer have my fingers on the pulses of all our operations like I used to.

"That is why I need you. A trusted, intelligent and well educated member of the family... a younger person who has stamina and a zest for getting the job done properly. There is no-one else who fits that bill, is there?"

She stared into his eyes to judge whether he was scamming her, but had to agree that there was no-one else to fulfil that function. "I know you're flannelling me, Dad, but it's hard to argue with you, so I'll do what you want me to, but I am determined to have a real job, not some silly excuse that you've made up for me. I am serious about wanting to make a real contribution to our business. I want to put something back. Do we understand one another?"

"Yes, darling, but you must understand this too: it will take a little time to bed you into this new rôle. It is not so much a new job, I used to check up on all my businesses as a matter of course every day or week as the circumstances dictated, but I have let it slide, so I want you to pick up from where I left off. However, it is a new rôle for you and it will take some time to teach it to you.

"Do you understand that?"

"Yes, Dad, when do I start? I can't wait to be working with you".

"Me too, love, but let's get you a new computer just for office work and a bigger desk. You can sort all that out and enrol yourself on some kind of accountancy course. Ask Manuel, our accountant, what he recommends and get the same software as he uses too". As John was saying all this, he realised that the ball was back in his court to give his daughter a meaningful function that she could be proud of doing well.

He still didn't want her to go anywhere near the dodgy things he did though.

∞

When Daisy sat behind her desk at nine o'clock the following Monday morning, she switched on her Apple Mac and stared at an empty accounting program. No-one came to see her, no-one sent her any data and no-one asked her for any advice. However, she was determined to make this job her own. She knew that her father was hoodwinking her somehow, but she was equally certain that he had been telling the truth when he had admitted that he had let things slide over the last few years. One way or another, she was going to reel in that slack.

However, faced with nothing tangible to do, she started her working life by filling in all the settings for the dozen or so programs on her new computer and then she went for lunch.

"How was your first day working for your father?" asked her mother.

"Oh, I set up all my programs and waited for someone to tell me what to do... or at least give me some information about the businesses I'm supposed to be scrutinizing - like their names and addresses, but no-one came. So, I just did what I could and came for lunch".

"That's the way, dear. You'll get there in the end. Slow and steady wins the race". She looked at her mother, who was often prone to inappropriately-timed, meaningless platitudes, but she was eating and not looking her way. Then she turned her gaze to her father, but he was avoiding her too.

"So, Dad, who is going to help me get started?" She was determined not to let the matter drop.

"Sorry, chicken, what was that? I was thinking. Before I forget, did Manuel send you the info I asked him to?"

"I don't know what info you're referring to, do I? However, since neither he, nor nobody else for that matter, has sent me anything all morning, no, he did not".

"Perhaps I forgot to ask him to. Just a sec". He pushed a few buttons on his phone and spoke to someone. "No, I don't know her new contact details. I'll let her tell you herself". He passed Daisy his phone, saying, "You need to get some business cards printed so people know that you exist and how to get in touch with you. I don't even know and I live in the same house as you!"

The point was taken. Whether people didn't know what to do with her or not, she was equally to blame for being inaccessible. That afternoon, she designed a business card using an on-line printer, cut the design out using Jing and emailed it to a local printer for immediate processing. A thousand colour cards would be delivered the following day. The only field that she had a problem with was her job title. She was determined not to be described as a bookkeeper or even an accountant. She liked the description she finally came up with though: 'Trouble Shooter'.

It matched the family's temperament, she thought, and sounded aggressive for a woman. Especially a pretty, young, blue-eyed, blond lady. It was perfect. Then she entered the names and details of her father's businesses and familiarised herself with where they were and what they did.

At dinner that evening, she presented her father with the list of fifteen businesses that she had been given.

"All right, Dad", she began, "I want to make myself known to the managers of each of these companies and state my intention of studying them. Do you think it is better if you take me around and introduce me or do you want to phone them first and take a letter of introduction from you?"

"Which one do you want to start with?"

"I thought that it would be better to start with the two smallest ones. Then I can perfect my technique before tackling the larger ones. What do you think?"

"That sounds fine to me. Is this list in any particular order?"

"Highest profit to lowest. Don't you even know that? The second column shows percentage profit of turnover".

"I get these figures every quarter from Manuel, but as long as they seem reasonable, I don't worry about them much". And it was true. He was a multi-millionaire and his legitimate businesses more than covered his lifestyle, but his other interests brought in far, far more.

"I will take you to meet the first couple on your list, no problem, but I can't guarantee to take you to all fifteen of them. What are you talking about, one a day?"

"That is the ground plan, but it really depends on what I find. Some could take much longer".

John nodded in agreement. "I will take my car and you can go in your own. Once I have introduced you, I will go about my business and you about yours. Is that all right with you?"

"Sure, that'll be perfect. There's no need for you to hang about twiddling your thumbs".

∞

The first on her list to be visited at eleven o'clock was a 'Cambio' - a place where people could exchange currency and cash travellers' cheques on the seafront in Los Boliches thirty minutes north of Marbella. As they drove there in their separate cars, Daisy explained her concerns to her father over their hands-free mobile phones.

"It is struggling, Dad. The rent is high for a kiosk, but the returns are negligible. It might be worth closing this business down and reinvesting the funds elsewhere".

"Whoa, girl! Slow down. Your assignment is investigative. You must bring your findings to me and then we will decide what to do. Don't start closing my businesses down before you discuss it with me. Is that clear?"

She hadn't quite meant it like that, but it was a lesson to her to choose her words more carefully when discussing sensitive issues. She apologized. "Sorry, Dad. That came out wrong. I was thinking aloud".

"Then that is another thing you have to learn to do. Be wary of telling people what you are thinking. It is acceptable with your mother and me, but on no account with anyone else. It's like telling people what cards you have. It's silly".

"OK, Dad, I'm reading you loud and clear". In fact, she had known that for a very long time, but she had thought that it didn't apply to her parents, as he had just said. However, apparently it did and so another lesson was learned.

John introduced his daughter to Paco, who was running the small shop, accepted a cup of coffee and then left them to it. Paco and John had behaved towards each other like old friends, but when the latter had left, he was wary of Daisy.

She questioned him about the number of transactions per day and the average value of them, the busiest times and the busiest days. She already had this information up to and including the end of the previous quarter, but she wanted to know how much on the ball Paco was.

At two o'clock, she feigned hunger and drove off. However, she only drove her ostentatious Porche out of sight and then walked back to a restaurant on the beach diagonally across from the kiosk wearing a headscarf and sunglasses in a mock-starlet disguise. She picked at her sea bass salad followed by ice cream for hours and photographed everyone who went to the kiosk with the zoom lens of her Nikon SLR camera.

She was excited about her findings and wanted to report them to her father over dinner that night, but she resisted the temptation because of what he had told her that morning. She simply told him that a full analysis would take several more days and that she would not be needing him to introduce her to the next business until the following Saturday, if he wanted, or the Monday.

She returned to the restaurant for a long lunch every day that week and wrote up her report on Friday evening. Her first analysis was complete and she was immensity proud of it.

She presented it to her parents after dinner on Friday night.

After a report lasting twenty minutes, she gave voice to her conclusions.

"My first impression was that the manager, Paco, was either often not open or massaging the figures. However, I am pleased to report that, although Paco seems to be losing his grip on the firm, he is honest, and does work all the hours he claims. However, it is a barely profitable concern because a) people are happy to withdraw local currency direct from their bank accounts using an ATM card, and b) sales of travellers' cheques have been in decline for years and that is affecting profits.

"On a purely profit-based motive, it would be reasonable to close this concern. The returns could be put into one of the other businesses, but I cannot yet say which". She sat down to applause from her mother.

"Didn't Daisy read that well, Johnny? Just like a real professional... and don't forget, 'A stitch in time saves nine! That's what I always say".

They both looked at her, nodded, smiled and then looked at each other. Daisy hoped for praise, but knew better than to expect it.

"Thank you, Daisy", replied John after a few minutes' reflection. "I think that you are correct in your analysis. Fundamentally, correct, anyway. Did you notice anything about Paco?"

"He was infirm, if that's what you mean?"

"Yes... his legs are mangled. He is, as you say, infirm. Theresa, do you remember Paco? The guy who runs the Cambio in Los Boliches?" She nodded and tears came into her eyes.

"How is the lovely man, Johnny? Is he well?"

"Yes, dear, he's fine. Daisy has been spending time with him all week..."

"Oh, there's a good girl, Daisy! Never forget your Uncle Paco".

Daisy was confused. She had never heard of an 'Uncle Paco' before. "Who is he, Dad?"

"I'll tell you who he is, chicken, he used to work with Tony. One day, a man tried to spray me with machine gun fire as I got out of the car in Fuengirola. Your mother was still in the car and Paco was holding the door open for me. He pushed me back inside and took five bullets in the legs.

"Five bullets meant for me, and possibly your mother too. I, we, owe Paco our lives. After that, he became infirm, as you rightly say, so we set him up in a little business to give him an income and some respect.

"I say this not to criticise your work, which is factually accurate, but Paco has a job for life... and he returns a small profit too, which your mother and I put into a fund that he is unaware of for him when he retires".

Daisy felt as if she had been set up to fail, but took comfort from the fact that she had made an honest effort to analyse the business within the framework of the knowledge that she had been given.

It took months to analyse the other fourteen businesses, but there were no more hidden pitfalls, although one of the bars was run by another ex-employee. John's legitimate empire in Andalucía consisted of three middle-of-the-range hotels, an 8-Till-Late convenience store, four restaurants, four bars, a travel agency, a tour operator and Paco's Cambio. However, she did find discrepancies with two of the bars and two of the hotels.

One afternoon, while passing the time of day with Tony in the garden, she asked his advice as she had done all her life; he was much more of an uncle and a confidant to her than any of her real ones.

"Uncle Tony, you have been with my Dad a long time, do you think I am helping the firm or just being fobbed off?"

"Little One, I have never lied to you willingly, but you have to be aware that my first loyalty has to be to your father. If he is telling you that you are helping, then who am I to argue? He has the global picture... I take care of security and a few other things. My advice is that you must trust your father's judgement. After all, he has done pretty well so far, hasn't he? But, if you can't see your way to doing that, then you have to follow your own heart. I'm sorry that I can't be of more help, but I will always be your friend, if you need me. I can promise you that".

"I know, Uncle Tony... I know that. You are a rock and always have been". She reached up despite her height, to kiss him on his craggy cheek. He put an arm around her shoulder and squeezed her.

"I'd better be getting on with my rounds, young lady", he said letting her go and walking away. She was the only female he hadn't had sex with who meant anything to him except for his cat, which he now regretted having named 'Pussy' every time he had to call her in.

4 DAISY FEELS HER FEET

Daisy enjoyed getting to know the managers of her father's legitimate businesses over the following months and collected a great deal of data, which she proceeded to analyse and convert into suggestions for streamlining and improving them. All of these outfits were between Marbella and Los Boliches, which is a reasonably short coastal drive. She was therefore quite surprised to find out how little most of them knew of each other's existence.

She had suggestions for each of the businesses individually and she had ideas for them globally as well. She wanted to be professional about her approach, so she scheduled a meeting with her parents, so that she could explain her plans.

"Should I invite Tony too, Dad?"

"No, he must know what we decide, but we do this as a family first and iron out any wrinkles. Then, when we are absolutely sure of our position, we can discuss it with others.

Never let outsiders see the insiders squabbling over details. The front that we present to the outside world, even to Tony, must be a united one. Even if we don't all agree on everything in private".

Daisy had heard it all before, but nodded solemnly. "I'll remember that, Dad"

"How's your course in Spanish accountancy law going? Are you still doing it?"

"Sure, I am. Why ever wouldn't I be? I told you that I was serious about helping and I'll prove it to you too in my presentation. In fact, I am enjoying the course, 'though many wouldn't. It's a bit dry, if you know what I mean".

"I can imagine, but someone has to do it, and that someone is you for the moment. Sorry, chicken".

"No apologies necessary. I asked for a job with responsibility, and now I've got one. I'm happy, really".

"Good…"

"I'm going out with a few of the girls tonight, Dad, so don't wait up for me. I'll see you in the morning at ten for the presentation. Bye, Dad. I love you". She put her arms around his shoulders, pecked him on the cheek and left looking very happy.

He smiled inwardly; he was so darned proud of her that he thought he might explode sometimes.

∞

In the morning, she had the chef prepare coffee and rich, chocolate cake for eleven o'clock in her office, because it was one of her parents' favourite combinations.

It took her to just after eleven to outline the individual modifications to the fifteen businesses, but she continued while her mother sliced the cake and poured the coffee.

"… and that brings me to the theme of 'Integration'. I feel that we don't encourage our businesses to make use of each other's specialities. For example, none of the hotels, bars and restaurants recommend one another.

"I find that very odd and shamefully wasteful. For example, one of the hotels and three of the bars do not provide any food other than toasties… and one does chips.

"I propose that we encourage the bars and that hotel to order take-away food from our restaurants, if they are within a reasonable distance of each other. My suggestions for link-ups is in paragraph seventeen. The five groups that you see, one hotel and four bars, are all within five kilometres of the restaurants in their group. Where two or three restaurants can be linked to one establishment, we could have special combined menus drawn up. There is no need to explain that the food is not cooked on the premises, unless the manager is asked, is there?"

It was a rhetorical question, but her father shook his head in agreement.

"The bar that is a little isolated could form ties with third-party restaurants for a percentage of the take". She looked up to see her father nodding at the page in front of him. It encouraged her, so she continued with a flourish.

"The next stage, we could call 'Globalisation'. Not the same globalisation as MacDonald's practices, but our own version. Only one of our bars has a decent website, and three of the other establishments have crappy ones. I propose that we create a first-class web presence for all of our businesses and include links to others where they could be beneficial. We can hire someone to do this for us, and I will monitor it.

"And finally, we come to 'Familiarisation'. What is this? It is my term for creating a mutually-cooperative, family atmosphere within your group. We could all meet for a chat, drinks and a meal once a quarter or twice a year... even once a year. Whatever you both think is best. You might even declare a group bonus of one or two percent of net profits across the board, but again, that would be up to you.

"Thank you for your attention, that is the end of my report". She sat down and both her parents applauded her.

"Well done, Daisy!" said her mother. "Wasn't our little girl wonderful, John?"

"She sure was, Teri. I knew you were special, chicken, but there is a lot more in there", he said waving the report in his hand, "than I was expecting and ninety-odd percent of it I agree with right off the bat. As your mother says, well done. You'll have to give us a couple of days to mull this lot over, but then we'll come back to you with any questions we may have. Is that all right with you?"

"Sure, Dad, anything you say". She was in Seventh Heaven.

"Let's go down to lunch", he suggested, looking at his gold Patek Philippe wrist watch.

∞

Her father was delighted with all of Daisy's proposals and told her so.

"The only one I'm not sure about, is installing wired money into Paco's place. I did look at it - Oh, ten or twelve years ago, but the figures didn't stack up. You can make fresh enquiries, if you like. The rest is great".

"So, what's the next step, Dad?"

He looked into space for a moment before speaking. "When we are ready, we will run it past Tony. Then, if he can't see any problems, we'll call all the managers in one by one and explain the new regime to them, and, in the interests of your 'Familiarisation', if you like, we'll hold an informal pool party, where we can discuss it with everyone and introduce them all to each other. Does that sound all right?"

"Yes, Dad, it sounds perfect. Shall I organize that or will you?"

"Let's talk to Tony first and then leave that to him. You are a new liaison officer, but it was always his rôle. You two have always got on well, so try not to upset him. Remember, no-one likes to feel downgraded... that they have lost a bit of power... especially to a newcomer, even if she is the boss's daughter".

"OK, Dad, I'll leave that one to you then".

∞

After she had explained the new structure of the family firms to Tony, and her parents again, she found herself with the Big Man in the garden, as often happened.

"Did you really approve of our ideas, Uncle Tony, or were you just accepting a new style of management?"

He was normally as guarded with his words as Daisy's father, but not as far as she was concerned. He had always told her as much of the truth as he felt she needed to know or could handle.

"I honestly approve of what you said in there. It's a sign of the times, I suppose... We wouldn't have thought of what you proposed... our style was to tell them, the managers, what to do and hassle them if the money wasn't right... But those ways are dying out... The police are nowhere near as corrupt as they were twenty years ago, and it has become unfashionable to batter uncooperative managers... So, all in all, I think that your way is a good update to the company's style... and to be honest with you, I'm pretty sure that your father agrees..."

"So, you think I'm doing OK, Uncle Tony?"

"More than 'OK', Little One, much more than that. You're a chip off the old block if ever there was one". Daisy took his huge bicep and hugged it to her cheek as they walked along. "There is something else though, I would rather you call me just Tony from now on. It doesn't change anything, but.... I don't know, it just sounds better to me..."

"No problem. 'Just Tony' it is!"

"There's just one other thing, if you're taking the gypsy's, I still might clout you... boss' grown up daughter or not".

"Message read and understood. Thanks for the pep talk. I'll see you later.

"Oh, Tony, there's one other thing, do you still have a few minutes?"

"For you? Always. What is it?"

"You know the Stranger's Arms in Los Boliches?"

"Yes, one of your Dad's".

"Yes. Well, I've been in there later at night, after most people's regular working hours, I mean, and I got the impression that some of the girls were 'working' in there".

"Isn't that the idea", he said but knew what she was getting at.

"No, I mean 'working' working... on the game. Does Dad allow that sort of thing on his premises?"

It was a difficult question to answer given the code that he had adopted when talking with Daisy.

"Let's just put it this way... My interpretation of your father's rules is that managers have a large amount of leeway, so long as their activities do not bring us into conflict with the police or the general public.

"Does that answer your question?"

"Sort of, but not really. Does he allow working girls to ply their trade from his bars?"

"If he doesn't know about it… and if neither the police nor the general public complains".

"Is that 'Yes' or 'No?'"

"It means what I said".

"So, that's a 'Yes' then?"

"That could be an interpretation, I suppose".

"Are the girls freelancing or do they work for us?"

Tony hesitated for a few seconds before saying, "They do not work for any of the fifteen firms on your list, if that is what you are asking".

"It was, but now I am asking whether they work for any of our firms that are not on my list?"

"Ah, now you have painted us into a corner. I cannot answer that question. Only your father can do that".

"I understand that I am putting you in an impossible position, Unc... Tony, but I cannot possibly do my job properly unless I know exactly what is going on. Don't worry about it. I'll ask Dad.

"See you later".

∞

When she spoke to her father several days later, he was expecting the question, because Tony had forewarned him. He had deliberated over what his response would be for many hours during the nights since.

"It is like this, chicken", he said as they sat in his large, airy, bright office, which had a whole wall of sliding glass that opened onto the pool, "... it really isn't easy to put it in a way that you will understand... When my father and I first came here to live, Oh, about fifty years ago, Spain was nothing like it is as you know it now and neither was I. Yes, we had money, but we, or especially I, still had dreams. Dad was rich and was satisfied, but I was still a young man and wanted to make my own mark... to prove myself too.

"I, or we, got into time-share, which was a new concept back then. Land was cheap and so was labour, but the locals still couldn't afford the prices we wanted to charge for the houses - villas and condo's, we called them - so we had the idea of bringing over loads of middle-class Brits to buy them by the week instead.

"That went smoothly, but then we realised that they needed something to do... especially in the evenings. They could lie on the beach with their wives or girlfriends all day, but after that, they wanted to do what their body clocks told them it was time for... an after-work drink. So we surrounded the villas, hotels and time-share apartment blocks with bars, restaurants and discos, which were the new thing.

"In those days, Brits were earning ten times more than the local Spanish boys and it didn't take long for the girls to cotton on. We had no choice but to cooperate with them. If we didn't allow them in our bars, they would hang around outside upsetting the female holidaymakers, and bribe the police not to move them on.

"Or, even worse, they would go to a competitor's bar where they were welcome and take our punters with them. The only sensible solution was to let them in, so that the customers could chat them up and buy them drinks. We did eventually get rid of the pimps, which the girls were grateful for.

"But it's about bums on seats at the end of the day. Customers sitting at the bar tend to spend more than those at a table, and sometimes, the bar stools were full of girls spending hours over a glass of water, so we had to charge them for using our bars as their offices. We eventually came to a working arrangement that was acceptable to all parties, and that worked well, but times and situations change, and businesses have to change with them.

"Nowadays, a lot of the girls are working the summer months to pay their university fees. Others might want a new car or a trip to the States... and some of the migrant girls just want to be able to send their families some money to help out... or to get them over here to be reunited as a family. Many are saving to bring their parents or even husbands over".

"But it's wrong, isn't it, Dad?"

"What is?"

"Prostitution... making money from girls selling their bodies..."

"The law says it is in some countries... but not in others. Prostitution, prostitutes... they are such horrible words, aren't they? I know about sticks and stones, and words and all that, but it is not true. Words can and do hurt. I'll tell you about my childhood one day, and believe me, they did hurt. Those words are overloaded with preconceived ideas put there in the past by middle-class people with safe jobs. Women who had never had to work in their lives and men who made use of the girls in the evenings after condemning them during the day. A wise, middle-class woman once said to me on the subject of working girls, "There but for the Grace of God go many women'. I urge you never to forget that you were born privileged, Daisy. Your position in life is not normal... you could have been born a pretty, penniless refugee as well. What would you exchange for food and lodgings then? Think about it long and hard... Your conclusions might surprise you.

"Anyway, I've already tried to explain that we would have gone under if we hadn't worked with them in the old days - but the same is still true. Men like a bit of nooky when they're on holiday. Surprising, isn't it, that even these lowly, penniless girls can shape business? Still, the only thing that has changed is the reason why the girls want money. In the Sixties, it was for was for life's basic essentials, and now it is often for luxuries... except in the cases of the refugees, of course. Is it wrong to help people achieve their goals? Is it not better not to criticize someone, unless you can honestly say to yourself that you have walked in their shoes?

"I don't think that it is wrong to try to understand and to try to help, especially when the people who are making the laws are also sitting in the bars of an evening with their hand inching up the bare leg of the pretty, young stranger sitting next to them. Most people are hypocrites, chicken. It's all 'Do what I say, not what I do'. You are still young, and I wanted to shield you from the crappier side of life, as I have done your mother, but I have realized that I was wrong. You are working in the firm, and Andalucía is not large. Now that you are living here and taking an active rôle in the community, you were bound to hear about our family reputation sooner or later".

"What else am I likely to hear?" She was all ears. Her father had never talked to her about his family, his past, or his business interests so openly before. However, she was shocked at herself more she was with him. She had expected to take the high moral ground, but she found that she was not. She also realised that the kids in school had been speaking more than a little of the truth, not that that made any difference to what she thought of them - they had still meant to insult her family after all and that was enough, whether they had been right or not.

John sighed. "Well, also back in the early days, the girls liked to smoke grass or dope. Many of the them came from Morocco, and the best weed and light-weight hashish comes from there... just across the water, in fact, from Ketama. You have to remember that these girls had watched the men in their families smoking it all their lives and it was cheaper than beer and safer than moonshine. It was also the start of Flower Power, Jimi Hendrix, and the Hippies. The possession of drugs was a criminal offence in Britain, and here, but the local police would look the other way.

"So, the girls would have their smoke, and share it with their clients... and some savvy hippies even came just for the 'scene' as they called it. It was inevitable, we got into supplying drugs to first the girls and then to others. That was profitable, I can tell you!

"We would send a Transit van, like a camping wagon. over to Morocco for a month, and it would disappear into Ketama for a week while touring. The farmers would dismantle the vehicle, stuff it with four or five hundred kilos of dope and rebuild it. A day later it would be on sale here. We could average £1 a gramme, so that was half a million a month in those days! And all for an out lay of fifty thousand!

"The problem was that it was so lucrative that others tried to muscle in. We fought off competition for years... that's how Paco got shot. I was shot twice on other occasions and escaped injury dozens of times more. Still, those drugs never hurt anyone. I used to smoke them myself and I bet your mother did too before we got married. We got out of drugs when the chemists moved in. A bit of coke or speed, even a trip was OK, but when they started enhancing the basic drugs, we stopped.

The Irish and the Russians control most of that now, and we just let them get on with it. They're forever shooting or blowing each other up... It's a mug's game... not for me and my family, but I won't deny to you that we did do it for about thirty years or maybe a bit longer.

"What else is there...? We smuggle cigarettes to the UK, where the government has taxed them so much that the ordinary smoker can't afford to buy legit cigarettes. Er, gambling... we do a lot of that. We have places where known clients can bet on horse racing and the like... mostly British races, but the Internet is eating into that... We have strip joints, but we are not involved with any other kind of porn... We don't do guns, except for our own personal protection. I suppose you could say that we do a bit of most things, but not the extreme stuff... any longer.

"Does that answer your question?"

"Yes... it gives me a lot to think about... Could you give me a list, like you did last time?"

"Yes, if you're sure. Give me a couple of days though and never let it leave the house".

She walked upstairs to her own office in a daze. Most of the bad things people had said about her family were true after all.

When she collapsed into the swivel chair behind her desk, she wasn't sure what to make of it all. She phoned down to the kitchen for a coffee and a cake, pushed back into her chair and put her feet on her desk. She was analysing her feelings and was surprised to find that there was no trace of disappointment. Her father had told her what had happened and why and it made perfect sense to her. They were different days, long before she was born; her father, and, no doubt, her mother had faced challenges and dealt with them in the best ways that they were capable of. It was easy to criticize people for what they did, but how would her offspring judge how she would deal with the problems that would one day come her way? Kindly, she hoped, but then didn't everyone want that too? Yet she knew that it didn't always work out that way.

She couldn't wait to see her father's new list and get involved with the people who were working with the businesses on it. It all seemed so much more exciting than the 'legitimate list'.

5 THE ILLEGALS

When Daisy had received the list of legitimate businesses, she had recognised the names of most of them, despite having spent most of her late teens in the UK in school and university. However, one name jumped out at her - a bar in the nearby hills with a salacious reputation amongst the locals. It was said to be a bordello, a brothel, and it was marked on the list as that - one of five such 'bars' or 'hotels'. There were seven 'madams', each running girls; twenty smugglers each running mules carrying contraband (mostly cigarettes) to the UK; three illegal gambling dens, an ex-customs agent who helped men obtain dodgy family permits for spouses who would otherwise not have qualified for a UK visa and a money laundering service, which charged a whopping forty percent.

She had no figures to work from, and based on her naïveté, the illegals didn't seem to be worth much, but she remembered that her father had said that they raised five times more than the legals did.

She needed another heart-to-heart with her father before she would get to the bottom of the businesses on the new list, but she was looking forward to it immensely. She broached the subject with him, guardedly for her mother's sake, over lunch and he told her to find him in the garden at three.

"Are you going for a walk in the garden with your father, Daisy? That's nice. It's a real picture out there. I'd love to come with you, but three o'clock... I'll be in the middle of my siesta. Why don't you make it later, say five thirty and then I can come with you? You know that three's company and two is, er, not', she said hesitantly.

"Perhaps we'll still be out there when you wake up, Mum. You have my mobile number, give me a ring and we'll come and get you".

It seemed to satisfy Teresa and she shrank back into her own little world, where everything was always lovely and the sun was always shining or the moon was always full.

∞

"If you are determined to go down the route of managing the other side of the firm, I want you to learn how to use a firearm and I want everyone to know that you know how to use one. I am scared to death of you entering this world, but if I died tomorrow, you would have to anyway, so you might as well do it with my help as without it".

"OK, Dad, I quite fancy that idea anyway... I always have. How do you mean to go about it?"

"I, no, you will open a legally registered gun club with you as the owner. Tony or someone he recommends can manage it for us, but I want you to be seen there at least twice a week, and whether you turn out to be a good shot or not, we will have the word put about that you are a marksman, er, woman. That will give you some protection, but we will also get you a weapon that you can handle well, whichever that is. Tony will sort that out with you. Just ask him".

She nodded, already feeling an adrenaline rush pulsing through her veins.

"These are all quite low risk businesses to be honest, but you never know when some upstart is going to want to get in on the act. The gun is not to be used to start trouble, do you hear me, only to defend yourself should anyone else start anything. Get it lodged in your brain right now, that you cannot win a turf war. Any old Joe Blogs from Liverpool could hire a hundred guns to come after you and you would be dead, and you would probably get your mother and me and Tony and his men all killed as well trying to look after you. Those old, black and white, American mobster films were just films. That is not how it works, at least it has never been like that in my time.

"It's the lone gunman that you have to be watchful for… or woman, I guess these days. I have had a couple of bullets and one hurts me every day, but nowhere near as much as the ones my men took for me. I think about those guys and their families every day. Never forget this: when you affect a person's life or even take it, you will change many lives including your own".

They both fell silent for several minutes. Daisy didn't dare break her father's mood, and he wanted to give his words chance to sink into his intelligent, but perhaps impressionable daughter.

He explained about the illegals, as he called them and where and how they operated, promising to give her the managers' names and addresses in the near future.

"When all is said and done, Daisy, the way I see it is, whether you like it or not, whether you're a feminist or not, there will always be a market for girls selling sex. Old men don't want to shag old women - that is not the way they think. They still want young ones, and at fifty, sixty or seventy, they get more of a thrill out of bedding a twenty-year-old than a twenty-year-old boy does. Much more… much, much more. So, as long as there are old men with money, there will be young women willing to sleep with them. It is not called the oldest profession for nothing. I see it as a sort of dating service. It helps both parties get what they want and some of the girls end up getting married too.

"So, that is one staple, and money laundering is the other main one. Arranging family policy permits to get girls into Britain used to be very profitable, but the vote for Brexit may have put the kibosh on that, we'll have to wait and see. Anyway, laundering money will always work, because there will always be newbies who don't know how to do it, 'though to be honest, even some of the big firms can't be bothered. They must factor the cost of laundering into their prices. In fact, it's a lot easier than you would imagine, if you know how.

"Any questions, am I going too fast for you?"

"No, I find it all fascinating... perhaps when everything has sunk in, and I have looked at the details you're going to send me, I will have a few points".

"Not send, chicken, handed. The illegals need to be dealt with with the utmost privacy. And that means no unnecessary records, not even between family, and even those notes have to be shredded or otherwise destroyed. Do you understand me? If you chuck a note from me into your waste-paper basket, the cleaner may find it, or the dustman, or someone at the landfill, but there might even be people, say, the Inland Revenue, looking for scraps of information... or the media. You have to train yourself to be meticulous when dealing with any potentially incriminating evidence. That, and security, which it is a part of, must be your main preoccupations. Have you got that?"

"Yes, Dad. You have taught me to be cautious, and careful about security all my life, so this is just taking it a stage further".

"Yes, but before I was mostly worried about you being kidnapped and held for ransom, now the worry is that you could land us all in jail. That might kill your mother, I might never see the light of day as a free man again, and you might spend years in the nick... not to mention the hundreds of other lives that would be affected if all of our businesses were to be closed down. Being the boss certainly carries privileges, but it also bears responsibilities... and they can be heavier than you can imagine at the moment..." He drifted off again, but she was still loathe to bring him back to the topic in discussion.

"Have you ever heard me called Micky the Bastard?" he asked suddenly.

She genuinely wasn't sure whether she had or not, but the epithet did sound vaguely familiar. "I don't think so, Dad", she chose to reply because she found it embarrassing. "Why's that?"

"Oh, it's a nickname that has followed me about for most of my life. It started even before I went to school. You don't know my family history, not really. You only know a potted, sanitised version of it. Your mother and I thought it better not to saddle you with it in the early days, but it is time you learned the truth now. Let's sit on that bench over there in the shade.

"To start at the beginning, I have to take you back to the First World War. The Germans invaded Belgium one day, so, many Belgians crossed the Channel to London. In the main, they were middle-class, but they had to leave most of their possessions behind. Within a short space of time, many of them were penniless. Most of the men amongst them joined the army and went back to fight, leaving the women to fend for their families as best they could. Some supplemented their incomes by working on the streets at night.

"An enterprising young Irishman called John saw an opportunity, rented a house and put a dozen of the prettiest girls into it. Well, to cut a long story short, he soon had several properties and scores of girls and within a few years he owned those buildings. My mother was one of the children of those women... a second generation Belgian, you could say, and she worked in one of John's houses. Most people who were willing to talk about my past said that she only looked after the girls - cooking, cleaning, washing and the like, but maybe they were only trying to be kind. I don't know, and it doesn't matter to me. I'm sure that she was only doing what she had to do.

"Anyway, John could not manage his empire alone and gave his family jobs to help him. One of these was one of his brothers called Dermot. Dermot raped my mother one day and I am the result.

"I know what that look is on your face, but don't feel sorry for me. Pity your grandmother, if anyone. She had me and I grew up with her and her mother. I don't know if her father came back from the war or whether he was already dead when they arrived in Britain. Anyway, my birth certificate said Father: Unknown. I don't remember anything about those days. Then, one day, when I was about two, my mother shot Dermot dead. Again, I don't know what drove her over the edge to do it, or whether she had just been biding her time.

"Two or three days later, Dermot's three sons burst into our rooms and shot my mother and grandmother dead. I don't know why they left me alive... perhaps they couldn't kill an infant in cold blood, or perhaps it was because I was their little brother - half-brother.

"The next bit is blurry, but the police must have come and put me in care. John, Dermot's older brother, the man I called 'father', then adopted me and brought me up as his own. He didn't have any other children.

"He had my name changed by deed pole to match his and I became John Baltimore. I don't even know what my original names were. John, Dad, never told me, never kept the original paperwork, and I never asked. It just didn't seem to matter. That makes you half Spanish, a quarter Belgian and a quarter Irish by blood, but half Spanish and half British legally.

"Anyway, back to my little story. Some people were envious of my good fortune at being adopted by the millionaire John, and referred to me as Mick the Bastard... 'Mick' meaning Irish, unless my original name had been Michael... or even Michel. Mick soon became Micky and I always imagined that 'bastard' came from 'lucky bastard', but maybe that was wishful thinking. Anyway, the nickname stuck.

"Kids can be so cruel, you know. They taunted me with that name throughout school and I cried myself to sleep most nights, until John found out about it. He made me take boxing lessons and the name-calling dwindled... to my face at least, but now the nickname certainly didn't refer to my legitimacy, but to my ability and readiness to exact revenge with my fists quickly and without mercy. Then the nickname suited my purpose. People don't use it here much, but they still do among the old crowd in the East End, although most of my contemporaries are dead now".

Daisy waited a while to see if he would continue, and then said, "Wow! I didn't have a clue about any of that. I'd heard vague rumours about Mafia and London gangland, but I never paid them a great deal of attention... well, I tried not to anyway".

"Like I said before, we tried to shield you from my past, but you have chosen to be a part of it. Still, you can ignore what I just told you, if it suits you better. It doesn't matter".

"So, if I Google your names, I might find something?"

"You might do. You may find some oblique references with regard to the Richardsons or the Krays, but we were not in their league. John, my Dad, had properties and girls and then just property. John was before those big gangsters' time... they were more my age... but we were in different businesses... there was a slight overlap perhaps. However, our solicitors have gone to great lengths to remove any references to me or Dad from the Internet. Google cooperated, and so did most of the other search engines, and we have been keeping a low profile since we've been living in Spain... certainly a much lower profile in any case".

"How did you meet Mum then? Was she a part of all that stuff too?"

"Your mother? No, Heaven forbid! I don't think she had ever even been abroad when I met her. Still, I think that that's her story to tell, so I won't go into it, but I can assure you that you were not a product of violence like I was. In fact, neither of us thought that we were capable of having children. I took a few beatings in my younger days, and the doctors said that I'd probably never be able to have any... and your mother said that she was past the menopause. Crikey, I was no spring chicken either! Your mother called you 'a gift from God' and I wanted to give you the name of a flower in memory of my mother, whose name was Fleur.

"Your mother and I were in love, er, and still are... and I am your real and biological father. See what a mess you're getting me into? That's why this subject is better left to your mother".

"OK, Dad", she replied smiling. "We all know that you don't do emotions very well. You know, I've learned more this afternoon than I did in any one week in uni. Thanks for telling me... I'm sure that it couldn't have been easy. I love you, Dad. Do you want me to walk you back to the house?"

"No, you run along, I'll just sit here a while and smell the flowers. Be careful, won't you. I would never forgive myself if anything happened to you".

"Nothing's going to happen to me. You worry too much".

"If you need anything, anything at all, just come to me or see Tony. Watch him and learn from him. He's a good man and can teach you a lot".

"I will, Dad. Don't worry. Shall I have Maria bring you out some iced coffee or ice cream?"

"No, I'm fine. I'll go in shortly. Is that one of Tony's new toys up there?" he asked pointing at an object in the sky.

"I'm not sure from this distance. It could be a bird or a drone. If you watch it a while, it's flight pattern will tell you. Yes, I think it's a drone, but I don't know whether it's one of his or not. Do you want me to phone him and ask?"

"No, I'm just curious, that's all. I'll just watch it and find out for myself. I'll see you later".

"OK, if you're sure. See you".

"Did you have a happy childhood, Daisy?" he called after her.

"Yes, Dad, very". Then she continued on her way.

"Good. I'm glad of that", he mumbled to himself. "I sometimes feel that I didn't spend enough time with you... I regret that, but just didn't know how to. Sorry, chicken".

She returned to her office, head swimming with her new knowledge. She picked up her mobile, activated it and pushed a button.

"Are we still on for this evening, Tony? Great. I'll see you at seven. Oh, Tony, were you flying a drone a few minutes ago? No? OK, it's just that we saw one between us and the hills to the north-west".

∞

Daisy was waiting on the front porch when Tony brought the Mercedes around and got in without more ado.

"Daisy, instead of going down the coast as you suggested, let's go to another bordello tonight - it's up in the hills near where you saw the drone. We've also got a casino between here and there that I can show you on the way back. We can do your two choices another time".

"Yes, sure, no problem. You saw the drone then?"

"No, not really. I saw a distant speck which could have been anything. I'll have someone look out for it tomorrow with binoculars".

"Could it be a threat then, do you think?"

"No, not really, but anything could be a threat. It's just best to be aware, stay alert and keep on top of things. I try to avoid surprises. We aren't having strife with anyone though, so it could be anything from hobbyists to drug enforcement.

"We practically own the little village we're going to now. There is a nice bar, which will hold twice the local population, a dozen girls working in it, a snack bar and a dance floor, where they also do karaoke three times a week. Not tonight, I might add. I hate karaoke".

"Me too".

"The bar has a couple of rooms upstairs, but most of the girls sleep at the guest house. Your Dad owns both establishments and everyone in the village works for us except two old ladies with small shops. They are all very loyal to the Boss, so it will be a good place to start. We have started making enquiries, on your behalf, regarding an old, disused mine nearby, which we could convert into an indoor firing range. We can drive past it, if you like".

"Yes, please. You don't let the grass grow under your feet, do you?"

"It's the way we've always worked. Take as long as you need coming to a decision, but once it has been made, get on with it, before someone beats you to it".

"The strategy seems to work. I'm just here to learn, so, please, teach me".

"OK. There's the village, Santa Amalia, up ahead to the left. It really isn't far out of town".

"What, those six or seven buildings halfway up the mountain?"

"Yes, and there is the mine on our right…" Tony swung the car around the next hairpin bend, "Right here". He stopped the car, but didn't switch off the engine or make any move to get out. "I know it doesn't look much at the moment, but it's close to the village, so it will become a part of the community". He drove on for a kilometre and stopped in a car park, which already contained half-a-dozen cars and a taxi. "The taxis're ours - part of the tour operators".

She nodded. "I take it you've warned Rick, is it, that we are coming? OK, so let me go in first, and you follow me in in five or ten minutes' time".

"Whatever you want; but are you telling me five or ten minutes. I like to know where I am".

"Let's say ten minutes, I want to get a feel for the place before they know who I am. Oh, and do your 'Hello's' before you acknowledge me, please". With that, she hopped out of the car and dashed around the front to the entrance. Tony set the alarm on his watch for nine minutes and scanned the skies.

Meanwhile, Daisy entered the bar. She was greeted by stares from the staff and the girls seated at the bar, where she proceeded to sit down. The lighting was on the dark side and there were quite a few even darker nooks and corners, some of which were occupied by couples. It was obvious that there was a lot of groping going on.

"Hello, Miss, are you lost?" asked a voice which surprised her.

"No, why do you ask?"

"We don't get many unaccompanied young ladies in here. How can I help you, Miss?"

"A bottle of San Mig, please".

"Certainly, Miss. With ice and a glass?"

"No, just the bottle, please".

He placed it before her. "That'll be seven Euros fifty, please".

"Put it on a tab, I'll probably have a couple more".

"As you wish. Would you like some company?" he asked thinking that she could be a lesbian.

"Later, perhaps. I just want to relax a few minutes". He took the hint and moved to the other end of the bar to talk to the girls, all of whom were about her age and just as pretty. Two of them looked Arabic; one was possibly Moroccan Rif. The door opened behind her and Tony emerged from the thick red cloth that was hanging just inside it She looked away before his head poked through. He passed her by and sat in front of Rick. She could just about hear them talking. Daisy caught the word 'lezzer' and watched them both turn to look at her.

"Hello, Tony!" she said holding up her right hand in greeting. She took great pleasure in watching Rick's features squirm as he realised his mistake. Daisy picked up her drink and clutch bag and moved to sit with them. Tony made the introductions.

"Daisy", she said. "Sorry about the subterfuge, but first impressions and all that".

"Rick", he said, nodding glumly.

"I saw a drone over this way this afternoon, did you see anything, Rick?"

"Me? No, but then, I don't go outside that often. This place can be a twenty-four/seven operation. You'd be better off asking some of the villagers, or I can ask the cleaners in the morning and phone Tony, if you like?"

"Sure. Thanks". The three of them and all the unoccupied girls looked at the red curtain as they heard the outside door open. The security camera inside the door showed a white male of about thirty years of age. He sat at the bar a few seats away from Daisy and ordered a pint, which one of the female staff provided for him. Minutes later, he was standing next to Daisy.

"Why don't you come and join me, darling? I haven't seen you here before".

"No, thank you", she replied, "and get your hand off my leg".

"Oh, playing hard to get, are we?" He began to stroke her thigh.

"I won't tell you again", she warned him. He tried to rub her crotch, and as she saw Tony get up, she lashed out with a backhanded chop to his carotid artery. He dropped like a sack of coal down a shute. Tony picked him up and carried him to a sofa.

"He's unconscious, but all right. Sorry about this, Rick. You can deal with this can't you? We'd better be going. Come on, young lady".

They hurried to the car and got in. "That was a dangerous thing to do back there, even though he was in the wrong".

"I wouldn't allow any man to do that to me in any bar. I would have reacted like that whether you were there or not, and whether I was in one of Dad's places or not".

"I believe you, but that's not the point. If you are going to punish someone, break his nose, knock a tooth out, but do not, ever knock him spark out on a tiled floor... or any hard floor for that matter. What if he had broken his neck on a barstool or banged his head on the floor, had a brain haemorrhage and died? You're up for man slaughter, not just assault. And that would bring the cops sniffing around and several people could go down with you. It was a stupid thing to do, Daisy! You should have let me give him a slap and throw him in a taxi. Please, don't do it again in one of our bars".

"Point taken. Consider me reprimanded. Are we still going gambling?"

"No, I'm taking you home. We'll go another evening".

She didn't say another word. She knew that he was right, but felt justified in hitting a man who was assaulting her

6 TERESA'S STORY

As she was getting dressed for breakfast the following morning, Daisy was thinking about the night before and how to best handle the situation. She didn't yet know whether the man she had hit had fully recovered or not, but she knew that Tony would have to report the incident to her father. She also realised that it would be awkward for him to bring the subject up, because it would mean admitting that Tony had told on her.

She concluded that the best thing to do, would be to admit it to him as soon as possible. She didn't mind doing that. People would realise that she had simply made a mistake, lashed out, and would be grateful for her honesty. *'At least, I hope they will'*, she thought.

"Good morning, Mum, how are you today? Lovely day, isn't it?" she said to her mother who was already seated. "Where's Dad?"

"He hasn't come back from his morning stroll around the garden, dear. Did you sleep well?"

"Like a top. Shall we start without him? He's probably talking to Tony".

"Yes, all right", she replied, but instead of going to the buffet, Teresa walked to the open French windows and scanned the garden. "I can't see him", she said, but it does look lovely out there". She helped herself to bacon, eggs and mushrooms and then joined her daughter at the dining table. "The Costa del Sol is so beautiful at this time of the year!" she said in the Andalusian dialect of Spanish.

"Yes, cool in the morning, warm in the afternoon, and cool again at night. I love the autumn too", she replied in the same tongue. Daisy had learned the local dialect from her mother when she was young, and then Catalan at school. She was fluent in them both and could switch between them and English mid-sentence. They tended to speak the dialect when they were alone or with the servants, Spanish when out, and English if John or Tony was with them. John could understand most things but spoke with an awful accent. Unfortunately, Tony's Spanish was still poor even after thirty years in the country. He was wont to say that he didn't need to speak Spanish, and life was proving him to be correct.

When her father entered the room a few minutes later, he looked in a good mood, so Daisy greeted him with, "Buena sera, Papa. Como estas?"

"Good morning, Daisy. It's a gorgeous morning out there. Now, what shall I have this morning?" he asked looking at the choices. The same as you, Teri, I think... and some toast. I suppose it's cold?"

"Yes, do you want me to ring for more, Dad?"

"No, there's no need, thanks. It's my fault that I'm late. Cold won't hurt", he added sitting down.

Daisy ate more than she usually would have and had three cups of tea, waiting for the opportunity to arise when she could talk to her father. Eventually, Teri excused herself to go to talk to the cook about dinner and Daisy seized her chance.

"I hit a man last night and knocked him out... in the Azure Club". John looked up from his newspaper, but didn't say anything with his mouth.

"I had asked Tony to start taking me to the businesses on the new list, and he chose that one so that he could talk to Rick about the drone and show me the proposed site for the gun club at the same time. I think that it would work there very well.

"Anyway, we were sitting at the bar talking to Rick, when this bloke started groping me. I warned him to stop, but when he didn't I hit him. He collapsed to the floor unconscious and Tony brought me home. I'm sorry if I caused you any trouble, Dad, but I can't bear men who think they can treat women however they like".

"You were sitting at the bar in a bordello full of working girls… what is a man supposed to think?" The reply surprised her.

"I did tell him to leave me alone, before I hit him…"

"Yes, but the music can be quite loud in the Azure sometimes, perhaps he didn't hear you".

"Oh, I'm pretty sure that he heard me all right!"

"'Pretty sure', but not absolutely sure?"

"OK, absolutely sure".

"Good, say what you mean, and mean what you say. There's a world of difference between 'pretty' and 'absolutely'. If the man had pressed charges, or died, a solicitor would have had no trouble gaining a conviction, if you said 'pretty sure' and he had witnesses to back him up.

"Thanks for telling me, although I suppose you knew that Tony would have had to anyway. In fact, that's why I'm a little late for breakfast, I was just talking to him in the garden. You will be pleased to know that the guy checked out of hospital this morning at eight with only a sore throat and a packet of lozenges. He's a regular up in the Azure, so Ricky will tear up his bar tab the next time he goes in there. I'm sure he won't cause any trouble about it, but you do have to be more careful.

"When I was young, if some bloke had touched my girlfriend like that, I would have done a lot more than you did, and John, my Dad, or Dermot even more again, but that's why we always had to be looking over our shoulders… and why some of us got shot.

"It's a mug's game. Leave it to the professionals. Tony would have sorted him out if you'd waited, and Ricky can leap that bar like an athlete. Next time, if there is one, make more verbal ruckus. Shout, scream, even pretend to be hysterical, but make sure that you have plenty of witnesses that can see that you are being molested or assaulted. They won't stand for it in Spain. There'll be macho blokes all around you in minutes prepared to defend your honour, and go to court for you for one of your smiles".

She smiled at him broadly.

"Believe me, chicken, it's true. Learn to use your assets and the characters of the people around you. They are useful weapons, don't leave them lying around going to waste.

"So, what are you getting on with today?"

"Just routine stuff like checking suppliers' discounts and deliveries against invoices".

"All right, well, off you go then. They won't check themselves. See you later".

"Bye, Dad, and thanks. You weren't hard on Tony were you? I'd hate to think that he got into trouble because of me".

"No, you've no cause to worry on that score".

∞

Tony didn't have time to take Daisy out for a few days and she didn't really have any friends in Malaga any more. The British children she had known in junior school were either still abroad in universities or working in Europe's cities, while most of the Spanish children she had known had polarised to people of their own nationality. It had been a recurring problem for her since she had gone away to private schools. School holidays and university mid-term breaks had been boring, and now her whole life was like it. If it wasn't for her job, she knew that she would have to move back to London for her sanity. It, therefore, came as a great relief when an old friend from school, Amy, called one afternoon.

"Amy! It's so lovely to hear from you! What a godsend! Where are you?"

"In my parents' house. I got back last night. How are you doing, darling?"

"I'm OK during the daytime, because I'm working for Dad, but the evenings are lethal. Until you phoned, the only person I knew to go out with was my Dad's bodyguard".

"Uncle Tony?"

"Yes, that's right. He's a sweetie and all that, but not really clubbing material, so I've been slowly going potty".

"Well, I'm here now, for about a week. Do you fancy going out tomorrow night?"

"Do I ever? I'd go out right now, if you said so".

"No, I can't tonight, sorry. Mummy has organised some terribly boring family get together for their twenty-fifth wedding anniversary. I'd invite you over, but I don't think it's your thing".

"No, nor do I. I'll give that a miss. Where and when tomorrow?"

"Do you want to eat first or later?"

"First".

"OK, how about the Alhambra?"

"Great choice, we haven't been there together for years. Seven o'clock?"

"Fine, I'll book us a table. See you tomorrow, Daisy, must dash. Daddy's beckoning me".

"OK, see you, Amy. Thanks for thinking of me".

She sat behind her desk staring out of the window towards the sea and thought about the life she had chosen for the first time.

She could see that it might be a very lonely life, if she were not careful. The Costa del Sol was densely populated around the seaboard, but her father knew so many people, that she had never been able to have any fun without it getting back to him. If she got drunk or kissed a boy, her father knew about it before she even got home. It had been like that since she was about twelve.

In the early days, she had mixed with Spanish and British equally, but as they had grown up, the two nationalities had gone their separate ways - grown apart. It had happened quite naturally, and she couldn't explain why. They still spoke when they bumped into each other in town, but there was no friendship. They didn't phone each other or invite each other to parties any more like they had done in junior school. She considered it a real shame, and then wondered whether the reason had been purely cultural, or whether it had been her fault for going away and not keeping in touch often enough.

She had to admit to herself that that might have had something to do with it. She had been mesmerised by London, it's lights and its speed of life. London never slept, whereas, Malaga slept at night and during the afternoon siesta. Not that there weren't places that were open all night, there were, but they were often full of drunken foreign tourists. It was ironic that the drunken foreign tourists that she and her friends so despised, paid for her family's affluent lifestyle, and that fact did not pass her by. She had often tried hard to disabuse herself of the feeling, but she had not succeeded so far. It was another reason why the summer was the worst season for her. The sheer volume of tourists in the summer changed the nature of the area considerably.

The man she had hit in the Azure had been a tourist, she knew it instinctively, because true ex-pats were more gentlemanly than he had been. Tony had said that he came to Fuengirola frequently, and she believed him, but the man still had the arrogance of the tourist. He still thought that everyone and everything could be bought, just because the poorer locals fawned all over tourists with their wallets stuffed with cash that they had had to save all year in order to be able to go on holiday.

They didn't know what the locals really thought of the two-week tycoons, and Daisy considered herself as much a local as anyone, although she was less sure whether she was Spanish or British.

It looked as if her Spanish friends had decided that she was British though, she thought somewhat sadly. She was half and half, but caught between the two stools, and it hurt.

It occurred to her that her father had carved out a life in the area and was happy. It was now her turn to try to do the same, but would that mean finding a Spanish spouse, like her father had done? If he had done it consciously. She felt the desire to talk to her mother about how she and her father had got together, as her father had suggested.

∞

That evening, while her father was otherwise busy, Daisy sat with her mother and watched television, waiting for the opportunity to talk about the subject that she was really interested in. She seized her chance during a commercial break after a particularly melancholy episode of a Spanish soap.

"Mum, after watching that, it makes me realize that I don't really know how you and Dad got together. Share it with me, please! I'd like to be able to tell my kids when they ask one day too. Go on, I bet it was dead romantic!"

"Oh!" she almost blushed, but her eyes became dreamy and distant. "You know that my parents and most of my family were killed by Franco and the fascists, well, I stayed with some old family friends in the hills around here and didn't return to the city until it was safe in about 1986. I mean to live, because I never stopped popping in and out of the towns to shop or do whatever it was that I had to do on behalf of myself or others in our community. It wasn't so dangerous by then either.

"Anyway, I eventually moved back to Fuengirola and worked in various shops and on the market selling farm produce. I also used to cook things to sell for myself... a tray of paella, some cakes... and pasties and pies went down well with the British.

"One man used to come every day there was a market, and he would buy half a dozen pies and half a dozen pasties off me every time. I thought he was the most dashing, handsome man that I had ever seen and when he smiled at me and complimented me on my cooking, I was so taken with him that I could barely speak! My colleagues used to poke fun at me saying that I used to go as red as a schoolgirl after her first kiss... but he was so... so exciting to be around".

"Oh, Mum, how romantic, please go on!"

"Yes, it was. Anyway, I gradually began to find out more about him, and one day, he asked me if I would consider working for him. He offered me good wages and my own room in his house - this one. I had never had my own room before. I was as happy as a hippo in mud. It wasn't long before I was made head cook and then housekeeper too. They were heady days for a woman with my background, and I was looking after the man I loved. All right, not as his wife, but that didn't bother me much. I would have done anything he asked me to and gladly done it for nothing. I even dared to think the unimaginable... that he might have feelings for me too, but I knew that he was the type of man who found it difficult to express his emotions, so I used to encourage him in any little way that I could".

"How, Mum?" she laughed.

"No... I cannot tell even you that... Everyone needs to retain some pride and that means keeping some secrets to oneself, but you are a woman, and if you ever need to know how to get the man that you love, you will find a way. I am sure of that. Let's just say that all women have their wiles when push comes to shove in matters of the heart.

"It took a while, and a bit of coaxing, but one day he asked me to marry him and then along you came, although neither of us thought that we could have children. You are our gift from God, the hidden pearl that we didn't know we had within us. You are our very precious Margarita, or simply, our Daisy".

"That's a lovely story, Mum, I hope that I have one like it to tell to my children one day. Thanks for sharing it with me".

"You won't have one just like mine, because I was poor and you are rich, but I am certain that your tale will be equally romantic and special to you and your children, when your time comes".

They hugged and kissed each other on the cheek.

"Are you happy here, working for your Dad, Daisy?"

"Yes, I think so. I would rather work for the family than anyone else".

"It's just that I don't see you having much fun. When I was a girl, life was very hard. There was oppression, hunger and death all around, but if somebody played a guitar or a fiddle at the camp fire, we all forgot our troubles for a while and danced and sang. I don't see young people having much fun these days... despite the fact that they, even the not so well off children, have more riches than we could ever have imagined. Why is that, darling?"

"I don't know, Mum, spoilt, I suppose. I don't really know much about other kids though... not even privileged ones like me. I've lost touch with all my school friends from around here... long ago. I didn't even notice it happening. Then I got back from London and there was no-one left to talk to. I am going out with Amy soon though. Do you remember her?"

"Yes, she was always a nice, polite girl. Is she still living around here?"

"No, she's just visiting, and then there'll be just me again".

"All right, I know that most of the British children have moved away to study or work, but what about the Spanish children you used to know at school?"

"That's what I was just saying, I didn't notice us drifting apart, and now there is no contact at all any more... unless we bump into each other in the street. Perhaps they feel that I abandoned them by studying in the UK, or perhaps they think that I have chosen to be British rather than Spanish, or fifty-fifty. Could that be it?"

"I don't know, my dear. I didn't have foreign friends, or not northern European ones anyway, when I was growing up. John was the first one who took an interest in me - and the only one, I might add, before your imagination starts to run away with you. After the war, the British always seemed too aloof, so… Oh, I don't know, aristocratic in those days. Then from the Seventies on, droves of younger people came… most of them Brits around here in the Eighties and Nineties, but they weren't very nice. They were often violent, drunk and disrespectful… They are becoming more polite again now. There was an arrogant element for a couple of decades. I'm glad to see they've mostly gone. Perhaps your Spanish friends' parents only remember that mob of hooligans… I don't know, it is not how I think.

"Don't worry… It will all turn out well in the end… it usually does, and you have the intelligence and… other resources to ensure that it does for you too".

"Yes, I'm sure you're right, Mum. Thanks for the chat and the pep talk. I have such special advantages being born to you and Dad, but sometimes… I don't know… I see other people of my age enjoying life so much more than I seem to be doing".

"Oh, my darling! Let me give you a hug. Happiness is a frame of mind… sometimes, you even have to work at being happy. You have the big resources that most people crave… you have intelligence, education, beauty, loving parents, heath and money, perhaps what you need to do is see the beauty in simple things like a flower, a cloud, the sea, good food, good music and even a pleasant smell. When you are capable of appreciating those things as well, find someone to share them with and you will be as happy as anyone on the planet.

"We, people, that is, were not meant to be alone. We live in families, communities, countries and continents. You have a generous heart, a lovely personality, don't be afraid to let other people see it. Maybe, you get that from your father... Let the Spanish side of you get out more... have some fun!"

They both laughed. "OK, Mum. I'll give it a try. Thanks again. I think I'll go and read a book in my room. Good night".

"Good night, darling. Just think about what we've been talking about, and you will see that it makes sense".

Daisy didn't really want to read a book. She brought her computer out of hibernation and opened up her Facebook page. She had nearly three thousand Facebook friends, but as she scrolled down through them, there were not many that she knew well, and even fewer from her pre-university days, and even with them, there were some whom she only recognised by their name or their pictures; the environments they were taken in were far less familiar. She looked through some of their profiles, but it only made her feel even more left out to find that many of them were married, and had not invited her to their weddings. Or had they, but she had been too busy to notice? She couldn't say with any degree of certainty, but she did find it depressing.

She abandoned the computer to switch itself off in thirty minutes' time, selected her journals from fifteen to eighteen years of age and flopped on the bed to flick through them. Daisy had never religiously kept daily diaries as such, but she had usually written down events that had been important to her at the time. She knew where she wanted to start - the day of her fifteenth birthday, when Juan Martinez Perez had stolen a kiss from her and made her blush. She had enjoyed it, but he had also embarrassed her in front of her friends. She had never openly forgiven him for that, and never told him that secretly she had liked it either.

She was surprised to be reminded how shocked she had been to hear the rumour that Sarah Butterfield had confided in her that Susan Perkins, a girl in the next form, had boasted about having sex with her boyfriend on the beach at sixteen. Daisy couldn't remember ever having been that prudish, but she was still well aware of what her father would have said and done, if she, Daisy, had been caught doing the same. She hadn't, and had never even really wanted to, but it had been out of the question anyway. She wondered whether that was the real reason why she had never let Juan know her true feelings about him. She concluded that it could well have been. He had been devilishly handsome, and she had liked him a lot... to distraction sometimes.

She moved on. A beach party just outside southern Fuengirola. The boys had encouraged the girls to go topless. Some had, but neither she nor any of her friends had. The entry had been finished with 'The SLAGS!' in red, highlighted in yellow. She knew that she must have been feeling jealous, but could no longer remember exactly why. Probably, a boy, she thought, or because the girls who did take their tops off got more attention, and she hadn't dared to, because of her father's reaction again, if he had found out. And he always seemed to know exactly what she was doing, and with whom and where.

Daisy didn't find being reminded about the distant memories upsetting, rather she wondered how she had forgotten the details of so many of them. Had she blanked them out subconsciously, or had events in London simply superseded them in importance in her memory? She didn't know, and pressed on with her memoires. However, she must have drifted off, because she awoke at two twelve a.m., pulled a sheet over herself and went back to sleep without undressing. She had been dreaming of a pool party in her family's back garden, where dozens of young friends of hers were dancing and swimming. She was standing on the lowest springboard getting ready to dive. When she checked the water below her for swimmers, she was surprised to see that she was topless. She felt liberated, spread her arms wide and shook her chest to make her breasts sway. She looked around herself smiling broadly, but no-one was paying her any attention except her father, who was scowling.

"Get down off there this instant and put some clothes on!" he shouted, and all the guests turned to look at her with shocked expressions on their faces.

7 DAISY'S NIGHT OUT

After breakfast with her parents, Daisy went to her office to prepare her paperwork for a day out with her father to purchase the mine for use as a gun club and shooting range. She was looking forward to an exciting day, because she had never been involved in the creation of a business from its inception and she was going out with Amy in the evening. When she walked out to the car with her father, she was a little disappointed to see that Tony was to be driving them, but it was not a complete surprise, since John hardly ever went anywhere without him.

They had already greeted each other that morning, so John simply acknowledged Tony with a 'Thanks, Tony' and got in the back of the Mercedes with his daughter.

"The mine first, is it, Boss?"

"Yes, let's have one last look at the old place, and then we'll go down to have a chat with Ramon". Tony nodded into the rear view mirror and eased the car into motion.

"Did you get a chance to look at the drawings Martinez y Martinez drew up for us, Daisy?"

She felt hurt that her father thought that there might be even a remote possibility that she wasn't giving the gun club project her utmost attention, but she tried to banish the upset from her voice when she said in reply, "Yes, Dad, I spent a lot of time looking at them. I made a few suggestions in my notebook too, if you would like to see them".

"Yes, of course, I would. Structural improvements, are they?"

"Yes", she confirmed, handing him her open note pad from her briefcase.

"Yes", he said after having read the five brief comments. "Yes, very good. Well, you can point them out to me when we arrive, and we can ask Ramon Martinez what he thinks later. So, you're keen on this project, are you, chicken?"

"Oh, yes, Dad! It's my first real taste of business and it's going to be my first project, and, best of all, I'm working and learning from you".

He put his arm around his daughter and hugged her. "Thanks, darling, that's nice to hear. Well, here we are". A heavy, fifty-odd year old man with black and grey hair, a drooping Mexican bandito moustache, a round face and a big paunch was sitting on a rock outside the already opened mine. There was a shotgun across his knees. He didn't get up until the trio had already gotten out of the car and taken a few steps towards him.

"Como estas, Carlos?" asked John.

"Muy bueno, señor, pero mucho calor!" He wiped his wet brow with a red handkerchief from his shirt pocket to emphasise the fact that it was hot. He had known Tony for a long time, but he eyed Daisy in a neutral fashion for some seconds, although not long enough to be rude. He had never met her, but he knew who she was.

"Daisy, I would like you to meet Carlos".

"Carlos, my daughter, Daisy. She will be in charge of the club".

"Carlos lives in the village. He will organise security for, er, ... with you". Daisy took his large beefy hand in hers, he had just finished drying it on his handkerchief, but she did not show any disgust.

"Nice to meet you, Carlos. I am sure that we will get along just fine", she said in Spanish, and then in English, "Do you speak English?"

"Yes, Carlos' English is fine", said her father. "Don't spoil him. It is, isn't it, you old rascal?"

"Si, señor", he smiled.

Daisy didn't ask about the gun, because a lot of Spanish men liked to hunt in the hills for small game. Carlos led the way into the mouth of the mine, which looked like a cave, now that the corrugated iron sheeting to stop children and tourists going inside had been removed from it.

The mine was made up of a series of tunnels, rather than shafts, that penetrated into the mountain not the bowels of the Earth, and the sunlight from the entrance illuminated the way adequately for some fifty metres, but they had also brought powerful torches. The main tunnel was about ten feet high for a hundred metres in, but it dropped from there on in. There were in fact two entrances some fifty metres apart and the tunnels from them converged twenty-five metres in and then went off at forty-five degrees from one another.

Once back outside, Daisy pointed out the main feature of her improvements. "Over there", she said, pointing at a space midway between the entrance tunnels, we could build a clubhouse, and we could use the tunnel we just looked at as a rifle range, because it is far longer, and the other one as a pistol range.

"Then, if you like, we could seal off the mouths to the tunnels and build our own entrances to them from the clubhouse. Two man-made tunnels, one going left and the other going right. That way, everything could be controlled from the clubhouse, thus reducing security risks and manpower".

"Two facilities instead of one, but controlled from one main entrance by Carlos and shotgun... Yes, I like it. Tony? You're not saying much".

"No, Boss, but I like what I hear. It is easier to control one exit and one entrance and we can construct that point to suit ourselves. Say using turnstiles to slow people down - electronically lockable ones, so that we can shut the place down securely easily, when we need to".

"OK, just making sure that you're paying attention. We might as well go down to see Ramon, and buy the place then. See you Carlos... Oh, by the way, any sign of our bird yet?"

"No, señor, but we will get it if it comes back and serve it up for you". All three men laughed. Daisy didn't know what they were talking about, although she was not prepared to display her ignorance in front of her first employee, so she just smiled.

"OK, Carlos, you can lock the place up again now, amigo. Nobody from our team will be back up here today".

"See you", he said after closing the car door behind Daisy.

"What big bird is that, Dad? The one you were laughing about back there..."

"Oh, that!? I have offered a thousand Euros reward to whoever shoots it down, if it comes back".

"That's a point", she said, "we could do clay-pigeon shooting on the ground above the tunnels facing the mountain".

"I like it! You'll go far", said John tapping her forearm with a smile. Daisy was beaming - the happiest person on the Costa del Sol.

John instructed the solicitors to proceed with the purchase subject to the police granting permission for the conversion of the mine into a gun club.

"Señor Baltimore, we have already put the plans forward to the Fuengirola city council and the police, and have been told on the QT, that they are sure to be passed. The only fly in the ointment, as you say, is the added terrorist threat to the local population. This has to be taken into account, but as I have said, everything should be all right".

John opened up his copy of the site drawings, picked up a pencil from the desk and began to sketch in Daisy's alternative plan. "In fact, Ramon, my daughter here was telling me about some security improvements that she has in mind just this morning. I wasn't sure whether to take them to the architect first or bring them to you, but we were going to see Raoul with them next.

"You, see, if we seal off both the tunnels and make them accessible only from a clubhouse... here, between the two entrances, and install electronic turnstiles and electric, reinforced shutters at strategic points, say here and here... security would be vastly improved. We could also build accommodation for a Spanish manager onto the clubhouse to improve security even more... and, we could allow free access to the ranges for all police personnel serving and retired. No terrorists are going to attack a club that could be full of armed police, are they?"

"I wouldn't, señor Baltimore, but then, I am not that way inclined and I am not a crazy terrorist. However, I am certain that these security enhancements will ensure that a positive decision in our favour will be reached more quickly. My suggestion is that you have your architect add your improvements to the drawing right away and have six copies sent over to me as soon as possible. We will get this through, Mr Baltimore, do not worry about that".

"All right, Raoul, thanks for that. We will leave you on that happy note and go for a spot of lunch. Would you care to join us?"

"Oh, I would love to Mr Baltimore, but I have a prior engagement. Thank you anyway".

"Oh, well, perhaps another time... when the deal goes through. Bye for now".

"Goodbye, Mr Baltimore, young lady, Tony".

"That was quick thinking, Dad", said Daisy outside.

"I had a gut feeling that the decision could go either way, but I couldn't have done it without your suggestions this morning. We make a good team". It seemed to Daisy that she was having the best day of her life. They drove on to the architect, where John explained the proposed alterations and why they needed them.

"Ramon Martinez Perez said that he would appreciate them ASAP, so that he can forward them to the planning and police departments. Will you take care of that for us, please?"

"Certainly, Mr Baltimore, it will be my pleasure. I will phone you some time tomorrow when they are ready for your approval".

"Thank you, Raoul. I can't ask for more than that. I'll wait to hear from you tomorrow then. Come on, Daisy, it's lunchtime for us. Sorry, Raoul, we are in a bit of a hurry, I forgot. This is my daughter, Daisy. She will be running the club at the mine".

The well-dressed and coiffured forty-year-old man stepped forward, took Daisy's hand and gazed into her eyes. "Enchanted to meet you, Daisy", he purred.

John had never liked him, but now he was certain of it. "Come on, Daisy, how about a champagne lunch at the 'Vino Tinto' on the old square in Fuengirola before we go home?"

She wanted to refuse but couldn't bring herself to break up the great atmosphere. There were only five hours before she was supposed to be meeting Amy and she had been hoping to save herself for that. John ordered a mixed seafood salad for the three of them to go with the bottle of Moët et Chandon champagne as an aperitif and proposed a toast.

"To my daughter Daisy's first business venture, may her chain of successes stretch far into the future. To Daisy's chain of successes!"

"To Daisy's chain of successes", repeated Tony and they drank her health. Then it was Daisy's turn.

"Thank you both for your good wishes. I promise that I will do my best not to let my family and friends down, and will try to build a chain of successes into the future, starting with the all-important first link that my father showed me how to create today. Cheers, Dad, cheers, Tony!" They clapped quietly and she sat down gratefully.

John and Tony had a steak and glass of red wine after the bottle of champagne, and Daisy had fillet of sea bass with white wine. When John suggested moving on elsewhere to continue the celebration, Daisy had to explain about Amy.

"That's all right, chicken, I understand about meetings and commitments, and I respect people who honour them. We'll go back home and I'll have a snooze in the garden. It'll be better for me anyway. We'll go out together another afternoon".

"Thanks, Dad, I'm glad you understand".

When they arrived home, Daisy, too, thought that a nap might do her some good, so she set the alarm, put on a DVD, lay on the bed a very happy young woman, and was soon asleep.

∞

On awakening, Daisy had the strange notion that it would be fun to meet Amy in a style that she was completely unknown for. She didn't think of it as a disguise, just a bit of fun. She was also hoping that it would shock Amy since they hadn't seen each other for years. Tony wasn't available to drive her there, but the cook's husband, Sal, the odd-job man, who lived in with his wife, had been trained to drive the big car. He was always more than happy to get behind the wheel of the five litre V8 beast. She looked at the thin, late-middle-aged man's happy face from time to time in the rear view mirror, and if he spotted her he smiled. Daisy could not help but smile back at the kindly man.

"Alhambra, no? Señorita?"

"Si, Alhambra, Marbella, Salvador". He smiled at her again, always pleased when she remembered his name, despite the fact that he and his wife had been with the Baltimore's for more than five years. He dropped her off and waited for her to get in safely, as were his standing orders when driving a member of the family. They gave a wave at each other as she went inside and Sal drove off.

The head waiter took over responsibility for her inside, although he did not know who she was. "Do you have a reservation, madam?" he inquired.

"I am meeting Miss Amy Fairwater here at seven".

He checked his book and showed her to a table by the window overlooking the yachts in the marina and the sea. Anybody could walk around the coastal area and the marina, but it cost serious money to have a boat in the water there. Most cost a million Euros and many ten times that and they came from all over the world - even the poor countries, where the élite were far from poor. She watched the all-female crew of one expensive yacht nearby frolicking on the deck trying to draw attention to themselves, which wasn't difficult being only partially clad in tiny royal blue bikinis. She couldn't hear what they were promoting, but the flags it was carrying were Russian and Panamanian. She watched her friend give the girls a glance and then the door opened and she was shown to her table.

"Daisy? Is that really you?" she asked sitting down. "I wouldn't have recognised you on the street. When did you start dressing like that?"

Daisy smiled. "I don't wear it every day, silly. This is my flapper girl look... you know from the Twenties? I bought it in London to go to a party when I was at uni there, but quite liked it. Don't you?"

She was wearing a period apricot cloche hat, a baggy, short-sleeved, chiffon, apricot Somerset dress to just above her knees with a white belt and white shoes. Her face was powdered white and her eyes and lips were heavily accentuated in black mascara and blood red lipstick. The look was finished off with a dozen chains and strings of cheap beads around her neck and wrists with costume jewellery rings on each finger.

"No, I like it... it just takes a while to get used to seeing you dressed as a flapper. You look good though. I feel rather under-dressed now".

"Oh, don't say that, Amy! I didn't put all this on to embarrass you. I only did it for a laugh. You look great too... much cooler than I do, in your Armani jeans and T-shirt. Daisy signalled for the waiter who had given up and left them to talk in private.

"What do you think, Ames? A bottle of ice-cold Chablis?"

"Yes, that would be nice. Let's leave the food for twenty minutes".

"Sure".

The waiter returned three minutes later with the wine, an ice bucket, a basket of warm bread and a bowl of black and green olives. Having done his duty, he left the young women alone to tend to other guests in the already half-full, fashionable restaurant.

They talked about school days, and university and whom they had seen and, just as importantly, whom they hadn't, while they finished the wine and the olives.

"More wine, let's get drunk!" said Amy.

"We've quaffed the lot!" giggled Daisy, but where there's smoke there's fire. They must have more". Daisy pulled a face and they both laughed again.

"How about half a lobster each to go with it?" asked Amy.

"We can have that with the third bottle - it takes twenty minutes to cook... More wine and caviare, while we're waiting for the lobster!"

"OK, I'm up for that", replied Amy. "You can do the honours". Daisy did as she was bid and they were soon back on the serious subject of catching up.

"How's work?" asked Amy. "Cheers, my dear!"

"Cheers! Excellent", she replied and told her about the day's developments. "How about with you?"

"Daisy's chain of successes, eh? That sounds good... I'm afraid there's nothing like that on the horizon for me yet. Congratulations!" They clinked glasses.

"Don't worry, Amy, something will turn up, but it's not as if you're hard up or anything, is it?"

"No, just a bit bored. I'd like a nice job in fashion. Vogue magazine, or something like that..."

"Well, you studied fashion at uni, didn't you? Perhaps someone can help you get in there. Have you asked your Dad yet?"

"Not yet, but that is sort of why I'm back here. I need to ask if Daddy can help. What a depressing subject... let's talk about boyfriends. Oh, wait a minute, I think those are our lobsters heading this way".

"OK, you sort out the lobsters and the Chablis, and I'll swim off to the Ladies.

"That's better", she said on her return, "any more and I would have wet myself. I'm a bit tiddly too. It creeps up on you... er, wine does, doesn't it? I used to drink buckets of wine and beer in uni, but it looks as if I'm out of the habit. Moderation in all things in Mum and Dad's house".

"Does that go for boyfriends as well?"

"Boyfriends at our house? Oh, no, there is no moderation there... there is only complete abstinence, I mean a complete, absence of boyfriends there. I suppose I mean both really".

"You mean that you haven't had one since you've been back?"

"I haven't had one for even longer than that..., hic, excuse me, not even a kiss".

"You had boyfriends in London though, didn't you?"

"Oh, yes, I had a few, but they all - all three - turned out to be tossers... as fickle as fairies... Is that what they say? No, as fickle as the wind. Fairies aren't fickle, they're nice".

Amy topped their glasses up, and they started on their lobster halves. "So, no love interest then? It must be a bit boring for you around here with no friends".

"Yes, it can be, but I have my job and I do enjoy doing that and working with Dad".

"Mmm, working with Dad, is not the same as cuddling with Chad, if Chad is a boy's name, is it, though?"

Daisy shook her head, picked up the claw and crushed it with the pliers. It spattered juice up the front of her dress. "Oh, shit! Look what I've gone and done now. Does it show?"

"It does now that it's wet, but it might not in thirty or forty minutes when it's dry. The colours are not a bad match". They both laughed and clinked glasses.

"How's your love life, Ames? I hope it's better than mine".

"Not really. There is one, but he's a plonker too. I'm thinking of going for the more stable older man. Have you tried them?"

"No, I don't think my parents... Oh, I don't know... maybe they wouldn't mind... But, no, I want somebody my own age or a little older. I'm all right, I'll get around to it one day. Have you got an older man in mind?"

"No, not yet. It's just an idea at the moment. What do you think about going to the Stardust on the marina and giving the younger blokes another chance first?"

"Yes, I'm up for it. I'll get this in celebration of the first link in my chain of successes" She held up her hand and pretended to write. The waiter nodded.

"Your Daisy chain of successes".

"What? Oh, yeah... my Dad has a way with words". She signed the credit card receipt and they stood up to leave. Daisy felt a little wobbly inside the restaurant, but when the fresh air hit her outside, she took her friend's arm.

"Wow! Are you sure that that wasn't sherry they gave us instead of Chablis? I feel a bit pissed. How are you?"

"I can feel the wine, but I'm fine. I could dance all night now. Are you sure you're OK?"

"Yes... I'll be all right... Let's go for it!", but they giggled the hundred metres to the club.

"Two, please", said Amy on arrival.

"The bouncer looked them over and replied, "You can go in, but your friend's too drunk".

"I'm not drink, er, drunk", said Daisy angrily.

"I watched you staggering along the quay. You would've gone in if it hadn't been for your mate. Come on, move on now. We don't want any unpleasantness, do we?"

"I tell you I'm not drunk, you wanker!"

"You've got vomit or food all down you, you're staggering and you're abusive. You look like some slag from Torremolinos. You're not coming in here, go on, shove off both of you". Daisy kicked him in the shin, but it didn't affect the big man who was probably wearing shin pads anyway "I'll call the police if you don't go, and you're on a security camera doing that".

Amy helped her friend away. Daisy was sobbing now.

"I'll have the bastard, you see if I don't", she promised Amy as she helped her into a taxi.

"Are you sure you'll be all right going home alone?"

"Yes. You go back to the club, if they'll let you in. I'll be all right. See you again".

Daisy felt humiliated as she let herself in through the heavy front gates, and then into the house. She knew that somebody would be watching her on a security camera, but she just wanted to get to bed before her parents saw her.

8 THE STRUGGLE FOR IDENTITY

The following morning, Daisy didn't have more of a hangover than two Paracetamols and a shower could take care of, but that wasn't ever going to be the problem anyway. She wondered whether her father would find out, indeed if he already knew, and if so, what he would say. She decided to put on a light, cheerful face as she entered the dining room.

"Good morning, Mum, good morning, Dad! What a lovely day, isn't it?"

"Yes, isn't it? Did you enjoy your evening with your little friend then, darling?"

"She's hardly 'little'", Mum, she's twenty-one, the same age as I am, but the whole day was marvellous. I enjoyed being with Dad and learning from him. I felt proud of the way my suggestions for the gun club were adopted. I enjoyed our lunch, and it was really nice to see Amy again. We went to our old haunt the Alhambra. It's not the same as it used to be, of course - nothing ever is, is it when you've been away for a while - but the food and the atmosphere were great and we had loads to talk about over a few bottles of Chablis".

"I do hope that you didn't drink too much, dear!"

Daisy saw her father look up from his paper, and replied, "Perhaps we did a little bit, but neither of us was driving. I did something stupid though! When I cracked a lobster claw, I forgot to shield myself and got covered in lobster juice! Stupid, eh?"

"Students in England probably don't eat as many lobsters as we do. You probably forgot what do to". John looked at his wife and then continued reading.

"No, they don't... Most of them don't have the money, and, well, you try to fit in, you know".

"That's right, dear. You don't want to go stepping on any toes when you're abroad".

Daisy used the pause to get some food. She would have skipped breakfast, if her parents hadn't still been there, but she knew that it was better to eat something. She chose what many students had told her was most likely to sort out any excess acid in her stomach: scrambled eggs on toast.

"Is there anything specific you want me to concentrate on today, Dad?"

He folded his paper in half, put it down and looked at her. "Let me see... at about ten, you could check that the revised drawings have been completed and sent over to the solicitor's; then you could ring them to make sure that they have received them in the quality and quantity that they require. You could also ask when they will deliver them to the relevant authorities and how long they expect it will be to get planning permission.

"When the drawings are ready at the architect's you could have them faxed or scanned over to us. Check them for detail and we can go over them after lunch. If they are correct, you can phone the builders and tell them to get over to the architect's to pick up a copy so that they can give us a revised price. Send a copy to the builder who came second in the tender too and ask for a revised quote.

"You never know. The sooner we get that project into the hands of others, the sooner we can get on with our next plan".

"What is our next plan, Dad?" she asked with the ring of excitement in her voice.

"I'm not sure that we have one yet, except for the standing order or making sure that everything is running smoothly, but that is not the point. Our job is strategy. We make plans and see that they are carried out by others, usually, and that releases us to come up with more ideas and, hopefully, some of those ideas will be good enough to turn into plans. We need time to think, and that means forming a good team who can relieve us of the details, so that we have the time to do that. Do you understand?

"It is not our job to be building inspectors, it is our job to decide what buildings we need and where and then move on... not that you can ever completely leave these things to others. You have to put in surprise appearances sometimes, and watch the figures... always watch the figures, and that is where you come in".

"Yes, I follow you, Dad. You have assembled a team that you can trust, and I met some of them yesterday. Tony and the others are also in your team, and now, so am I..."

"Yes, but I would say that your rôle in the team is not just as a paid employee, is it? Even though you do receive wages".

"No, I didn't mean that... I wasn't getting funny about my position... or my status in the firm. I was thinking aloud really..."

"I have warned you about that, haven't I? When you are thinking something in your head, you have the luxury of knowing what you are thinking about, but if you then think a few words aloud, they are open to misinterpretation even by your closest family and friends, which is why thinking aloud is not a good idea unless you are standing alone in the middle of a field.

"Anyway, your mother and I are going out for the morning and lunch, but we should be back by two. Ring me if you need me, we are not going incommunicado", he smiled.

"He's having his feet done at the chiropractor, and I'm going to let them have a look at mine too, but your father is embarrassed about it".

"Chiropodists, Teri. The word is chiropodist, and I am not embarrassed about it, I just don't think that it is anyone's business but mine... or ours. Anyway, come on, let's get going. She you later, chicken".

"Yes, see you later, darling", and they started to leave. "You're a fibber, you are embarrassed about your feet. I keep telling you there's no need, but you don't listen..."

"Have a nice day!" Daisy shouted after them with a loving smile. As she finished her last piece of toast and drained her teacup, first one idea began to form in her head and then another, but it was only as she was walking to her office that she saw the link between them that might have created the second one.

Sitting alone at her desk, she no longer had to pretend that everything was going swimmingly after the night before. She strongly resented the bouncer calling her a 'tart from Torremolinos' and she strongly resented his suggestion that she might have been sick down her dress... that all bothered her immensely, but the thing that she could not forgive him was that he had said it in front of the couple of dozen others waiting to get into the club. He had humiliated her in front of others on purpose, and it made her blood boil.

The solution to that had been the second idea that she had had at the dining table, the first had been that she should start to build her own team now, and the link was that then they could deal with nasty shits like the bouncer. Her problem was that she had no idea where to choose members for such a team from. Certainly not from those she had known in school or university, and the only friend she had was Amy, who was hardly a femme fatale.

It was a big problem, but one that would have to wait until she was on her own time. She picked the architect's card out of her bag and dialled the number.

∞

Her first attempts at recruiting were ham-fisted. She went to clubs and bars and hoped to find disgruntled ex-bouncers and strong men whom she could lure with the suggestion of sex, if not the deed, but she was not good at playing Mata Hari and had no success. It took almost a month to realise that a more fertile recruitment ground might be the gymnasia and Dojos which proliferated the area.

This she found much easier because she was fairly proficient at several martial arts, such as Karate, boxing and Aikido. She was already a member at the East Wind Dojo, at her father's insistence, but she hadn't been to any others and there was no likely material there, so she put herself up for competitions. At the level she would be competing, many of the bouts would be held either home or away, and that was her key to meeting other types of fighters.

A month later, the gun club was granted planning permission, the property had changed hands and Daisy was training for her first bout. Her trainer said that she had improved a lot since the first day she had decided to take up the sport competitively, and she felt that that was true. He also said that she had a good chance of winning her bout, which she was less confident of, but she decided to go all out for positive thinking and believe that victory was within her grasp.

She put her heart and soul into her training and her father supported her, even if her mother had her reservations. "You are such a beautiful girl", she would say, "why do you want to risk getting a broken nose or being scarred?" to which she or her father would point out that surgery could fix those problems these days.

∞

Daisy and her father put the first shovelful of concrete in the founds of the gun club building and laid the first concrete block, although it was only for Daisy's sake, since the exterior was going to be clad in local stone to match the hillside. They planned to have a more formal and more visible plaque on a boulder outside the main building when all the construction work was complete.

She enjoyed paying the site a visit in person, with or without her father, every day, and when she knew that Tony was flying one of his drones, she liked him to fly past so she could take a look. The only problem there was that the unknown drone had still not been brought down yet, and Tony risked having his shot down by mistake

"Why don't you tell them that yours will fly between ten and twelve and two and six every day?" she had suggested, but Tony had not been impressed.

"Because that lot would not know how to keep that information to themselves, and soon everyone would know that they could do whatever they liked outside those hours". Tony eventually settled for painting his in yellow and black bands like wasps.

∞

Six weeks after her first win, about halfway through the construction of her gun club, Daisy won her second friendly bout under the name of La Femme Fatale and both teams of competitors went out for a meal afterwards. She and a man from the other club spent such a lot of time talking and laughing that she wondered about his potential not only as a member of her team, but as a lover too. Claude was a handsome six foot two, eighty-kilo Frenchman, a fourth Dan Karate expert and a keen shooter too. He was noticeably impressed when Daisy took him to visit the site.

"And this will be yours?" he asked in a heavy French accent.

"My family's, but I will be responsible for it", she answered honestly.

"I am impressed, may I join, when it is finished?"

"Of course, you may, Claude. I'd love to have you as a member", and she squeezed his large right bicep. If he hadn't been in love with her before, he was head over heels now. From that day on, Daisy and Claude were frequently seen in public together.

On the day of the topping out ceremony, and opening of the Daisy Chain Shooting Range, Claude was within feet of her as she and her father unveiled the boulder that bore her and the club's name, and it was to him that she held up her first celebratory glass of champagne. Both her parents noticed but their opinions differed. Her mother was happy that her daughter seemed so obviously in love, but her father told Tony to have him checked out.

Several other astute people noticed her new romantic attachment as well.

That night, after a meal involving the family, some friends and some of those involved in the project went for a meal at John's expense, but it finished early at seven, so Daisy and Claude went on the town together. However, if Claude thought that it was going to be his lucky day, he was very much mistaken

Daisy claimed that she was a virgin, which was untrue, but she was not experienced, and said that she would only sleep with the man she was married to. Claude immediately went down on one knee, professed his eternal love for her and asked for her hand in marriage on the dance floor of the night club they were in at the time.

Daisy acted as if it was a huge shock to her that Claude felt that way, helped him up, not that he needed it, and led him to their table.

"I'm sorry, Claude... I, I had no idea that you felt that way about me!" she said holding his hand.

"How can you say that, Daisy? I have been mad for you for months... not mad, er, crazy for you for months. Did you not see that I love you more than anyone or anything?"

"I saw that we are friends, good friends, and that our friendship is growing steadily deeper, but I did not see love. Love is not something I know much about... I saw deep, deep friendship, perhaps that will turn into something that I will understand as love.

"Oh, my dearest, dearest Claude... if I have led you on, I am deeply sorry about it and if you decide to walk away right now and give me up, I will understand..."

"Is that what you want? For me to abandon you?"

"No, no, you are my best friend! It is the last thing that I want. I am just saying that... if you feel that I have been giving you false hope, and you want to leave, I will understand". A few tears ran down her cheeks, but she made no attempt to remove them. She wanted to see whether Claude would.

"Do not cry, mon petit choux..." he said, stoking the tears away gently with the side of his index finger. "I understand that you have principles... they are unusual principles for these days, but I respect them and I respect you. I will not leave you, so long as you want me as a friend, and one day, perhaps as a husband".

She squeezed his hand. "Thank you, my darling, Claude. I am so in need of you and your friendship, especially at this moment in my life. I think I want to go home now, Claude, do you mind? It has been a very tiring day for me".

"Non, but of course not. I will accompany you to your villa, if you will permit me".

She nodded, "Yes, I would like that, Claude". They held hands in the back of the taxi, and he kissed her on the cheek before she got out, but he made no other move on her. He was smitten, and believed with Gallic pride that, if she were not already in love with him, then she would be soon.

∞

At breakfast the next day, her mother wanted to know all about the handsome stranger that her daughter had taken to the opening.

"Oh, mother!", she exclaimed with a measure of false exasperation, "You have seen me with him before. He has dropped me off a couple of times and even been in the garden at least once. You remember him from the construction site, don't you, Dad?"

"Yes", he said lowering the newspaper, "but you have never introduced him to me before. I don't know anything about him yet. Who is he? What does he do for a living?"

"His name is Claude Bouvier, he's French, but came here to teach martial arts six years ago. He is in charge of the club where I had my last fight".

"Oh, I have seen him before, I am not saying that I haven't. He's a striking young man... and in more ways than one I take it, but what is his interest in you?"

"Oh, charming! My own father cannot understand why a man might be interested in me!"

"I didn't mean it like that!" he said grimacing, because he realised his mistake too late, "Of course, you are a beautiful and talented young woman. Everyone can see that, but you are also wealthy, which means that you have to be extra careful".

"So, because my family has money, that means that no man can like me just for who I am? Is that what you're saying?"

"No, and I think you know that I'm not. Don't play games with me and don't put words into my mouth".

"He says that he loves me, and he actually asked me to marry him in public last night. He went down on one knee, Mum, in front of hundreds of people and asked me!"

"How romantic!" cooed her mother.

"Bollocks!" broke in her father, "most gold-diggers would cut their right arm off to land a catch like you. Sorry, Daisy, but going down on one knee doesn't cut it with me".

"Well, although it was nice to be asked - my first time, I might add - I turned him down. I said we could stay friends. So, you needn't worry; the family jewels are still safe".

"Good", said her father picking up the paper again. "I am very relieved to hear it. Did you know that the local press phoned last night for a comment on 'the obvious love affair' between you and that man?

It caught me on the hop, I can tell you. I didn't know whether it was true or not, so I gave them the usual 'just good friends' statement. I'm glad to hear that I was telling the truth.

"It is very important that we maintain a united front on issues like this, Daisy, so next time you bring someone to one of our dos that might possibly be seen as a paramour by the press, please warn us first".

"Yes, well, I am not in love with him, but I am very short of friends, so Claude is firmly in that bracket. Now, if you will excuse me, I have to get to my office and then up to the gun club to welcome the first joining members. I probably won't be back for lunch, I'll get something up there, but I will be in for dinner. Bye for now".

"Take care, darling", said her mother, and then, "What a shame! He was such a tall, handsome, fit-looking young man too".

John lowered the paper enough to look at his wife, shook his head slowly and raised it again.

Daisy left for her office with a smile on her face.

9 A PLAN COMES TOGETHER

Over the following couple of weeks, conjecture mounted as the local press and friends speculated whether Daisy, the only child and heiress of multimillionaire, John Baltimore, was in love with the handsome manager of a nearby martial arts centre. John's solicitors were able to keep it out of the papers, but it was becoming increasingly difficult, especially after one reporter showed him photographs of them kissing outside a nightclub.

However, John and Daisy continued to deny that there was anything more than a 'strong bond of mutual respect between the two friends'. Nevertheless, despite her assurances to her father to the contrary, she continued to fuel the rumours in public by giving Claude signs of deep affection, if no more. She was behaving like a wannabe starlet, and the local press was lapping it up.

The floodgates opened one Sunday morning, when the photographs of Daisy and Claude kissing appeared in a British tabloid newspaper under the headline of: 'Daughter of Multimillionaire Costa del Crime Boss Falls KO for Penniless Gallic Fighter'.

John laid copies of the newspaper at Daisy's place at the breakfast table and waited for her to arrive. The atmosphere was tense to say the least. She could feel it the moment she breezed in with a cheery 'Good Morning!'.

"Is it really?" asked John.

She kissed them both, but only got a reaction from her mother, then she helped herself to breakfast. "What are you both looking so glum about? Has someone died?" she sat down, saw the photos and the headlines on the centre spread, and let out an "Oh!"

"Oh? Is that all you have to say, young lady?"

"Well, I haven't finished reading the article yet, give me a chance".

"Give you a chance? You've had more chances than a million kids of your age put together!" He waited and stewed.

When she had finished, she glanced at her mother, who was studiously reading the colour supplement from the offending tabloid, so she looked at her father who was staring back. "How can I help what the press publishes?"

"How can I help what the press publishes?" quoted John mockingly. "I don't see you objecting to him cleaning your tonsils with his tongue in public!" he exploded.

"John, please! There's no need to speak to Daisy like that. Please moderate your language".

"Moderate my language?' Well, I like that! Why don't you tell your daughter to moderate her love life in public? Listen, you two, and especially you, Daisy! My father and I came here about sixty years ago to get away from all this crime boss nonsense and I have managed to keep a lid on it since he died forty years ago, and you have fucked all that up within a year of leaving college!"

"John!"

"Sorry, Teri, but her irresponsible behaviour has got me angry. We haven't heard the last of this… Oh, no. this is just the beginning. The local and regional guttersnipes will be all over this by tomorrow. In fact, I bet they are writing tomorrow's headlines already. In fact, it was a local photojournalist who took those pictures of you and lover boy, he showed them to me a couple of weeks ago and asked what they meant.

"Like some sort or limp dick, I said that you were 'just good friends' and now this. How do you think that makes me look?"

"Like a caring father looking out for his beloved daughter?"

"Don't get smart with me now, this is not the right time".

"Sorry, Dad, but it will all blow over. I am not in love with Claude, and we have never slept together. We are 'just good friends' – very good friends – and that is all. And that kiss might look like a deep throat, but it wasn't, I can assure you".

"You can assure me? That's a laugh, after this lot and all my advice…"

"I'm sorry if I have caused any distress to you both. Can't you sue them or something?"

"I doubt it. Look at the photos. Read the quotes 'from friends of the couple'. Anonymous friends, of course".

"Who got paid, if they exist".

"Yes, well. True or not, this has raked a lot of mud up into the water, and what will happen next is anyone's guess. I don't want you leaving the house today, Daisy, and don't talk to anyone unless I put them on to you… especially the press. Do you understand? Tony has someone intercepting all in- and outward bound phone calls, but I am talking about mobiles, Skype, email and the Internet. OK. We are going to batten down the hatches until we have worked out what to do".

On the way to her office, Daisy, sent one simple text message: 'Sorry, can't come out to play today'.

Later that morning, John called a family meeting with their solicitors in the drawing room, and they drew up a strategy of dealing with the home and foreign press, which basically boiled down to the Baltimore's saying 'No comment' to anyone's questions and Martinez y Martinez issuing injunctions and a press release denying the affair. However, they all knew that the damage had already been done. They were just trying to stop it getting any worse.

∞

When she was allowed 'out to play' again two days later, Daisy went straight to meet Claude in a hotel in Benalmadena. They were disguised and arrived separately, but if anyone had been following the British press, they would have recognised them without much trouble.

91

"I thought it better to meet here than at my place", said Claude holding Daisy in his powerful arms. He kissed the top of her head, and she began to cry. "Don't cry my little darling, if we were married, none of this would be happening. Why don't you say 'Yes' and make me the happiest man on Earth?"

"I can't Claude, you know I can't… not yet. We have been through this a hundred times, and now we have another setback. Did you see Sunday's story about us?"

"Yes, but who took those photos?"

"A local journalist, weeks ago… Apparently he showed them to my Dad, who denied all knowledge, and then he sold them and his story to the Sunday People"

"If I knew who he was I would break his arms and stuff his camera up his backsides!"

"Backside, not backsides… Would you? Would you really do that for me?"

"I would do anything for you, Daisy! Anything in the world. Just say the word, not even that, just hint at it, and it shall be done".

"Oh, Claude… you are so sweet and kind to me. I don't know what I would do without your love, support and friendship".

At those words, he squeezed her tighter and looked around them as if looking for a monster to slay for her to prove his love. He released her and put his finger to her lips, then he sprang at the door and yanked it open. He grabbed a man who was standing outside their door and threw him against the wall.

"Why are you spying on us?" he demanded.

The middle-aged man was terrified and between wheezes managed to get out, "I wasn't, honest. I just stopped to get my breath back and look for my key". He held up a hotel key to a room three doors down.

"I'm sorry", apologised Claude.

Daisy interjected, "My husband is a famous French footballer. We are on holiday, but the media never leaves him alone. It gets to him sometimes. We are very sorry".

The man muttered something about understanding and hurried off, but not before his suspicions about their sincerity were aroused by giggling from behind their closed door.

"He was lucky, because if he had had a camera around his neck, it would be up his backsides, er, backside now!" smiled Claude and they both laughed.

"You're my hero, Claude", she cooed, echoing the words she had often heard her mother say to her father. Claude's chest swelled with pride.

∞

After one of John's informants had told him that Daisy was meeting Claude secretly in hotel rooms, he was not best pleased.

"Daisy, is it true that you have been meeting lover boy in hotel rooms?" he asked one afternoon in her office.

"Yes, Dad... not to have sex, just to talk. I thought it would be better than meeting here or at his place..."

"Sometimes, I wonder what goes on in that head of yours", he said walking over to the open French doors. "Did you give any consideration to how bad it would look if the press got wind of this?"

"Yes, but, as I said, we thought it was better than meeting here or at Claude's – the best of three evils, if you like".

"How can you possibly think that? I mean, have you taken leave of your senses? I don't know whether he ever had any, but you did... at one time. I just can't figure you out any more. Sleazy hotel rooms... Mr and Mrs. Smith... don't the old clichés mean anything to you?"

"Yes, Dad, but what else was there?"

"How about a restaurant, or a good old fashioned pub?"

"Journalists, Dad! Telephoto lenses, long-range listening devices. At least in a hotel, we have some privacy".

"OK, I get that, but what do you need so much privacy for? What do you get up to that you want to keep secret?"

"Nothing!"

"So, why don't you do 'nothing' in public?"

"Because of prying journalists".

"I give up… no, I don't. All right, you can bring Claude around here for your private chats, but I want you to stay away from him in public until I've had a chance to think about it. Deal?"

"Deal, Dad, but how long can we not be seen together in public?"

"I don't know, chicken, give your old Dad a break will you? Let's say two or three days for now".

"All right, my dear old Dad, three days for now it is, and I will probably invite Claude around for a chat the day after tomorrow. OK?"

"Yes, darling, OK.

∞

That night, at nine o'clock, she told her parents that she was going out for a meal with some friends, which did not include Claude. Tony dropped her at the Alhambra, waited for her to go inside and watched her take a seat at an empty table by the window. He thought she looked stunning in that apricot flapper outfit as he waved and drove home.

In fact, Daisy wasn't seeing any friends at all that evening, although she was hoping to meet someone later on. She ordered a bottle of Chablis and half a lobster with salad. She felt awkward being dressed in exactly the same outfit that she had worn at exactly the same table eating exactly the same meal all those months ago, but she didn't show it. She laughed and flirted with the waiter and drank her wine steadily. She was on her second bottle by the time the main course arrived. She took care not to splash herself with juice this time and she finished off the meal with a brandy and coffee.

"That was wonderful", she said accepting her credit card back from the waiter and smiling broadly. "I'm supposed to be meeting friends in the club on the quay, but I don't know whether I've got the energy now".

"The Stardust is very good, so they say, señorita".

"All right, I'll give it a try then. Thank you and good night, señor".

Before she rounded the corner on the way to the Stardust, she rearranged her clothing slightly so that it looked untidy and took her place in line to go in. When she was standing before the bouncer, she burped in his face and giggled.

"Sorry… Oh, no! Don't say you're going to stop me going in again, you fat bastard! You've got something against me, haven't you? You banned me last time!"

The memory came back and he said, "Drunk again, eh? You're not coming in this time either, now push off!"

Daisy started to cry and walked off a little. "Last time I came here he called me a drunken Torremolinos Tart. I reckon the fat pig fancies me. You do, don't you? Or are you gay?" People were looking, but they just wanted to get inside away from the embarrassment.

Daisy walked to a bench, sat down and called Claude still sniffling.

"Oh, Claude, I feel so miserable".

"What is the matter, mon choux, where are you and why are you crying?"

"I am down by the Marina. I was feeling lonely without you so I went for a meal at the Alhambra. Then I thought it would be nice to go dancing with my friend Amy. She likes the Stardust and it's only around the corner, but the bouncer wouldn't let me in. He told me to 'eff off' or something. I think he recognised me from the last time I went there. He wouldn't let me in then either and called me a drunken Torremolinos tart.

"I'm not a tart, Claude, you know that. Why would he say such horrible things about me and in front of so many people on the street?"

"I don't know, my darling. Wait there and I will come and take you home".

"No, Claude, my sweet, you cannot, I promised Dad not to see you in public. I'll just get a taxi home. Don't forget we're meeting at our home the day after tomorrow at three. I can't wait".

"I will not forget. Are you sure I cannot take you home?"

"Positive, I don't want to upset Dad any more than I already have".

"As you wish, text me when you get home and I will call you tomorrow. Good night, sweet dreams, darling".

"Good night, Claude".

She dried her cheeks, got into a taxi on the rank and went home.

∞

Daisy didn't say a word about the events of the previous evening to her parents over breakfast, and they didn't ask where she had been and with whom, because John for one was trying to build an atmosphere of trust between them. However, there was something in the air, and her mother picked up on it.

"Daisy, you know that whatever problem you have at any time, no matter what it is, you can always come to us. We will never willingly fail you". John looked over his paper and wondered where she was going with this. "That's right, isn't it, John?"

"Yes, most certainly... Why what has happened?"

"Nothing that I know of", said his wife.

"Daisy, is there anything that we ought to know about? Anything you want to tell us?"

"No, I assume Mum is just talking in general, aren't you, Mum?"

96

"Yes, in general. It is just that sometimes, when people get older, they forget that their parents still want to help. It is natural for children to run to their parents when they have a problem, but when they get older they think that they have to do everything alone or they are not fully grown up, but it is not true.

"Every day that your father and I live, we will be as much older than you as the day that you were born. That age gap will never diminish. I was forty-two when you were a day old and now that you are twenty-one I am sixty-three. We are equal in the eyes of the law, but in nature I have a lot more experience than you. Your father was sixty-odd at the time, so that is a hundred years more knowledge you can draw on than you yourself have.

"Do you see what I am saying, darling? Do not waste that knowledge if you need it".

John lifted up the paper again and shook his head. "No kids listen to their parents. They all think they know better", he said.

"Well, if your cynical old Dad is correct, then try listening to God. I was a Catholic, but I gave up on God when my parents were killed. John was never a church-goer, but I want to give you some advice that has helped me when I most needed it. If you ever get to the stage where you don't have a clue what to do next, just go into a church - any church - sit quietly somewhere and think about what is bothering you. Even ask for help, even if it is just in your thoughts. You don't have to ask God, or Jesus, or Mary, or your Guardian Angel, if you believe in one, just ask for help or guidance.

"The results might surprise you. As I have said, it has helped me, but I didn't have any parents to turn to. I beg you to remember my words, if you are too big to turn to us for help, or we are no longer here, turn to yourself in the serenity of a church".

John closed the paper, looked at the two women in turn and said, "Right, I had better get some work done", and left the room.

Daisy stood up and hugged her mother. "Thanks for that, Mum, but I'm sure that you and Dad will be around for decades yet, and I know that I can come to you. Now, I'd better get started too. See you later. Love you".

"Yes, darling... love you too". Tears formed in her eyes, so she dabbed at them delicately with her napkin, so as not to ruin her make-up or get mascara on the beautiful imported Irish linen.

∞

Claude phoned at a little after ten, as she had expected him to.

"How are you today, my little darling?" he asked.

"I'll get over it", she simpered, "what other choice do I have? He is a big, strong man, and I am just a woman doing my best in a man's world. The strong can do what they like and the rest of us just put up with it as best we can. It's the way things are".

"They don't have to be like that for you, my darling".

"I'm sorry, I don't know what you mean, dear. Why should things be any different for me?"

"Because you have me to take care of you. If you will accept my help, no-one will ever hurt or abuse you ever again. Just say the word".

"What, you will be my Sir Lancelot?"

"Yes, that is he, Lancelot du Lac. Lancelot of the Lake and like that great knight, I will protect and honour my Rèine Guinèvre".

"Queen Guinevere... me?"

"Yes, just say that you want my protection and you shall have it".

"Yes, my darling, I want your protection. Wow! What an idea! Are you still coming around tomorrow?"

"I would not miss it, I have thought about nothing but you since last night. I will be there at three. Au revoir, ma chère, Guinèvre".

"Au revoir, Claude, I mean Lancelot".

∞

Daisy was playing football with the three Rottweilers in the front of the house when the gate opened to admit Claude on his Kawasaki EN 500 Vulcan Classic. She gave the ball one final hard kick and walked over to her guest as he was putting the bike on its stand. She kissed him on the cheek and bade him follow her to her office.

"You're never alone out here, there are cameras and Dad's men everywhere". As they looked around, Daisy spotted the drone in the hills. "And there's that thing", she said pointing at it. "Do you know whose it is?"

"No", he replied shaking his head and looking perplexed. "Some kids?" There was the muffled sound of a distant volley of gunfire and a wing came off the drone causing it to tailspin down. They looked at each other and laughed. "Fate is smiling at you today", he said.

"I guess someone else is fed up with its snooping around", she said without letting on.

"It sounded like several guns to me, not just one..."

"I've no idea. Come on, let's go inside. Can I get you something to eat and drink?"

"I have eaten already, thank you, but I would very much like a cold beer and some olives with a little bread".

"Certainly". She placed the order over the phone, showed Claude where to sit, closed the French windows, and sat on the matching sofa opposite him. Minutes later, there was a knock on the door and a girl wheeled in a trolley with the food and ice. There was always beer in the office fridge. "Thank you", she said in Spanish, "that will be all". The girl did a little curtsey and left.

Daisy laid out the food, opened two beers and sat down again. "Where were we? Oh, yes! How are things with my Sir Lancelot du Lac?"

"Very well, my Queen Guinevere. I have news that I hope will please you".

"Really? I'm all ears. What is it? Cheers!"

"Cheers! Eh bien", he said sheepishly, "I am not sure where to start... OK, I will just tell you and throw myself upon your mercy.

"When you phoned me two nights ago and you were crying, I flew into a wild rage. I started to smash cups, plates, chairs and even a table, until I had the good sense to go out into the garden. I exercised all night, but still I could not sleep. It is lucky that my *Finca* is outside the village or I am sure that someone would have called the police to deal with the mad man that was I.

"Speaking to you the following morning, yesterday morning, it seems so long ago, put me in a calmer frame of mind, but I was still enraged with the man who had made you cry. I wanted revenge for you, so I formed a plan and enlisted the help of my two most trusted friends.

"In short, we followed the scum home. I attacked and rendered him unconscious, then we bound, gagged and blindfolded him, bundled him into a van that we had stolen and took him to my farm..."

"You kidnapped him, the bouncer from the Stardust?"

"Yes, that is so. He is bound and gagged in a couple of sacks in my garage at home".

Daisy finished her beer, and watched over the top of the bottle as Claude did the same, which was unusual for him because he didn't normally drink much. She held up her empty bottle.

"Another?" Claude nodded. "What are you going to do with him?" she asked feigning shocked horror as she handed over the bottle.

"I thought that I'd leave that up to you".

"Did he see you, or does he know where he is?"

"No, not a clue, I am positive about that. Cent procent!"

"So, we could let him go and no-one would be any the wiser..."

"Or we could kill him and it would be the same..."

Daisy was trying not to show that she was becoming excited. "This is shocking news, Claude. You understand that I had no idea you would do this crazy thing, don't you?"

"Yes, Daisy. The responsibility is all mine. Have I displeased you?"

"I can't say that, my darling Claude. It is very flattering, but it is also, I don't know, er, shocking. I'm stunned, overwhelmed".

"But not displeased?"

"No, I will not say displeased. Come here, you, Lancelot!" she said standing up.

He moved to her and she threw her arms around him. She felt his muscled arms and was aware of the bulge in his trousers pressing on her stomach. She allowed him to feel her left breast and squeeze her bottom through her short skirt. She felt him quiver as he did so. It took a great deal of will power to push him away when he made a move to unhook her bra, as a desire had started to grip her that she had not felt for a very long time and in a magnitude that she had never known.

"I am sorry; I went too far. My apologies".

"Don't worry about it this time", she said, straightening her blouse, "I was getting carried away myself too for a moment. Go back over there, it's safer. We have to decide what we are going to do next".

It took them two more beers each to formulate a basic plan, which involved keeping the man alive, if he didn't cause any trouble, which it was impossible for him to do anyway, according to Claude. Daisy walked him to his motorbike, told him to be careful and went back to her office.

She sat behind her desk, massaged her breasts, and then slipped a hand into her panties. She was climaxing as a knock came on the door.

"Who is it?" she panted a few seconds late.

"Shall I clear away, miss, if your guest has left?"

"Yes, come in", she replied testily, but she was already beginning to feel a lot more relaxed, although it wasn't the last time that she would climax on her own that night at the thought of what someone had done for her, and that she held another man's life in her hands.

10 THE FALL GUY

Daisy had had a few more beers in her office and in her room after dinner with her parents, but, although she thought that mild levels of alcohol helped her think, because it relaxed her, she was no nearer a solution concerning the bouncer than the day before. She put the matter from her head, had breakfast and lunch with her parents and then phoned her father.

"Dad, I'm going to spend the afternoon and evening at the gun club, is that all right?"

"Yes, sure, but why?"

"Oh, no real reason, but I want to keep on top of things and I can work up there on my laptop".

"Yes, I know you can, but that isn't what I meant. Is there a problem?"

"Oh, no, not that I know of… I just want them to know that I am watching, that's all. By the way, congrats for shooting down that drone!"

"Oh, that? I knew that Carlos and his men would get it one day. OK, are you back for dinner?"

"I'm not sure, I might eat out, but I'll let Mum know. See you, Dad".

She knew the gun club inside out, but she had an idea that she needed to stress test. At first, she sat in her small, but adequate office in the club and allowed Carlos' wife, Isabel, to bring her cakes and coffee. Then she moved to the pistol range and practised with her Colt Python .38 revolver, which she now carried on her person or in her bag all of the time.

The club provided storage facilities for customers who wanted to leave their weapons or/and ammunition there, but it was impregnable. Even the state police were impressed. Then she borrowed a hunting rifle and fired a few dozen rounds, but it hurt her shoulder and she felt more comfortable with her thirty-eight.

When the club closed to the public, Daisy told Carlos that she wanted to inspect the bunkers – the areas behind the targets where hundreds of tons of sand stopped the bullets. Carlos was happy to accompany her to show how well he and his team managed the site, and Daisy complimented on it.

"Look, Carlos", she said in Spanish, "why don't you go and have your dinner and a bottle of wine? You deserve it. I just want to have a little poke around, there's no need for you to come with me. I'll tell you what, you lock up the clubhouse as you normally do, drop all the shutters and everything else and when I'm done in the firing ranges, I'll lock up behind me and give you a bell to turn on the rest of the security system."

Carlos trusted his boss, and wanted his dinner, so he had no hesitations in agreeing.

The clubhouse could be sealed in its own right, because that was where the guns and ammunition were stored, but the firing ranges were less secure, because there was nothing to be gained by breaking in there. Daisy walked along the maintenance track of the twenty-five by one hundred metre pistol range, and inspected behind the tons of sand that stopped the bullets, then she locked that range up, and entered the rifle range from outside.

It stretched two hundred metres, but she walked it and checked behind the sand pile. There was no light that she didn't carry with her, and no sound so deep into the mountain. On her way back, she turned the security camera away from the maintenance entrance and pointed it at the club door, then she locked up and left without phoning Carlos, who, she assumed, was still eating and watching TV, since the danger zone was secure.

Once outside, she phoned Claude and told him that it was safe to proceed. He and his men, whom Daisy had never met, arrived a few minutes later.

"In there, quickly, yes, behind the van, don't forget the camera up there scanning the drive! Get the van out of here now!"

As the van was driven away, two men pushed a man in a sack into the shadows.

"In here", whispered Daisy. She re-opened the maintenance door, and they made their way to behind the sand pile by flash light. The man in the sack was whimpering, but not loudly, not that there was anyone who could have heard him in the rifle range.

As they had agreed, everyone spoke with a small handkerchief in their mouth, and as little as possible. The bouncer also had wads of wax stuffed in his ears. Daisy showed Claude and his assistant, François, where she intended to hold the man, and then left with Claude. It was François' job to look after him for the night, but he had food, wine and blankets to see him through his shift, whereas the bouncer only had his own excrement.

Daisy went back outside, and they drove off in her car, then she phoned Carlos. It went to voice mail.

"Sorry, Carlos, I didn't phone because there was no signal. I'm nearly home now. Thanks for everything, good night. See you tomorrow, Daisy".

She dropped Claude home, refused an invitation to go in, but stroked high on his thigh as he kissed her and squeezed her breasts again. She shooed him out with promises of 'tomorrow', and then drove off exhilarated. She didn't want to go home, but she had nowhere else to go although it was only just past nine o'clock, but that didn't matter to her. She now had four strong men under her control, and she liked it.

She put her foot down and laughed as the powerful Porche threw her back into her seat.

That night, lying in bed, Daisy was a very happy woman. Her short term plan of getting revenge on the bouncer was in hand (she only had to work out what she wanted to do with him) and so was her medium term goal of piecing together her own team of reliable personnel.

∞

Daisy scanned the local papers eagerly at the breakfast table, but there was no mention of the missing bouncer. Her father noticed her sudden interest in local news and commented on it.

"Oh, I got to thinking last night that I should take more interest in local current affairs, and I heard a rumour the other day that Amy might be getting married", she lied.

"Oh, that's nice, dear. To a local boy, is it?"

"I don't know, Mum, but I think so. That's why I thought I'd check the Costa Sun. There's nothing here though. Perhaps it was just a bit of gossip".

"Aw, I hope she finds a nice young man… I like Amy. I hope you do too one day and give us some beautiful, chubby grandchildren to spoil.

Daisy groaned inside and could imagine her father shaking his head behind his newspaper.

"All in good time, mother", she said, "all in good time".

"That's it, my girl, don't you go rushing into anything you'll cause us all to regret at leisure. The future of this family is in your hands, so make sure you have a steady grip on the wheel. How did it go at the gun club yesterday?"

"Oh, really well. I get on well with Carlos and his wife. I like working up there. In fact, it makes a nice change from my office, and I can do anything up there that I can do down here. I was thinking that I might go up there again this morning. I think that the members like to see me there… it makes the club more personal".

"Yes, I'm sure you're right. When I was younger, I used to spend a lot of time socialising in our clubs and bars. You can ask your mother".

"Yes, too much time", she added.

"I told you then and I'll repeat it now; it was necessary for goodwill. You just heard the same from your daughter without any prompting from me".

"Perhaps, but you enjoyed it too much as well".

"You can't win, can you?" he said to Daisy. "Some people just can't imagine having a job that they enjoy doing! If you aren't miserable, and up to your knees in crap with an aching back, it ain't work. The only problem with that philosophy is that nobody who has a job like that lives in a house like this!"

Daisy got up. "I can see that this is a long-running dispute, so I shall leave you two love birds to your tiff and get on with my job, which I also enjoy. See you tonight".

Daisy went to her room and stuffed her flapper gear into a carrier bag, which she put into her briefcase. She considered that it had been worn for the last time and needed retiring. Her first thought was to burn it, but then she decided 'to let someone else have it'. She took it out of the bag, folded it neatly as if it had just been bought and repacked it.

The club was open from eleven in the morning to seven at night, but being in Andalucía, those hours were flexible, and few members arrived before two anyway. She wanted to get there at about ten or ten thirty. On her way out of town, she stopped at Mercadona's, a large supermarket, and bought some supplies, which she wheeled to her car in a trolley. After unloading her shopping, she put the bag with her flapper costume into the trolley and pushed it to the trolley bay. Then she hurried back to the car and left.

She phoned the club, "Good morning, Carlos. Lovely day, isn't it? I'll be there in ten minutes".

"Everything is open, Miss Daisy. See you soon".

Then she called Claude, "Good morning, handsome. Look, I'm on my way to the club with some supplies… I don't suppose your man has any signal in there, has he?"

"Morning, beautiful, no, nothing at all. I haven't heard from him. do you want me to meet you there?"

"No, it isn't necessary… not yet, but you could come up for some target practice after lunch".

"About two?"

"Yes, that would be fine. See you later, I'm there now, she said parking her car in the shade by the service entrance to the rifle range. She looked in through the door. The range supervisor wasn't in yet, so she grabbed her bags from the boot of the car, switched on the lights in the narrow service passage which ran along the length of the range and hurried down it, she glanced at her watch; she would have twenty minutes, if she was lucky.

She tapped the door in the two-foot thick wall that separated the sand pile from the rest of the tunnel. It opened an inch, and then further. The area, about five metres square was dimly illuminated by two Calor gas lamps, and she could just make out a heap in a corner.

"How are you? I brought you these", she said handing over the bags.

"I'm OK. It's a bit boring though" said the gaoler in his French accent. "There's no signal and the batteries on my iPad have run out".

"Give it to me, I'll get Claude to recharge it for you and load a few films. You will be relieved between eight and nine tonight. How's he doing?"

"He's alive, but he has crapped himself a few times. He stinks to high Heaven".

"Just keep him alive. Is it cold here at night?"

"No, it's not so bad. Just boring, and creepy. There are noises sometimes from deeper down".

"Rats?"

"That's what I thought, but what would rats live off?"

"I don't know, other rats? Anyway, keep it up. Bye"

"Bye-bye, Mademoiselle. Thank you for the supplies".

She nodded, smiled, looked at the bouncer in his sacks once more and hurried away. When she reached the customer end the supervisor was at his desk eating.

"Oh, I didn't know you were in there, Miss Daisy", he said in Spanish.

"I was checking the target pulleys. I'm thinking of automating the game targets that pop out from the openings in the service ally. At the moment, it is expensive to have them operated manually, so hardly anyone is using them".

"Good idea, señorita. Can I get you anything?"

"No, no thanks. I'll be in my office for the rest of the day, if anyone is looking for me".

"Right you are, Miss Daisy". She left him to his tortilla and bread.

Carlos' wife included Daisy in with the lunch she prepared for the gun club staff every day, so she took her a tray with anchovies in tomato sauce, bread, green salad, olives, olive oil and red wine into her office. After lunch, Daisy changed the plan and called Claude to tell him.

"Instead of coming here this afternoon, Claude, arrive at six forty-five with a replacement for the guy whose here at the moment. Get him a tool bag and set of worker's overalls. Better make that two of each and make them identical... caps too. We are thinking of making some alterations here, so we can pretend that he has come to measure up. Oh, and tell, er, Charlie, is it, that he might want to bring an extra battery pack and films, or a book to read? The man you have here, what? François? OK, François says that there is no phone signal and it's pretty boring, which I would have thought he could have guessed, being under a mountain, but there you go. See you later".

The time passed quickly as she followed her routine work of checking the weekly takings and expenditure of the various business looking for trends and anomalies. Time only slowed to a snail's pace between six thirty and Claude's arrival sixteen minutes later, when Carlos showed the two men into her office.

"Thank you, Carlos. I'm sure you remember my friend Claude, well the other gentleman is an associate of his who is going to give us a quote on some minor alterations I have in mind". They nodded at each other but Charlie held his head so that much of his face was hidden by the peak of his cap.

"We need to look around the rifle range, so could you make sure that everyone is out of there at seven, please and for safety, please drop the shutters at your end and I will lock the service entrance from inside. We don't want anyone shooting while we're on the range, do we?".

"Certainly not, señorita, I shall attend to it right away". He nodded to her, turned on his heels and left.

They entered the tunnel to the rifle range and waited for the electrically operated roller shutter to be lowered behind them before continuing to the range and locking the service entrance.

"OK, Claude, the first thing I want to do is impair the image collected by that security camera above the picture window. Don't stare at it! Here's what I want you to do. Come into the service passage both of you. There is no surveillance here. Hold out your arms, Charlie... as if I were going to give you a baby". She placed her case on them and clicked it open. She took out a small paper bag such as is used for children's sweets, and a spray as is used for aphids, passed them to Claude and retrieved her case.

"There is ordinary road dust in the bag, and mildly soapy water in the bottle. While I am distracting Carlos, spray the camera's lens with water, pour some dust onto the palm of your hand and then blow it onto the lens. We can't disable the camera or they will repair it, but if we just blur the picture they probably won't get around to cleaning it. It's seven oh five, now; do it in exactly five minutes and I'll be straight back. OK?"

"OK".

She spread the fingers on her right hand, nodded, and left. As it happened, there was no-one at the bank of screens in the foyer of the gun club, because Carlos had locked up and was having his tea. She watched Claude carry out her instructions until the image went misty then she tapped on the door to Carlos' living quarters and waited.

"Sorry to disturb you, Carlos", she apologised, "I just came to get three beers. Put them on my tab, will you, please?"

"Certainly, miss". He unlocked the fridge behind the counter with a key on a bunch hanging from his waist and handed her the bottles".

"Thanks, Carlos. I won't be disturbing you any more tonight. You go back to your tea, and I'll lock the service door to the rifle range when we leave. Good night".

"Buenas noches", he said, locked the door behind her and activated the roller shutter thus effectively sealing his wife and himself in.

Daisy returned to her team and locked the door behind her.

"Good job with the camera, it's like looking through fog. Let's go and see how they're getting on."

They trotted down the narrow service passage and tapped the door. They heard movement; then the door opened and they went in cautiously.

Although the tunnel extended another three to five hundred metres into the mountain range, the part that they were occupying was starting to smell foetid, because there was very little circulation of air. The prisoner was still in a large sack, but his head and shoulders were sticking out now. He had a towel over his head held in place by a pair of headphones.

"Can he hear us?" asked Daisy.

"Non, I don't think so", replied François.

"OK. I want to release him at this time tomorrow, but first I want to scare the living daylights out him. Can he see?"

"He has duct tape around his eyes, hands and ankles, so no", said Claude.

"Good. Cut him out of that sack, and then..." she said opening her case again, tie this rope around his ankles and hoist him up to the rafters". She pointed at the wooden beams spanning the roof of the tunnel in case Claude did not know the word. The smell of excrement was bad when they cut the sack open. They hoisted him up until his head was about three feet off the ground.

"Now cut his clothes off". The men hesitated. "What, all of them, miss?" asked Charlie.

"Every last stitch!" Claude went to work and the others helped. The smell grew steadily worse. His buttocks and legs were covered in it. "Take the towel and headphones off him, and the tape from his mouth", she ordered, taking a small pair of gardening shears from her case. "I'm going to cut this limp dick's limp dick off". She opened the blades and snapped them shut again several times. She moved forward and poked his tackle with the open blades. She wanted to hear him scream for mercy, but he said nothing. He moved, but there was nothing he could do. He crapped himself again and Charlie looked away at the moment he thought she was about to castrate him, but there was a stay of execution.

"No more shagging for Mr. Limp Dick after tonight, eh, boys? The only problem is that it's so small, it looks as if someone has cut some of it off before. We're going to have to stretch it so I can see what I'm doing!"

While she turned back to her case, the three men looked at each other. Claude was starting to feel decidedly jealous that the prisoner's dick was getting more attention than she had ever shown his own and Charlie was beginning to feel queasy about what he might have to witness. François alone seemed unperturbed by the events playing out before them. Daisy turned back to them with what looked at first like a cat collar on a long piece of string. Except in size, it closely resembled a choker chain collar for a large dog with spikes like barbed wire pointing outwards.

She threw the collar over the rafter, caught it and put the chain around the base of his testicles. Then she turned the spikes inwards and pulled on the cord. Slowly at first, but then with a sharp tug. Blood trickled from several wounds and the man's face contorted with agony. She jerked the cord a few times as if playing some mutually acceptable, sadomasochistic game with him, then pulled it tight and tied it off around his wrist.

"What the Hell is that, miss?"

"It's called a tawse, Charlie, a tawse; meant for inflicting pain, but usually on oneself as a display of devotion".

"Oh, I see. Never seen one of them before. Do you need me for anything right now, miss? It's just that I will be cooped up in here for over twenty-four hours and I'd like a bit of fresh air before you go".

"No, you'll have to wait. We won't be long. Claude, give François the overalls, cap and tool bag. François, put those on, then go outside and wait for us. Your cover story, if anyone challenges you, is that you came to measure up for a job. We'll be along in a minute. Wait by Claude's car".

"Right you are", he said dressing. Then he nodded to the other two men and left. Five minutes later, Daisy was ready to leave too, so Claude gave Charlie some instructions and they entered the passage closing the door behind them.

Daisy gripped Claude and kissed him hard on the lips, grinding her pelvis along his thigh. She squeezed his buttocks and the back of his head and he responded, but this time she didn't refuse him. She undid his trousers and massaged him then turned to the wall and stuck out her bottom. He pulled her panties down and entered her. They didn't have long, but they didn't need long either. Daisy was noisy and she hoped that Charlie could hear her through the door.

It was the best sex she had ever had, and Claude forgave her for playing with another man's genitals.

11 DAISY'S MISTAKE

Claude met Daisy at the hotel restaurant in the village near the gun club at two o'clock the next day for lunch because it would not be busy during the siesta.

"What did you do last night, my darling?" he asked when they were seated.

"I went straight home, made myself a sandwich and went to my room to sleep. I was worn out". He smiled, taking that as a compliment and put his hand on hers. "What did you do?"

"Oh, François wanted someone to go for a beer with him, you know after being in the cave for so long". He paused and removed his hand as the waiter approached. They ordered a seafood salad and a glass of white wine each, and then he continued. 'I didn't stay long though… an hour. I had two beers with him and then some of his mates came in so I went home. I enjoyed being one with you last night very much".

"Er, yes, me too… the same. I want to let the Croatian go tonight. What do you think?"

"Yes, I think so. He has suffered quite enough for not letting a stranger into a night club".

"And humiliating her, don't forget that".

"No, of course not, I was not belittling your reasons".

"In fact, I had nothing to do with his abduction, if you remember. It was all your idea".

"Yes, I know, my love, but I did do it for you and I think you have to admit that you were enjoying yourself tormenting him last night…"

"I wouldn't go that far".

"The tawse?"

"Somebody gave me that for a birthday present years ago as a joke. They'd bought it in a sex shop in London's Soho. It's not meant to hurt really".

"Perhaps not, but where you put it, it probably did. You are not a man, but I think that it would be painful".

"So, you noticed that I am not a man then?" she said trying to change the subject.

"Oh, yes, darling, you are every inch a woman, a beautiful, sexy, intelligent woman, and I love you very much".

"Good, I'm glad we got that sorted out. Now, how are we going to release you know who?"

"Uninjured?"

"Yes, in his current state. Do you have any chloroform?"

"Pardonne? Where would I get that from and why would I need any?"

"OK, just thinking. Rhohypnol?"

"The dating drug? No, I have never needed that either".

"OK, I'll pinch a few of Mum's sleeping tablets. We can crush them up and put them in a glass of water for him. When he's asleep, we can take him somewhere where he'll be found and leave him".

"On the outskirts of town, where people going to work in the morning will spot him".

"Yes, but not somewhere where there are likely to be security cameras. We don't want to slip up now".

"I think I know just the place, but I'll get François to steal another van just in case".

After lunch, they went their separate ways. Daisy had to go home for the tablets and Claude had to speak with François about that evening, but they arranged to meet at the club again at six forty-five.

At five o'clock, she left her office to check the camera from the rifle range. The image was still poor, but she could see that the superintendent was alone, so she went down the connecting tunnel to speak with him.

"Paco, I need to go down the service tunnel a little way to check on something while the place is empty, so why don't you go and get yourself a cup of coffee in the foyer and make sure no-one comes in here for ten minutes?"

"Thank you, Miss Daisy, I'll take you up on that. I could do with stretching my legs", he said in Spanish. She watched him disappear into the foyer and then trotted down the service passage to what had become known as 'The Cave'. She tapped on the door and heard the rock being removed from behind it.

"Charlie", she said, "I won't come in. Cut him down, take off the tawse, crush these sleeping tablets into a glass of water and give them to him to drink at six o'clock. We'll be letting him go as soon as it's dark and we want him asleep. Have you got that?"

"Yes, Miss Daisy".

"Good, we'll be back at seven". She hurried back up the passage, but stopped at a service entrance to the range halfway up and cautiously looked up the range. There was no-one there, so she continued another fifty metres and tried again. This time Paco was just retaking his seat. He held up his hand in greeting and she waved back, then re-joined him. "Those contractors are coming back tonight... I just wanted to make sure of something. It's all clear now, but could you get everyone out punctually at seven again tonight, please?"

"Certainly, Miss. I'll be glad to".

Daisy returned to her office to work for a few hours.

∞

When Claude and François arrived, Carlos directed them to the range and alerted Daisy personally. She finished what she was doing and then went to see them, as one would expect.

"OK, Paco. We might as well close a few minutes early. I've got my stuff from the office, so if you go back that way, you can drop the shutter and leave us to it".

"Right you are, Miss. Good night".

"Good night", she replied, "see you tomorrow", and watched the shutter roll down. "Right, all clear. You've got about forty minutes to get him ready. It'll be dark by then. Is the van outside?"

"No, it's hidden about two kilometres from here. I'll take Charlie to it just before we are ready to leave".

"Good, but there's no need for you to do that. I've no need to go back to The Cave, so you go and help François get the Croatian ready and I'll drive Charlie to the van". Claude agreed and left them for The Cave.

Daisy sat directly under the camera where she was invisible to it. She saw Charlie looking at her legs and the hemline of her short skirt and got a warm feeling from it. "Don't stand over there, anyone watching the security footage will be wondering what you're doing. Come and sit by me where they can't see us".

Charlie, a handsome young man, who was closer to her own age than Claude, was sitting on the chair but one next to her on the left.

"I won't bite, you know?". Charlie moved up closer. "That's better. They can't see us now". She put her left foot on her right knee, giving Charlie a better view of her legs. "I think I've got a stone in my sandal", she said handling her foot. She wanted to laugh at the expression on Charlie's face, he was so mesmerised by her hemline.

"Have you got a girlfriend, Charlie?" she asked, her knee touching his briefly. "There, I think that's shifted it", she said putting her foot back on the floor. "Come on then, I suppose we can get going now. Silly me, I should have asked you to get it out for me, shouldn't I, Charlie?".

He followed her through the door and waited while she locked it. Then she clicked the doors of the drop-top Porsche open and they both got in. As she slid into position behind the wheel, her hem rose up to reveal her panties. "What do you think of her?"

He looked at her and then down, as she wriggled and adjusted her skirt.

"The car, I mean, you naughty boy!"

"It's beautiful", he said, "just stunning…"

She didn't take him all the way to the van in case someone spotted her, but she dropped him close enough. She would claim he was a hitch-hiker, if she ever had to explain herself. "I won't be coming back to the club. Here's the key to the side door. Let yourself in and lock it. Let yourselves out and relock it. If anyone sees you, say I was called away. Unless they see you with the Croatian, then I have no idea what you're doing.

"When you've loaded him into the van, drop the key into the letterbox of the main building. I'll get it in the morning. Good luck, Charlie. I'll phone Claude later, but don't worry, I won't tell him that you were staring at my legs or what you were thinking" and with that she sped off leaving him in a cloud of dust.

She drove down the mountain to the beach in Fuengirola and then turned left to Los Boliches. She wanted a busy bar/restaurant and one that her father owned so that the manager would remember her being there. She imagined that the Sandcastle not far past the Yaramar Hotel would fit the bill nicely. She parked the car out the front as it was still early, went in, sat at the bar and ordered a cold San Miguel. It was twenty to eight.

One of the waitresses warned Sammy the manager that the boss' daughter was at the bar, and he soon made an appearance. They chatted pleasantly for ten minutes and Daisy assured him that she was there for pleasure only, not business. She explained that she had gone for a fast drive after work and was choking on dust, so she had fancied a few cold ones before going home. He offered her a meal to go with them.

She looked at her watch, eight o'clock, they would be on the move by now.

"I couldn't eat a full meal, Sammy, but a plate of tapas would be nice. Something to soak up the beer so I don't get nabbed by the police. I want to be home by about nine anyway. Thanks".

"I'll see to that myself right away! We've got some lovely, really fresh prawns, a few marinated abalone, some Palma ham and some special old cheese… OK?"

"Perfect, Sam".

"And I'll send you over another San Mig as well".

She smiled at him as he walked off and scanned the dozen or so people in the bar. She didn't know any of them, but that didn't matter.

At eight twenty, she received a text message on her phone: 'Where are you? JD'.

'At home. See you for lunch tomorrow same place', she texted back.

She was glad that that episode was behind her although she had found it exciting at times. She wondered how some people could live every day of their lives with that kind of stress, but supposed that it got easier with practice. She also wondered whether she would miss the thrill of having a man with whom she could do with whatever she wanted, and what her newly-formed team was going to do next?

∞

"You're late. That's not like you. Anything happen?" asked Claude when she eventually arrived for lunch.

"No, just work, sorry". The truth was that she was glad it was all over and forget all about it - pretend it had only been a bad dream.

"Have you ordered yet?" she noticed his glass of mineral water with gas. She knew that he only drank alcohol when he was with her.

"No, I was waiting for you".

"OK, well, I'll have a chicken salad and half a bottle of white wine".

Claude doubled the order for the two of them, and started his story as soon as the waiter had left.

"Those tablets didn't put him out completely, so I had to hit him, but then we got him into the van and drove down to the roundabout on San Cristobal and de Coin in Fuengirola. It was quiet, so I stalled the van while the other two dragged him into the central bushes, then I picked them up on the other side of the roundabout. Oh, we left him still taped up, but I put his arms in front of him so he could pull the tape off his mouth and use his teeth to free his hands when he woke up.

"Good idea".

He nodded at the compliment. "Then François drove me back to get my car, and Charlie dumped the van in in the car park at the Miramar, and presumably went for a drink, knowing him. I went back to my club, which was locking up, picked up a load of papers I didn't need and went for a meal – alone. I was hoping that I might share it with you, but if you were tired, I understand. Did you sleep well?"

"Not really. I didn't know how things had gone, so I was worrying that you'd get caught..." she lied.

"But I told you by text that we had finished. JD, 'job done', no?"

"Yes, I understood that, but I still worried about you".

"Oh, how sweet", he put his hand on hers, but she slid it out to pick up her fork and continue eating.

"So, that's it then. I owe you all some money. How much?"

"I do not want paying! I did it because I love you, but you may pay the others, if you like. They will not refuse and will help again next time you have a problem".

"Sure, a thousand each?"

"Perhaps two... it was very unpleasant in The Cave".

"OK, two thousand each it is. I'll let you have it tomorrow. Can you pop by the office after lunch to pick it up?"

"I would rather pick it up here and have lunch with you".

"Yes, all right. At about the same time… I have a heavy schedule this week…"

"Is everything all right, my sweet? You look tense, nervous… uncomfortable. Have I done anything to upset you?"

"No, I'm fine, really I am", she said tapping his hand with her palm. "Don't worry, about me, I'm just glad it's all over, that's all. The release of nervous tension, I expect. Can you order me a half carafe of house wine, and then I had better be getting back to work".

He did so, but thought it strange. Daisy had never before asked him to order for her, yet this was the second time in one day. He knew that something was wrong, but couldn't work out what. However, Daisy didn't know either, so what chance did he have?

∞

The next morning, she was still not feeling any better. She knew that something was wrong, but had never experienced an illness like it. The pit of her stomach was churning, as if she were about to sit an important examination and her head ached as if she had a heavy bout of the flu, but she was anxious as if in a hangover after a drinking session that she could no longer remember. It crossed her mind that it might be food poisoning. She had that before, several times, but could not remember it being like this. She thought that there might be gradations of food poisoning, with perhaps shellfish being the most serious and bread on the turn the least.

She hoped that a hearty breakfast would settle her stomach. She greeted her parents, put ham and scrambled eggs on her plate and picked up the local paper., which she glanced through as she was eating, until she saw the bottom of the second page.

'Naked Man Found on Fuengirola Roundabout Delirious'

Palpitations of the heart were now added to her list of ailments. She read on.

'A naked man covered in excrement was found by early morning commuters on Tuesday wandering on the roundabout on San Cristobal and the Camino de Coin. Police and an ambulance were called. He is still in a state of shock in an undisclosed hospital, but is said not to be in danger. It is not known whether his condition was due to the use of recreational drugs. The police are asking that anyone who has any knowledge about the case presents themselves to the Local Police Station in Fuengirola, where all information will be treated confidentially, or rings the Police Freephone Line anonymously'.

"What is it, dear? You've turned as white as a sheet!" said her mother.

"Oh, nothing, Mum. I haven't been feeling a hundred percent for the last two days, and reading this piece about a drugged man in Fuengirola has sort of upset me, but Heaven knows why it should".

"Show me, dear", her father lowered his paper and awaited his turn to read it.

"A drug-crazed, drunken bloody holiday-maker, no doubt. Probably from the UK too. They usually are. it makes me ashamed to be British, it really does. Pass it over here, when you've finished, love".

"It doesn't say that he's British".

"Maybe not, but he probably is – they usually are, aren't they?"

"Excuse me, I feel sick". Daisy rushed out of the room covering her mouth.

"Not pregnant, is she?" asked John.

"I don't know, dear… I shouldn't think so. She hasn't said anything".

"I hope not, that's all we bloody need!"

Daisy resisted the advice of her mother to stay at home for the day, so that the doctor could come and take a look at her, but she did promise to come home after lunch if she wasn't feeling any better by then. Her mother gave her a strip of Paracetamol tablets and bade her take two right away, which she did just to please her.

"Take two more with your lunch, dear. I hope they do the trick", she said as Daisy left for her car. Her first stop was at the bank to pick up some money. She withdrew five thousand Euros after a sudden panic attack that the police might check out everyone who had withdrawn four thousand that week, which her two men might claim they were paid, if they were picked up because they had somehow given away their identity to their captive.

Driving up to the club later, she had to laugh at herself for worrying about such an off-chance. She sat in her office and opened her laptop, but she had no power of concentration, absolutely none. In stark contrast to the day before, she couldn't wait to go to the restaurant for lunch, or start drinking wine anyway. By eleven o'clock, she could take it no longer, told Carlos she was going for an early lunch and grove down to the hotel, where she ordered a bottle of red Rioja, then she went to call Claude, but thought better of it. She would sit alone until he arrived in a few hours' time.

The manager tried to talk to her, but she got rid of him politely, and stared out of the window, an open newspaper in front of her as a decoy, because she wasn't reading it.

∞

Daisy was just finishing her second bottle of wine and had already eaten by the time Claude arrived although he was on time. It was quite plain that she was not happy.

"You do not look like my happy little cabbage today. What is it?" If he had been hoping to bring a smile to her face, he had seriously underestimated her mood.

"I am nobody's bloody cabbage today or any other day, got it? Did you see the paper this morning?"

"Got it. Yes, I did, but what is the matter?"

"I don't know, I'm not a bloody doctor either. I just feel awful, that's all... all over. From head to stomach. I'm just waiting to get, thrush, the trots and an ingrowing toenail and I'll be a complete wreck. I think it might be food poisoning. How long does that take to show itself?"

"Different types, different times. With shellfish it is usually within hours, but with campylobacter it can take two, five, even ten to fourteen days".

"Jesus, how do you get that one?"

"I got mine from rice that had been kept warm, but not warm enough, for too long. It is very serious, the public health inspector had to check the hotel I was staying at. It is almost as serious as salmonella".

"I've probably got that then, at least I feel as if it's serious".

"In that case, you need to see a doctor, my dear"

"Yes, all right, you sound like my mother now. I'll have another bottle of wine, and then you can drive me home in my car. Someone will drop you back up here for yours".

"I sound like your mother because we both care about you. If you are going to see the doctor, do you think you ought to do it on three bottles of wine?"

"Señor, mas una botella vino, por favor!" she shouted.

"OK, OK, you win, I give up".

"Don't ever tell me what to do, Claude. There are only two people in the world who have the right to try to do that and you are neither of them. Now, order your meal and we'll leave when you've finished".

∞

Dr de Souza examined Daisy in her bed at home that afternoon.

"I can't find anything wrong with you Daisy, so I'd like you to undergo some simple tests at the local hospital. Obviously, you cannot do that today because of your high level of intoxication, but take this note to give them any time tomorrow, and they will know what I want them to do. All in all, it should take about an hour. One further question, before I leave you to rest. Have you had a fall recently, or bumped your head?"

"No, doctor, why?"

"Some of your symptoms resemble those of concussion: nausea, vomiting, headaches. Do you feel stressed or confused?"

"I always feel stressed, doctor, but I don't feel confused. I have felt anxiety a few times... as if I've forgotten to do something important or I'm doing something the wrong way... like panic attacks, I suppose".

"Yes, well take these mild sedatives, they should help that, and a couple of sleeping tablets, but only if you need them. An omelette without spices, or milk and cornflakes might help your stomach. You can have an early breakfast, but nothing after eight am. No diarrhoea, is there?"

"No, doctor, I'm expecting that at any moment".

"Why?"

"Oh, it was just a silly joke. I told a friend that if I had thrush, the trots and an ingrowing toenail, I would be a complete wreck".

"Oh, yes, I see. Very good, well, let's hope we can stop whatever it is before it gets that far. The sooner you have those tests done, the sooner we will get the results and the sooner we will be able to help you, Daisy. I'll see myself out. Bye".

Teresa waylaid her in the hall, but the doctor had nothing to tell her, so she walked her to her car. "Er, doctor, you don't think that Daisy is, er, in the family way, do you?"

"I don't know, I didn't test for pregnancy. There are plenty of OTC test kits in the chemists, you can do that yourself, unless you would like me to add it to the list of tests for Daisy to undergo tomorrow?"

"Yes, please", smiled Teresa, "it would be nice to know for sure".

"Sure, I understand. I'll phone when we have the results... perhaps tomorrow, but probably the day after. Make sure she gets plenty of rest until then. Bye, Mrs. Baltimore", she said and waved her goodbye.

Daisy waited for her mother to come in and ask her how she was, told her what the doctor had recommended she have for dinner and asked for it to be served in her room. Then when her mother had left, she opened the fridge, took out a bottle of wine and lay on the sofa in front of the satellite TV to watch a film and drink it. She had bad feelings about everything, but alcohol seemed to push them to the back of her mind - at least for a while.

"We should have killed him, that was our one big mistake, our only mistake", she said to herself quietly. "You hear the advice in all the gangster films - dead men tell no tales. Next time there will be no loose ends.

12 REPERCUSSIONS

Daisy's hangover prevented her from eating the breakfast that she had ordered for seven thirty, but she ate a fresh one at ten thirty and enjoyed it, then she got ready and a gardener drove her to the hospital in Marbella. Ninety-five minutes later, she was sitting in a taxi on her way back home and looking forward to something to drink. She fancied lounging around the pool with a few beers and a book. At least nobody would bother her there, as it was her parents' day for the chiropodist again.

She put on her bikini and some sun cream, and phoned the kitchen to bring her a cold box of San Miguel's and a plate of tapas to go with her two Paracetamol tablets. It was a relaxing afternoon, but her brain was racing and she couldn't shake off the fear that something was wrong, although she still had no idea what that might be.

At one point, it got so bad that she had to talk to herself aloud to calm herself down. Sometimes, she even fancied that she could hear voices, but she managed to persuade herself that it was only her conscience. When she tried to remember later what the voices had been saying to her, she could not. It was as if meanings were being conveyed to her without memorable words.

She felt like crying several times, but just poured the beer down her throat until she fell asleep in the warm afternoon sun.

When her parents returned, she retired to her room to continue drinking and dozing in front of the television.

She had left her mobile in the bedroom, because she knew that Claude would pester her and she told the man on the gate to admit no-one who wanted to see her. On her way to the bathroom, she checked the muted phone: there were thirteen calls and messages from Claude, but she wasn't interested.

∞

At ten o'clock, bored with watching films, she checked her Facebook page. There wasn't much new except adverts and a private message from Claude. She sighed, opened it and read: 'I need to see you ASAP, something serious has happened.'

She replied with a simple 'OK, lunch?''.

She really couldn't think what it might be, but in her highly-strung state of mind, her imagination wandered far and wide. It really was the last type of news that she needed so late at night. She took another beer from the fridge and tried to follow a new film, but it was very difficult. Until gone five in the morning, she drank, dozed off, woke up from some shocking dream or nightmare, and watched television, then at eight, her alarm rang for breakfast. She cursed for not having switched it off the night before, disabled it, and went back to sleep.

When she woke up hours later to use the toilet, she noticed that the time was one fourteen. She checked her Facebook. There was another PM from Claude: "Meet me in Raoul's, Mijas at two'.

'Make it three', she replied. It wasn't far, but she was in dire need of a shower before heading to the secluded restaurant. Few other than locals knew about it. It was the kind of small, cosy, atmospheric venue to take a secret lover. She hoped that wasn't the reason for their meeting.

She got ready to go out, tip-toed through the hall, noticed a letter from the hospital, but left it there and hurried to her car. She wasn't in the mood for pleasantries with anyone. Once on the road outside, she stopped, took two Paracetamols from her bag and drove on.

"Hi", she said in greeting sitting down. "I hope all this was really necessary. I feel like death warmed up".

"As it happens, that is a rather apt choice of words". The waiter stepped up and Claude indicated that Daisy should choose first.

"A carafe of chilled house white and a raw steak with green salad, please".

"Chicken and salad for me, please. Two glasses for the wine".

"Why apt and which ones?"

"Charlie is dead, and François has disappeared".

"How… er, why?"

"I don't know all the details, but there are rumours in the Underworld. It seems that Charlie went on a binge when he was paid off and started telling his friends about what happened in The Cave. We don't know exactly how much detail he gave, but the barman in the Pegasus overheard him saying something about his boss putting a dog's collar of barbed wire around the bloke's balls and pulling it tight. He said that his boss had called it a tawse, but he and his mates had nicknamed it Daisy's Chain. François said that by mates, he was referring to me and him. So, François left last night. If they link me to it, then it will soon become obvious who Daisy is, won't it"

"What happened to Charlie?"

"You don't want to know?"

"Don't tell me what I want!"

"He was found on the same roundabout, covered in blood and bruises. He had been castrated and then shot through the head".

"The stupid bastard… the poor, stupid bastard". Her eyes never left Claude's, but there were no tears in them and he couldn't read them. "Are you going to leave as well?"

"I have thought about it, but I have many connections in the Dojo, so I think that I will get advance warning if there is going to be a strike on me".

"And on me?"

"I don't know, sorry…"

She put her knife and fork down and drained her glass. Claude refilled it for her and topped up his own. She sat back in her chair and let out a long, pitiful sigh. Then Claude could see tiredness, stress and confusion in her eyes. She was way out of her depth and was beginning to realise it.

"Surely, you father would hear if something was about to go down?"

"Perhaps, but I would have to alert him to the possibility, and that would mean telling him what we did... and I don't fancy that idea one little bit".

"No, I don't suppose you would, but it might be safer".

She didn't react. Her mind was racing with possibilities, but seemed frozen in time too. She knew that she was thinking, but couldn't remember what she had been thinking about even seconds before. It was as if her thoughts were playing on a short, continuous, garbled loop.

What Claude interpreted as deep thought when he looked at her face, was in fact a reflection of 'nothing going on' - inaction and turpitude.

His hopes that she would come up with a solution were doomed to be disappointed.

"What do you think we ought to do?" she asked.

"What, me or you?"

"Well, both, but whatever happened to 'us'?"

"I have already told you about me. If I hear any whispers about me, I will probably take off, and if I hear anything about you, I will tell you. However, I am bound to say that I think that you and your family are in a better position to weather a storm than I am alone. C'est vrai, ne-c'est-pas?".

No reaction, simply because she didn't know.

"I think it would be a good idea not to be seen in public together though. It might delay a connection between us, if one of us falls under their suspicion".

She readily agreed, but not for the reason he gave. She had been looking for a way to dump him for a while, and this was his own suggestion. "Yes, OK. Who do you think 'they' are?"

"I'm not sure. He is Croatian and the night club is owned by Russians, but he could have been working for anyone. I'm trying to find out, but you can't be too obvious, or people will wonder why you're interested".

They kissed briefly in the foyer of Raoul's, little knowing that that would be the last time they ever saw one another. Once off the mountain, they went their separate ways.

Daisy went back to her sofa, television and beer, but had nightmares when she slept. At three fourteen, the alarm of a message arriving on her phone woke her up. She had not switched it off, because all messages now were potentially very important. This one certainly was. It read:

'I have hit the road. Watch the news. Love C'.

She returned to the television and flicked through the local TV stations: Marbella, Mijas, Malaga, Fuengirola, but there was nothing. Not fifteen minutes later, there was an urgent news flash:

'There are reports of an explosion at a martial arts centre in Fuengirola. We should be able to go over to our reporter on the scene now. Hello, Paco Perez, can you hear me?"

"Yes, Jesus, I can hear you loud and clear. I am standing outside the Samurai Sword martial arts centre in Fuengirola. There are flames and smoke from an unexplained explosion that took place approximately twenty-four minutes ago. No-one is thought to have been inside, but the fire is still too hot to go in and check, although fire fighters are already on the scene'.

There followed footage of smoke billowing out of non-existent doors, and flashes of yellow fire inside. Firemen were running around still organizing themselves.

She picked up her phone and replied to Claude's text. 'It's on TV now. Gutted. Are you OK?'.

'Yes, kilometres away and moving fast. I will dump this SIMM after this message to prevent tracking. Suggest you do same. Goodbye, my love. C.'.

She swiftly replied with: 'Goodbye, love'.

She didn't love him and felt hypocritical writing it, but she wanted him to gain some comfort from her. He was, after all, the closest thing she had had to a friend for some time. She removed the SIMM from her phone, wrapped it in toilet paper and flushed it down the loo.

Now she had some serious thinking to do. Her team had evaporated and she was more isolated than ever.

She took another bottle from the fridge, and resumed her place on the couch. They were still reporting on the blaze, but they were only repeating themselves. They still knew nothing that she wanted to know, or they weren't making it public, if they did. She turned the volume down low, and remembered the hospital letter, but thought that it could wait.

She decided to review her situation. The first thought that she had was that she was on her own.

"I'm on my own, all on my sodding own", she said out loud. She repeated it over and over using various different descriptive swear words. She found it difficult to get past that first observation of isolation. She eventually could see three possibilities, but none of them was attractive. She could stay put and hope for the best, flee the country on the pretext of wanting to work in London, or she could tell her father the truth and risk losing his respect. The last option was the most fearful, because everything that she had ever done had been to gain her father's attention and respect.

She had realised that years ago in university, and it was no less true now, although how she arrived at thinking that punishing a man in such a way for being rude to her would impress him escaped her. What could she have been thinking? If he was Micky the Bastard, then she should be Daisy the Stupid Bitch. None of it made any sense to her now. One man had already died, possibly tortured to death because of her, and two men's lives had been disrupted. To say nothing of what might happen to her, because she was now completely alone. '*I could stay in the house for the rest of my life,*' she thought, '*and direct operations from the centre of my web like a spider, a big Black Widow... a widow before I have ever even been married*'. She laughed at the thought of being a Miss Havisham, spurning contact with the outside world except a trusted confidante, her own Stella, although she didn't have a Stella, because she was all alone.

Those two or three thoughts revolved around her brain until it hurt, and she sought release in more alcohol.

∞

She awoke at eleven thirty-three with her now customary hangover, showered, put on her bikini and went into the garden with the letter from the hospital, but before she opened it, she rang the cook for lunch and a cooler box of beer at the pool. She asked the teenage girl who delivered them, where her parents were and was told that they had gone to meet friends for lunch, but she didn't know where. It was all the information she wanted anyway; if she had wanted details, she could have phoned them and asked.

"Thank you, Maria", she said smiling, "that will be all". Maria curtseyed, smiled and skipped off.

The letter gave her the all clear for all the tests, but suggested that they carry out one more - an MRI scan to see whether she was growing a tumour that was affecting her character. It also noted that her blood pressure was higher than when it had been taken at her house.

Daisy took her phone from her bag to make an appointment at the hospital, but remembered that she had no SIMM. She trotted into her office and used the land line. She had no intention of going that day, so agreed on the following at three. Then she returned to the pool.

She decided that flight was out of the question. It was not only not in her character, but it would mean living away from her beloved parents and abandoning the family business, which she felt destined to take over one day. That left whether to tell her father or not.

She hatched a scheme whereby she wouldn't have to admit any liability. She would ask him whether he had heard about the arson attack on Claude's Dojo, and then innocently ask whether that might have implications for her, because of their well-publicised friendship, and ultimately for the family. She reckoned that if she worded it correctly, she might even score points for alerting her father to possible dangers, however slight they may be. She decided to concentrate on that avenue. She could also mention that Claude had fled the country for some unknown reason. That was sure to please him, since he had always considered Claude an opportunistic gold digger anyway.

Happy that she had found a reasonable way out, she ate some more of her lunch and went to sleep

∞

"Señorita Daisy! señorita Daisy!" she woke up to. "The police want to speak with you urgently. They are at the front door".

"What do they want, Maria?"

"I do not know, señorita, they said that it is of a personal nature, but urgent. Please come quickly".

Daisy stood up and Maria handed her her robe, then she followed the girl through the house.

"Hello. How can I help you, officers?" she asked sweetly.

"There has been an accident, miss".

"What kind of an accident?" she asked assuming that Claude was in trouble.

"It would be better if you came with us, Miss Baltimore. We can wait here while you get dressed."

"No, please step inside, I won't be a minute". She rushed to her room, pulled on jeans and a T-shirt, and returned. "OK, I'm ready".

"Are your parents both Catholics?" asked the female police officer, her pen poised over a clipboard".

"My mother, yes, but not my father. What is this all about, officer?"

"There has been an incident involving your parents and their driver, a Mr Anthony Walters. They are in hospital. I'm afraid that that is all I can tell you at the moment".

The police car pulled into the hospital in Marbella and Daisy jumped out. The female officer took her by the arm and led her inside at a trot.

They boarded a lift and were transported up. The officer pushed a button, and when they exited the lift, Daisy saw the words 'Intensive Care Unit'. Her skin turned ashen, and the officer took her forearm.

"They are still alive as far as I know", she said encouragingly, "It's through here". The officer spoke briefly with the nurse behind the desk, then they both led Daisy to a private room.

There were two beds, and her father's had an oxygen tent around it. Neither of them seemed to be conscious.

She looked at the nurse, who had no advice, so she approached her mother first. She took her hand and said, "It's all right, Mum. I'm here now. You and Dad are going to be all right". She felt like a liar or a hypocrite, because she had not a shred of evidence that that was true, it was just something that she had heard people say in films. Her mother did not respond.

She moved to her father and was shown how to enter the tent. She took his hand, but there was no response from him either.

"Dad, I'm here now. I love you so much. Please, please, get better". Again, there was no response. The nurse beckoned her away.

"You can sit here", she said, pointing to a chair between the beds. There will be a nurse on duty twenty-four hours a day as well. The coffee machine is down the corridor to the right, and there is a canteen on the ground floor. Your parents are stable, but seriously injured. Your mother is doing well, but it is more of a challenge for your father because of his advanced age. That is what the doctors are saying, but in my opinion, they should both pull through with a lot of love and prayer".

Having said that, she squeezed Daisy's forearm, and went outside to join the police officers. Daisy watched them chatting through the large window, then the nurse, whose duty it was to sit with her parents throughout the night, came in. They acknowledged each other and sat next to each other on the bench seat under the observation window, but did not exchange a word or a glance more.

Daisy could not shake the thought that this was all her fault.

Then she remembered Tony, but the choice of staying with her parents or not for now was simple.

The nurse who sat with her parents read a book as she waited for a monitor to alert her to potential problems, but Daisy did without. Her mind swam with what could have happened, but it wasn't until she had to go to the toilet that she found out more, because there was an armed police officer sitting outside their room.

"Why is there a need for an armed policeman outside my parents' room?" she asked when she returned from the Ladies'. The woman looked at her and stood up.

"Didn't they tell you what happened?"

"No, but I didn't ask either".

She considered for a moment, and then replied. "It will be all over the TV by now anyway. Your parents left a restaurant just outside Las Lagunas and their vehicle was attacked by gunmen on its way back – presumably, home. I am sure that you will need to answer a few questions when you have come to terms with what has happened".

"How do you mean, 'answer a few questions'? Why would I know anything?"

"I'm sorry, I didn't mean it like that. I only meant that the Special Branch will probably want to ask you why you think this happened".

Daisy shook her head and said, "Yes, of course. I understand. I will be only too pleased to help catch the people who did this to my parents and our driver Tony. He has been with our family for thirty-odd years… I have known him all my life". Tears started to flow again. "Do you know where he is?"

"Certainly, Miss. Just across the corridor".

Daisy stepped across the corridor and looked in through the window, but Tony was silent in a tent like her father. She went inside, nodded to the nurse and entered his tent.

"Tony, my dearest Uncle Tony", she sobbed, "I am so sorry that I brought this down on you and my parents. Please forgive me". She kissed him on the forehead, but there was no response, so she left and went back to her parents.

13 THE PRICE OF FOLLY

Daisy had a lot of time that night to think about what she had done and what she was going to do next, despite the fact that she kept going to see Tony. She had asked the nurses in both wards to tell her the moment one of them came around, but like a teenager constantly checking for messages in spite of the warning the phone gives, she could not sit still and wait. And the reason she could not sit still was not because she loved all three of them, which she did, it was because she had a sneaking suspicion that what had happened to them was linked to her, although she still didn't know exactly what that was.

At eight pm, there was a tap on the window, to which the nurse responded.

"There's a police officer outside who would like a word with you, Miss Baltimore".

"Thank you, but please call me Daisy, everyone does".

The nurse smiled, nodded, scanned the monitors and went back to her book, while Daisy left the room. A detective in plain clothes introduced himself as DI Rodriguez and offered her a seat at the small table where she had seen a uniformed officer sitting earlier.

"I was supposed to be going off shift at eight o'clock… It's my little boy's birthday, and I'm late already. Do you mind if I ask you a few questions before I leave?"

"No, of course not", she lied, her stomach twisting into knots. "How can I help?"

"May I call you Daisy?"

She nodded and smiled, "Yes, please do, I prefer it".

"Thank you, Daisy, why do you think this happened to your parents and Mr Anthony Walters, who is your family's chauffeur, is he not?" he asked consulting a note pad about Tony.

"Tony is more than a chauffeur, detective inspector, he is my father's right-hand man, and has been more of an uncle to me than any family all my life". The DI was making notes. "But as far as what happened is concerned, nobody has told me what happened yet".

"Oh, I see", he said consulting his notes again "That was probably because you were so concerned about the victims' state of health. It seems that your party was involved in some kind of a shoot-out with unknown assailants. Do you have any idea who they could possibly be or why the shooting could have started?"

"No", she lied, "where did it take place?"

"Up in the hills above Marbella. A witness who was minding sheep a little way off, said that your father's vehicle stopped at a cross-roads to allow another vehicle to pass first and was then fired upon. That sounds like a classic ambush to me. Mr Walters returned fire with his handgun and sped off, but was hit, causing him to crash the vehicle which gave rise to your parents' injuries. One of the attackers was found dead at the scene, but the interesting thing is that the calibre of the bullet that killed him was not the same as Mr. Walters' Colt Python 38, which was loaded with .357 Magnum rounds.

"Does that help you think of anything that might help us, Daisy?"

She hung her head and shook it. "No, I'm sorry, it doesn't. There has never been any violence in our family, not that I know of and I'm twenty-one".

"Why do you think that Mr, Walters would feel the need to carry a weapon then, Daisy, albeit a licensed one?"

"In case something like this happened, I suppose!"

"Yes, quite, but as you say, it has never happened before…"

"My father is a very wealthy man, detective. He has warned my mother and me for decades to stay safe from kidnappers by following his rules and Tony helped him enforce them. He insisted on driving me everywhere whenever his other duties allowed. Rich people are always subject to extortion, inspector, it is one of the advantages of being poor that they are not – not in Europe anyway".

"Yes, I see. Well, that's enough for now. Time for my jelly and blancmange, if it hasn't already melted. Here's my card, call me if you think of anything, won't you? Day or night, any time. I hope your parents and friend make a speedy recovery, Daisy. Good night".

"Thank you, good night, inspector", she said taking a few seconds to recover before looking in on Tony and resuming her seat with her parents.

She knew that the ambush had something to do with her and the Croatian, but was she going to admit it to anyone else? Was there any point in doing that? These were the two questions that raced around her mind like puppies chasing one another. At least she now understood why there was a police officer outside the wards. They obviously suspected that there was a chance that the assailants might return to finish the job they had started.

She had already forgotten about the mysterious other bullet, at least for the time being, but she did consider blaming everything on the three men. After all, she hadn't asked them to kidnap the bouncer, although they had done it for her and she had derived pleasure from his suffering. She found that last part hard to believe now. It seemed that that person had not been her and it seemed so long ago. Ancient history about some mad abductress in a Latin history book.

She decided that she would tell her father everything, come clean completely, once he was better and could be released from hospital, where he was safe, which meant that home was less safe and all this mess could start all over again.

Thinking about why they had hit her father and not her, she realised that they had made the connection between her and Claude, thanks to something that Charlie had said either in the bar or under torture, but they had assumed that her father, and not she, was ultimately responsible for the kidnapping. That struck her as odd. Why would they think that her father would want to do that?

She couldn't work that one out. To avenge his daughter's wounded pride? That seemed hardly likely… So why?

It always came back to the same thing: they should have killed the bouncer. Then the thought came to her that it was her own man, Charlie, who had given the game away. Killing the bouncer would not have prevented that, and it might even have made his protectors even more determined to have revenge.

'Even more determined?' she asked herself. 'How could it get any worse? Her parents and 'uncle' were at death's door, and her team was no more. If she had felt alone before, she hadn't known what loneliness could really be like, especially if the gunmen wanted to annihilate her whole family… which meant that she would be next. It was a terrifying thought.

Now she had no father, no Tony and no team to advise and protect her and she was only twenty-one! She wished that she had weighed up the possible consequences of getting involved in that dangerous world, before she had entered into it. She remembered her father's words. She should do, he had said them often enough: 'The deeper the water, the bigger the sharks' and she was certainly in very deep water now.

"Will I be able to stay here all night, nurse?" she asked.

"Of course you will, Daisy", she said smiling, touched by her concern for her parents. "This is a private ward. Think of it as your hotel room in a hospital", but what she didn't know was that Daisy was fearful for her own life as well as theirs.

At nine o'clock, a nurse entered the room with bedding. She made up two simple beds on the sofas at the foot of each bed: one for the night nurse and one for herself. The nurse got into hers immediately, propped herself up on two large pillows and continued to read her book, but Daisy was content to sit in her chair a while longer. She was watching the television on the wall between the two beds without any sound, but that didn't matter, she wasn't interested in the story anyway, the moving pictures were just something to help occupy her mind, which was still racing.

At three fifteen, she awoke in the chair and decided to visit the loo and go to bed herself. She glanced at her parents, but they had barely moved an inch in hours, and went across to look in through Tony's window. The officer at the table started when he heard her footsteps on the floor and smiled at her in embarrassment. She smiled back thinly, but was not concerned. Tony was still out too, so she returned to their room. First she took a closer look at her mother and touched her hand, but there was no reaction, then she went to her father. She slid one hand under his and lay the other on top.

"Oh, Daddy, Daddy! Please get better! I'm so sorry for all the misery I've caused…"

His eyes flicked open. "Daisy?"

"Yes, I'm here Dad", she replied quietly lest she wake the nurse and have to share these precious moments with her. "You're going to be fine, Dad".

"Teri?"

"Mum's all right. She's asleep in the next bed. Just shaken up, that's all. Look, she's right here". She was about to help him move his head to the right, when she noticed the neck brace. Tears formed in her eyes, but she went to her bag, took out her compact and held it at such an angle that he could see his wife. "I love you, Teri", he murmured as tears filled his eyes too. "Letters… look in the safe". Daisy clenched his hand and he smiled, then closed his eyes.

Daisy suddenly had the most dreadful premonition of her life, seconds before she heard the most awful sound of her life too – a loud, long monotone beep. It was the flat line warning from the heart monitor. She screamed for the nurse, but she was already approaching. She pushed the panic button and began resuscitation. Seconds later a doctor and assistant charged in through the door with a defibrillator and tore at the oxygen tent and John's pyjamas.

Daisy lost count of how many times they tried to resuscitate her father, but she only knew that she wanted them to try again. Eventually, the moment came when the doctor looked at her, shook his head sadly and deactivated the machine. She hugged her father and wept. She later had no idea what she had said and hoped that she hadn't incriminated herself. She looked to her mother for comfort, but mercifully, she had slept through the horrifying ordeal.

The staff allowed Daisy a few minutes alone with her father before covering him over and wheeling him away. Daisy transferred her attention to her mother and wept uncontrollably, but her mother was oblivious to that too.

When the doctor returned to check on Daisy and her mother at the request of the nurse, he was concerned that Daisy might distress her mother, so gave her a sleeping tablet. She slept on the sofa soon after, but it was a restless repose, in which she dreamed that her parents were drowning but she couldn't get to them quickly enough because there were no oars in her dingy. The nurse heard her cry out several times, but put in her report that the words were unintelligible.

Later, Daisy would remember the dream and tell herself that it reflected her opinion that she had let her family and best friend down by re-embroiling them in a world of terror that they had spent so many years trying to escape. She further felt totally and solely responsible for her father's death and the injuries of the others. At least two people had died now because of her choices and there might yet be two or three more including herself.

∞

When she awoke a little after ten, her mother had already had her bed bath and was showing the first signs of recovery. A lot happier with this news, she went to look in on Tony but there was no change there. He had lost a lot of blood before the ambulance had arrived, and, despite a transfusion, he was still suffering from his body's shock at the loss and the impact of the bullet.

Daisy thought that it was time to do something positive, so she reached into her bag for her phone, before remembering that she still hadn't replaced the SIMM. She took the elevator down to the shops on the ground floor and had a look around. She soon found a mobile phone shop, bought a card, and went to the hospital café to install it over breakfast

She called the cook at home, gave her the sad news about her father, asked her to make up a case for her, her mother and for Tony, and then have Sal bring it in. She was quite specific about what she wanted for herself and her mother, but left it to Maria to decide for Tony.

"I shouldn't think that they will be leaving here for at least a week or two", she explained, "but they will appreciate having some of their own things around them as they recover".

Maria asked if they could receive visitors through her sobs, and Daisy promised to let her know the minute they were allowed to".

∞

When Sal arrived late that afternoon with the bags, a hospital porter helped him transport them to Daisy's room. He had tears in his eyes as he gazed through the window at the motionless bulge in the bed that was her mother, but he wept openly when he saw his friend Tony and heard what had happened to him - a bullet inches from his heart, crushed ribs and a broken leg, plus multiple bruises and concussion.

"Don't worry, Sal, the doctors have assured me that they are out of danger and should come around this evening or tomorrow morning". He took both her hands, blessed her and then left.

147

Daisy was grateful for a change of clothing and took them into the en-suite to shower and get changed. As it began to get dark, Daisy decided to take a stroll. She was still worried about reprisals, but she figured that with the clothes she was wearing and in the poor light, nobody would recognise her anyway. She didn't have any particular goals in mind as she wandered the streets, except to get some of her mother's favourite peanut nougat in chocolate and something nice for Tony. Her mind inevitably turned to self-guilt again and sickening depression soon followed. She also realised that she had spent all day in hospital and forgotten to go for her MRI scan. The staff had probably tried to reach her on her old number she thought.

Her meandering eventually brought her to The Plaza de Los Naranjos and she stopped dead, for there in front of her was a church, the Ermita de Santiago, and with the sight of it, came her mother's advice. She hadn't put foot inside a church since her school days, but she knew her way about. The handsome young priest turned to look at the door as it creaked open. He was straightening the candles in their sticks at the chancel of the church. He looked as if he was going to come to welcome her, but he continued his work when she avoided his eyes, slipped into a pew at the back and then moved over into the shadows. He had seen that kind of behaviour before and knew that that person wanted to be left alone, at least for a while.

He finished quickly and then moved away from the chancel so that she had an unrestricted view.

Daisy still remembered her prayers and her Hail Mary's, but that was not what she was there for. She clasped her hands together, rested them in her lap and closed her eyes.

Before leaving for his vestry, the priest looked at Daisy from afar. Her pale face reflected the little light there was and looked quite angelic, he thought, in the shadows of the grey stone walls.

Without addressing anyone, she asked for guidance in the physical absence of the person whose advice she most respected. She asked how she could right the wrongs she had perpetrated and how she could make life more bearable for her mother and Tony. She asked nothing for herself, because she was absolutely certain that she deserved no help, not now or ever again. Her irresponsibility had been the cause of the death of her father and the hospitalization of her mother and best friend. She would happily have given up her own life to undo the events of the past weeks, but how many millions of people had said that in the course of history knowing that it could never happen?

She became aware that a steady stream of people was beginning to fill the foremost pews. She checked her wristwatch. It was gone seven thirty and the congregation was arriving for the evening service. She had been there an hour, but if her watch had told her that she had been there ten minutes, she would have believed it.

She slipped out quietly before the service began and went back to the hospital. She still didn't have any solutions, but she did feel better in some indefinable way.

When she entered the room, the doctor was examining her mother behind a screen, but the nurse had some good news for her. Good and bad news for her. The good was that her mother had opened her eyes and spoken, the bad was that she had asked after her husband. The nurse had dodged the question and called the doctor who had arrived ten minutes before. She motioned for Daisy to sit down and then she put her head inside the screen and announced that Daisy had returned, presumably to help break the bad news of her husband's death.

Daisy was quite aware of this and sat waiting to be called to bear the bad news. She saw it as the first task in her quest to atone for her unforgivable behaviour, but she was surprised at how quickly her prayers, or pleas to be of assistance were being answered, as she saw it. She had not expected anything to come of her visit to church and still wasn't completely convinced that the two events were linked, although she had to admit that it was a remarkable coincidence if they were not.

14 RECOVERY

Her mother had been extremely upset by the bad news and had had to be given a sedative just minutes after coming around from more than two days sleep. When Daisy realised that her mother would not awaken until the following morning, she decided to go home and get her the letters that her father had mentioned when he had thought that she was his wife. There was a resemblance, but she had always thought that she took after her father more than her mother. John had obviously been aware of her mother's good looks in her.

She phoned home to warn them that she would be there in thirty minutes and left. She had to deal with the grief-stricken staff at home who had all lined up in the foyer, despite the time, to express their condolences and grief. It was touching to see how much they had loved and respected John, so she felt obliged to stay with them a while. However, she wanted to retrieve the letter and get back, so she promised to return in a day or two, depending on her mother's health.

They gave her cards and presents for both patients and expressed their hopes to be allowed to visit them soon. Daisy left them still tearful, opened the safe and took out two letters: one addressed to her and one to her mother. There was also a stack of paperwork in there, which she and her mother would surely have to go through one day. She relocked the safe, said 'Goodbye' to the staff and left.

She was tempted to park somewhere to open her letter, but she resisted, thinking that it might be nicer if she and her mother read their letters at the same time.

As she was parking her car in the hospital's underground car park her phone rang. It was the hospital. She didn't answer it, but fearing the worst she ran for the elevator and clicked for her mother's floor. There was a doctor and a nurse coming out of Tony's room so she hurried to speak to them.

"What has happened, Doctor?"

"Don't worry, Daisy. It's good news. Mr. Walters has woken up".

"May I go in and see him?". The anxiety on her face was being quickly replaced with a big smile.

"Yes, but he is still very weak. Perhaps it would be best not to tell him the sad news about your father unless he asks specifically. However, he has been told that he is not to try to get out of bed under any circumstances. We don't want his stitches rupturing. His hips will probably be sore anyway despite the analgesics.

"Try to make him feel good… I'm sure that a pretty young woman such as yourself will have no problem on that score". Daisy smiled at him, knowing that he had meant it as a compliment to lift her own spirits and opened the door to Tony's room.

Tony was lying flat out watching her coming in, and the nurse was watching him watching her coming in. Perhaps, he had heard her talking in the corridor.

His face was ashen, his lips a pale pink and his eyes had the same look of world-weariness that she had seen in her father's seconds before he had died. She couldn't help herself, she burst into tears and ran to him. The nurse jumped up worried that she might upset the drips and other monitoring equipment that he was hooked up to, but she was too worried about causing any more damage to him to touch anything.

His eyes brightened visibly when she touched his hand and tears dripped onto his bed.

"Hey, come on, girl. You have to be strong or you'll get me going as well", he wheezed with obvious discomfort.

She smiled and squeezed his hand. The nurse sat down again and picked up her magazine.

"How are you coping, Daisy?"

"I'm fine Uncle Tony, don't give me a second's thought".

"No, threats against you then?

"No, nothing. I've been staying in my parents' room across the corridor…" she hesitated and he caught something in her voice.

"How are they?"

"They're safe and in good hands", she said carefully but with as much cheer as she could muster.

He never took his eyes off hers and knew that she wasn't telling him everything, but he didn't want to push her into saying anything she didn't want to. At least not at the moment.

"I have been ordered to stay in bed for now, but I will go and visit them tomorrow even if I have to crawl there".

"I sent for a few of your things yesterday. Sal brought a bag over. It's in the corner over there, and I went back to the house today. Everyone there sends their love and best wishes. You can borrow my phone to ring them later… well, tomorrow, if you like".

"Tomorrow…" said the nurse.

"Yes Miss Ratchet!" said Tony under his breath, but she either didn't hear him or missed the reference to 'One Flew Over the Cuckoo's Nest'.

"I'm afraid I'm going to have to ask you to leave now, Daisy. Mr. Walters is going to have a bed bath, some food and go back to sleep. You may come back in the morning".

Tony poked his tongue out and they both smiled.

"OK, well, I had better go. You be a good patient, Uncle Tony. I'll see you in the morning. Good night".

"Good night, Daisy, I do feel a little tired".

"Bath and doctor's rounds first" interjected the nurse.

They exchanged smiles again and Daisy returned to her mother, who, she could see through the window, now had her head on the pillow".

As she entered the room, the nurse pointed at her mother, so she went over.

"Mum, are you awake?" Her eyes opened. Daisy could see that they were bloodshot and still damp, but she didn't turn to face her daughter. "Are you all right, Mum? I mean are you in pain?"

Teresa shook her head an inch. "Why would someone want to kill my John and me? I don't understand it... I have never seen any violence around him before... Oh, I know about long ago, but not since before you were born... Why has it started all over again?"

Daisy wanted to tell her and apologise, but didn't have the courage.

Her mother looked tired and distraught, so she kept her news of the letter for the next day, knowing that she would soon be given a sleeping tablet and settled down for the night.

"Tony came around a short while ago, Mum. That's good news, isn't it? I just had a little chat with him, but the nurse asked me to leave because they want to give him some food and a bath and then put him back to sleep. He's already making rude jokes about his nurse. Never changes, does he? He said he's going to come over and see you tomorrow, even if he has to crawl..."

"Does he know about your Dad?"

"No, the doctor warned me not to tell him yet, but he's very sharp. I'm sure that he suspected I wasn't telling him everything".

"Probably. Your Dad used to say that Tony could read what mood a tree is in".

"It takes one to know one. Dad was pretty much the same".

"Yes, they had to be, especially in the early days... but the moment they let their guard down, after twenty-odd years of peace, this happens".

"They are not to blame, Mum. Like you said, who would expect trouble to flare up again after twenty-odd years?"

"It did though, didn't it? If you live by the sword, you shall die by the sword. It's a very old expression, but nonetheless a true one. What goes around comes around, Daisy. You remember that".

"I will, Mum. I will. I remembered something else you told me today and sat in the Ermita de Santiago".

"Did it help, child?"

"Yes, Mum, I'm pretty sure that it did..."

"I won't ask you how, because the messages are for you, I'm just glad that you tried it and got something out of it. It proves that I'm not such a stupid old codger as everyone thinks I am".

"I have never thought that, Mum".

"Oh, get away with you! All children think that about their parents at some time... I did about mine too".

"All right", she smiled, "maybe I did once for a minute".

Her mother managed a weak smile.

"I bought you some of your favourite nougat today, and had your toiletries brought from the house. They're in a case over there with some clean clothes if you want me to get you anything else, just say".

"Thanks, darling, you're a good girl. Perhaps tomorrow. I would love a small piece of nougat now though". Daisy went to her bag.

"Can my mother have a small piece now, please?"

The nurse looked inside the paper bag and nodded. Daisy offered her a piece and she took one smiling. "I like chocolate nougat too. Oh, and this is the best... the chocolate is so thick and crisp". Daisy offered her a second piece and then took one out for her mother and herself. At this rate, she would have to buy another three hundred grammes the next day.

"Shall I swing the TV around for you, Mum? We can sit and watch it together".

"No, I'm not in the mood for all the bad news they show on there. I've had enough recently to last me a lifetime". Daisy straightened her sheet, kissed her, bade her 'Good night' and went to her bed on the couch. She flicked on the TV, but found that it didn't interest her either.

∞

When Daisy awoke the following morning, the doctor was examining her mother behind the screen, so she went to use the toilet in the foyer and have breakfast. When she returned half an hour later, she was surprised to see her mother sitting on her bed trying to put some weight on her feet. The doctor and a nurse were assisting her, but her face showed the pain she was experiencing.

"I am going to use the toilet in the toilet", she was saying. "No more bedpans for me! They're demeaning. I have to walk again some time, so it might as well be now".

"You will walk again, Mrs. Baltimore, there is no question about that, but your legs and hips are still badly bruised..."

"I don't care, doctor..."

"At least let me send the nurse for a walking frame..."

"I don't have that long to wait. I want to go now!"

Daisy stepped forward smiling. "I'll help Mum get to the toilet now, doctor, if you send for the frame for her to walk back". She took her mother by the waist, and Teresa supported some of her weight on Daisy's shoulders. Together, they hobbled to the en-suite, and Daisy came out again. "She's always been proud and independent", she said.

The doctor nodded slowly. "They make our job more difficult to do by the book", he said, "but in my experience, they are the patients who get well fastest. The walking frame will be here in a few minutes", and she left to continue her rounds.

Tony fared less well. He wouldn't be walking or even crawling anywhere that day, but Teresa and Daisy paid him a visit. He knew as soon as he saw Teresa that John had passed on.

"I am so, so sorry, Teresa. I will never forgive myself for not spotting that ambush".

"How did it happen? Nobody has told me yet" asked Daisy.

"We had been invited out for lunch by some old friends and Tony drove us. When it was over, at about three, we started back..." began Teresa.

Tony took up the story. "We came to a junction, where we didn't have the right of way, so I slowed right down as an old pick-up cruised across the road in front of us. Then it appeared to stall... anyway, it stopped. I saw the bonnet bounce up an inch, so thought nothing of it when a man jumped out. That was when I should have just driven around them and shot off, but I didn't, I waited. Then the man behind the bonnet started firing and two guns opened up from the bed of the vehicle. I put my foot down and fired through the closed front passenger window. I saw one man go down, then I was hit and lost control of our car. I don't know why they didn't finish us off there and then, but I don't remember anything else until after I woke up last night".

"A DI asked me yesterday what I knew, which was nothing", said Daisy, "and he said that there was one dead man at the crossroads, but that he had been shot with a calibre other the 357 you were using".

"Really?" asked Tony. "You mean that one of them hit their own man?"

"The DI didn't say. He had to rush off to his son's birthday party, but I bet he'll be back today now that you two are awake.

"You don't think that the meal was a set-up, do you, Tony?"

"I think it must have been. Either that or someone followed us up there and put the ambush together PDQ, but that's possible as well. What do you think, Teresa?"

"I don't know... I don't like to think badly of the Johnston's, but I suppose they could have set us up".

"I wish I wasn't stuck in here!" growled Tony. I could get to work on this, if I could get about, but nobody is going to talk to me over the phone".

Daisy hoped that neither of them spotted the relief that that sentence gave her. She didn't want Tony to investigate the whys and wherefores of the shooting in case it led him to her.

"Is there anything I can do?" she asked.

"No, definitely not!" said Tony with too much force for his condition. "You are to stay out of this. Is that clear, Daisy?"

"Yes, you listen to your Uncle Tony, and do what he says".

She had every intention of keeping out of it, she had only wanted to appear willing.

The DI arrived to interview all three of them individually that afternoon, but Daisy had nothing more to tell him. Tony's description of the ambush was almost identical to that given by the shepherd who had witnessed the event, and Teresa was closely questioned about their relationship with the Johnston's, whom she described as old, but not especially close friends, although John had never had bosom buddies, he had not been the type. They had been asked to help them celebrate their twentieth 'wedding' anniversary, and had gone because they had no reason not to. The DI had seemed to be satisfied with their stories and had left, promising to keep them informed of progress. Tony had grumbled that if he was mobile, he could find out more in a week than the police could in a month.

It was Daisy's good fortune that he was bed-ridden. However, the thought that he would be released from hospital one day in the not too distant future worried her more than the ambushers did.

After the police had gone, Daisy went to her mother's side and told her about her husband's last few moments. "He was very concerned about you", she said. "He wanted to see you but couldn't move his head, so I held up my mirror for him and pointed it at you. He smiled and said I love you, Teri'. Then he closed his eyes and passed away".

They both had tears in their eyes and couldn't hold them back any longer. They cried in each other's arms for several minutes until Daisy pulled away.

"There's something else. He told me about a letter in the safe addressed to you. I picked it up yesterday, but there was one there for me too". She reached into her bag and extracted them. "Here they are". She handed Teresa hers.

Teresa studied the handwriting as if it were an old friend all in its own right, and looked at her daughter.

"I'll leave you to read yours, and I'll read mine on the couch". Her mother nodded and slit the envelope open very carefully with a nail file from her bedside cabinet. Daisy also opened hers carefully, but with the keys of her car.

John told Teresa how the last twenty years had been the happiest of his life, and that he only had her to thank for that - her and the wonderful baby daughter that she had given him. He told her how he had been bored with his life before she had agreed to marry him, and that she had taught him what it was like to be a loving, caring human being, even if he had been a difficult pupil.

She found his letter touching, and could not remember him ever being so romantic or eloquent in person. He poured his heart out to her, often admitting things that that she had known, but he had never told her. Strangely, she thought later, the letter did not make her want to cry, only to be with him and hug him as a mother would a crying son.

∞

A few days later, the patients were allowed visitors and the first and most frequent were the members of their household staff, who always came bearing flowers, fruit or chocolate.

Teresa enjoyed these visits more than Tony, who didn't like a fuss, and she made a rapid recovery once she had started walking albeit with a frame. Within a few more days, she was going down to the foyer for a newspaper and a coffee, accompanied by Daisy, and could have gone home ten days after waking up, but she chose to stay a little longer to keep Tony company. Tony was also recovering, although he looked ten years older than the man in his mid-fifties that he was in reality. On the day that Teresa and Daisy went home, he was allowed to get around in a wheelchair and Teresa promised him that one of them would visit him every day, and that the moment he could be released, she would hire a pretty, young nurse to take care of him until he was his old self again.

"I'll hold you to that!" he said and he meant it.

He was released from hospital fifteen days later on the strict understanding that a fully-trained nurse would take care of his dressings and physiotherapy at least twice a day, but Teresa went better than that by giving the nurse a room in the main house until the doctor said that Tony no longer needed her.

∞

A week after Tony was back, Daisy unveiled her own surprises. The first was that she had organised her father's funeral with the help of the young priest, although they had only made provisional plans so that Teresa could personalise them; and the second was that she had booked the three of them and the nurse on a three-month world cruise. The nurse, Lisa, had already agreed to go, if Teresa and Tony wanted, and they would be leaving a week after the funeral.

Teresa looked at Tony in his wheelchair and he shrugged back. He was pretty sure that Teresa would have difficulties walking on a rolling ship, but he knew for certain that he would not be able to manage it. Still, it was not his decision. He would go wherever Teresa wanted him to go, but it did strike him as annoying that he would again be prevented from investigating the attack on John.

Daisy's nervous breakdown and the MRI scan, which she had been recommended, were rendered almost unimportant in the light of the events going on at the same time. She did not exhibit any signs of a brain tumour and her odd behaviour and symptoms were deemed to be understandable in the light of what subsequently happened, although they had preceded the ambush and death of her parents. Daisy was happy to let it all be forgotten and pretend that her illness had been the result of a slight case of food poisoning.

15 THE CRUISE

Teresa toned down the style of the funeral for several reasons. Firstly, she knew that John would not have liked a fuss, but secondly for reasons of safety. She had talked it over with Tony first and then with the police and they had recommended that it be for invited guests only in case somebody was planning a hit on them. The service in the Ermita de Santiago and the burial at Ojen memorial ground was touching, then the guests went back to the house where a marquee was stuffed with food and drink, the only stipulation that John had made.

It was a sad day, naturally, but John's body had been 'on ice' at the hospital mortuary for weeks, and the funeral put an end to his mortal remains, so that everyone could continue with their lives. The cause of death had been attributed to an inability to recover from the trauma caused by the car crash because of his advanced years. Teresa was happy with that explanation, it sounded less painful and embarrassing than what she thought they might have written.

After the clean-up operation, which was carried out by the caterers and overseen by household staff, they turned their attention to the cruise which was to depart from Malaga in seven days' time. Teresa was determined that she would not need her walking frame, and Tony was hoping to get out of his wheelchair; they were both reasonably confident that they would manage it.

They had to inform the police that they were going away for three months. DI Rodriguez was concerned, but since none of them were under any suspicion whatsoever, there was nothing he could do to prevent them leaving. They did want to co-operate fully with the investigation though, so consented to any number of interviews and said that he may contact them at any time on the cruise by telephone or Internet, which they had been assured was fully functional on board.

DI Rodriguez was determined to make as much use as possible of the time that he had with them, so scheduled their first interviews to take place the day after the funeral.

Nothing had occurred to Teresa that would help him solve his case, but he did have a specific question for her: 'Had the Johnston's visited them in hospital, sent a card with their condolences or attended the funeral?'. To which she replied that they had not. She also added that it hadn't occurred to her to find that unusual, because she hadn't expected them to do anything.

"We have never been that type of friends", she said, but as the words left her mouth, it did seem rather strange that they hadn't rung or sent a card since they were two of the last people to see John alive. "I don't know", she said, suddenly looking worried. "I don't know what to think, I really don't. John didn't encourage people to be pally. He liked to keep his distance. I was surprised that he even went to their anniversary in the first place, but I suppose he did it for me… I don't get much of a social life being stuck in here all day. At least he had his businesses, meetings and such like. He was a kind, considerate man underneath, he was always doing little things like that for me, but he didn't like other people to see him doing them. Ironic, eh, look where thinking about my social life got him".

"You mustn't allow yourself to think like that, Mrs. Baltimore. None of this is your fault. I don't think I need trouble you further today, except to ask you to think about your relationship with the Johnston's and see what you can come up with. For example, years ago, was there ever any hostility, bad feeling, ruined business deal… something like that.

"Anyway, we will talk again before you go. I wish I was coming with you. I don't mind telling you. I could do with a break".

"Perhaps, after you have caught my husband's murderer, Inspector", she said enigmatically.

"Yes, perhaps. Would you send your daughter in now, please, Mrs. Baltimore?"

"Good afternoon, Miss Baltimore".

"Daisy, please".

"Of course, Daisy. Please take a seat. Listen to the cheek! Here I am offering you a seat in your own house. Sorry, I usually conduct interviews down at the station".

"I quite understand, please don't concern yourself about it. How can I help?"

"Has anything occurred to you?"

"No", she shook her head. It hadn't. nothing new anyway. She had had a good idea who the gunmen were all along. She wasn't precisely sure who they were, but they had to be supporters of the bouncer, but she wasn't going to tell him that. In fact, she was going to obstruct him as much as possible without making it obvious.

"Nothing at all, Miss?"

"No, why should anything have occurred to me? How could it? I wasn't there or involved. I don't know any gunmen and I didn't want my father dead. I loved him".

"Yes, I don't think that your love for your father is in question".

"What is then?"

"We can't understand why the attack took place unless somebody provoked it... and the only two likely to have done that were you or your father, but your mother says that he had given up all violence more than twenty years ago".

"So that leaves me".

"It is a possibility that we need to look into. Have you upset anyone, let's say even inadvertently while taking over your father's affairs?"

"No, not that I know of. Tony watches my every move like a hawk, so if I had slipped up somewhere, he would have told Dad, and Dad would have sorted me or it out".

"Yes, it is rather the 'sorting of it out' that I am talking about".

"I'm sorry, Inspector, but I don't think that it had anything to do with any business mistake that I made, but if it did then Tony would surely know about it".

"Yes, I can see your logic, Daisy, and I will be asking Mr Walters about it in a few moments. There's just one more question. You have been frequently photographed by the press recently in the company of a Frenchman… a Mr Claude Bouvier, who fights under the name of Claude the Damned, whose Samurai Sword martial arts club was bombed not long ago".

"Yes, I know who the man is, what about him, Inspector, please get to the point".

"Yes, was he your lover, Miss Baltimore?"

"That's none of your business, but as it happens, no he was not. We were just good friends. Why do you ask?"

"He was six or seven years older than you, and certainly not as well off…"

"And?"

"Did he ask for your hand in marriage and did your father refuse?"

"Oh, I see. Did he kill my father because he refused to allow me to marry him? No. I would never have married him. I was not in love with him".

"He confided in some of his friends that he was hoping to marry you… and now he has disappeared. Do you know where Mr. Bouvier is, Daisy?"

"No, I don't even have his phone number. Here, you can check on my mobile phone". She took it out of her pocket and held it out, but was shocked when the inspector took it.

"Thank you, Daisy", he said passing it to an officer sitting behind him, who seemed to be there for that precise purpose.

"You may go for now, Daisy, but please do not leave the grounds until my colleague has finished inspecting your phone. Would you ask Mr Walters to step in, please? That will be all for now".

Tony hobbled in on crutches and sat down. "Good afternoon, Inspector, what can I do for you?" They had met briefly before John's death, but not in connection with a case.

"I was relying on you to help me further with my enquiries, Mr Walters. The ladies don't seem to know much".

"Tony, please... not even my bank manager calls me Mr. Walters. Why did you expect them to know anything, and why do you expect me to know any more than I have already told you either for that matter?"

OK, Tony, call me Dan. We are both men of the world, and in a way, we are in the same business. I protect the public on behalf of the state, and you protect the Baltimore's. You are in the private sector and I am in the public one. It is also my job to find out who did this and why, and then bring them to justice, and I am sure that you want the same I only hope that our definitions of justice are the same. Are they, Tony?"

"One step at a time, Dan, let's find out who did it and why first".

"Well, that is where I run into a problem, Tony. I would like us to pool our resources and work together - share our Intel - but I cannot do that if I cannot trust you not to mete out your own form of justice when we apprehend them. Do you see, what I mean?"

"We could just work separately", he replied pointing with his chin at the other officer who was tinkering with Daisy's phone. DI Rodriguez nodded.

"Rico, why don't you get yourself a coffee from the kitchen and do that in the garden?"

"Right out this door, and follow the passage round to the right. You can't miss it. Say I said it was all right", said Tony. The officer left them willingly.

"Where were we? Yes, but I think that we would do better together. I have more resources than you do, and you probably have more reliable snouts than I do. Let's say we'll work together and leave the courts to deal with the bastards who did this to you and the Baltimore's. Come on, Tony, what d'you say? Shall we shake on it. You're a man of honour, I know that".

"All right, Dan, you have my word that I will help you get them to court, but then the deal is off. If they are set free or get a lenient sentence, the deal is off. I will not allow whoever is responsible to buy their way out of this or send the gunman abroad for a few years".

"That's a deal, I don't want that either. The only snag is, that this is a gentlemen's agreement between us... No-one must know about it".

"That suits me too, Dan"

"So, what is your opinion of what happened?"

"A grudge, but I can't work it out. John hasn't gone against any of the others for decades. If he had, I would have known about it. It was, is, my job to know about these things so that I can organise security to prevent anything like that ambush. That's how they got us, because I was not aware that we had a problem".

"Could Daisy have upset anyone?"

"I can't see it. They would have complained to me or John and he would have warned me. I would have known".

"A pre-emptive strike?"

"That's all I can think of, but for what? John wasn't into smuggling drugs or trafficking people. That's where the big money is and the reason for most turf wars, as I'm sure you know. John never dealt in people and stopped the drugs about twenty-five years ago. John was an old man. He had pots of money and all he wanted to do was enjoy his old age with his wife and daughter".

"So that brings us back to Daisy".

"What more can you tell me about the ambush, Dan?"

"How do you mean?"

"Who was the rifleman? Where was the body he shot? What calibre round did he use? That sort of stuff".

The DI hesitated, he had been hoping to get more information than he divulged. "I was hoping that you could throw some light on him. All right, we don't know who he is. We haven't found the round or a casing yet and probably never will, but judging by the entrance and exit wounds, ballistics say that we are looking for a high-powered rifle. Probably a high-velocity 6.5mm hunting rifle like a Nosler M46 Patriot and the deceased was lying face down about halfway between the crossroads and your vehicle. He had been shot in the back, but straight through the heart".

"So, is it possible that he was running over from the pick-up to finish us off?"

"That's how we read it. Someone saved your lives".

"So, it is likely that the pick-up took off because they saw their man go down".

"Yes. We have found the pick-up. It was stolen, of course, and had been torched, but it had seven bullet holes in the bodywork... all in the left-hand side. Four of them were 357 calibre and three were 6.5mm".

"Wow!" whistled Tony realising the implications immediately. That means that the rifleman was behind our car at the crossroads and shot the man on foot through the heart from some... two hundred metres?"

"I am informed that if the rifleman was ten metres behind your car at the crossroads, the shot would have been two hundred and nineteen metres. But he wouldn't have been standing that close to you? Would he, Tony?"

Tony started and looked the DI squarely in the eyes. "I shouldn't think so or I would have seen him".

"Exactly, so that puts him even further away".

"That man should be in the army".

"Perhaps he was at one time, or still is but on leave, nevertheless, what was he doing there at that precise moment?"

"I don't know; he wasn't working for us. If I had suspected an ambush, I would have advised not going out. I wouldn't have put a marksman in a field on the off-chance that we might need him!"

"No, I don't suppose you would have. I was only hoping..."

"You have a witness though, don't you?"

"Yes, an old shepherd who was grazing his flock on the hills. He says that he saw your car, then saw it stop for the pick-up, saw the fighting and that was it. Apparently his eyesight is too poor to see any detail over that range and his doctor confirmed that".

"So you are looking for someone hunting in the hills?"

"Yes, probably a lone hunter, and who's going to come forward and say he shot a man dead, even if it was justifiable homicide? I wouldn't, would you?"

Tony shook his head, realizing that was one of the reasons why he was wanted on the team. "I hope you're not expecting me to shop the man who saved our lives, if I find out who it was?"

"No, not really. I didn't think you would".

"Good, as long as we've got that sorted out".

"Well, I don't have any more questions, unless my colleague has found anything on Miss Baltimore's phone, so I think we'll call it a day. See you, Tony. Er, which way is it again?"

"Go out through this window, and walk to the right, Dan. You'll probably find your man sitting by there somewhere. Oh, before you go, were there bullet holes from the rifle in the cab?"

The DI consulted his pad. "Er, no. Yours were... the rifle holes were in the side of the bed. Why?"

"I was just wondering why you hadn't found a rifle round in the cab. There were two shooters on the back of the cab, any unexplained shooting accidents?"

"Not locally, but I get your point. They could have been taking cover behind the panelling when the van took off. See you soon".

When the police had left, the three met up over coffee and ice cream to pool their knowledge. Daisy thought it best to tell them everything that the DI had said to her. "He seems to think that this is all my fault for upsetting a business rival, but I told him that if that were the case, then Tony or Dad or both would have known about it. That's right, isn't it, Tony?"

"Yes, protocol usually means that you put your grievances to the offending party before taking violent action. It saves resources. Anyway, I can confirm that I am unaware of any conflicts with any of the other families".

"Then he suggested that Claude had attacked you, because Dad had refused him my hand in marriage!"

"He never asked!" said Teresa, "but John would have forbidden it. The man was a common gold digger... a gigolo!"

"I agree; I don't think that he could have organised this".

"He wants me to consider why the Johnston's didn't come to the funeral, but I told him that I had never expected them to. We just weren't that close. We went for the meal just to give me someone to talk to... if only..."

"Don't torture yourself, Mum", said Daisy putting an arm around her.

"Well, that's all we have, so we need to think about the matter whenever we have time. I'm sorry, but I have to go now, Lisa wants to change my dressings at five".

"Wooo! Lisa now is it?" Daisy teased, but he wasn't biting and left with a smile on his face.

∞

Daisy could feel the pressure building up in her again, and so went for the MRI scan that had somehow been forgotten about. She obtained the results the following day. It reported lesions in the brain, which were causing high blood pressure. The increased pressure in her head was then thought to be causing anxiety. The immediate treatment was to reduce the blood pressure with tablets and see what effect that had. However, Daisy was sure that her anxieties were not being caused by hypertension, rather that her anxiety was causing the hypertension, so she had no expectation that the treatment would work and it didn't, but then she hadn't confided in the neurologist that she was responsible for at least two deaths including her father's.

She tried to blame Charlie for the deaths, and even Claude, but she was not stupid. She knew full well that she could have ordered the bouncer's release, but hadn't. She felt as if she were on a slippery slope and picking up speed.

It didn't help matters two days later when the DI appeared at their house with a court order forbidding Daisy from leaving the country, which effectively meant that the cruise for all of them had to be cancelled.

"I don't understand it!" she said to the DI, "You didn't find anything on my phone, you couldn't have because I haven't been in touch with anyone you may suspect".

"But that in itself is suspicious", he replied. "Why did you change your SIMM card so recently, Daisy?"

"So that Claude couldn't contact me again". she said quite naturally.

"But why would you want to do that? You told me that you were good friends".

"Yes, we were, but after his club was bombed, he decided to run away. He begged me to go with him, but I had no intention of doing that. He kept phoning and emailing me, so I bought a new SIMM and changed my email address. I haven't heard from him since".

"Why didn't you mention this before?"

"I didn't think it was relevant. Someone had a grudge against Claude, but that had nothing to do with me, and I certainly didn't want my father to find out what a poor judge of friends I was... not in light of my new job as an executive in the company".

"Do you still have the SIMM?"

"No, I flushed it down the toilet".

"What was your number?"

"Sorry, but I have no idea, I never phoned myself".

"All right", he said, "a lot of people don't know their own number, but I should be able to find out what it was".

Her whole world was starting to fall apart again, she thought, as she watched the police officers driving out of the gates.

16 THE INVESTIGATION

As the inspector had pointed out, he had more resources at his disposal than Tony, so his investigation proceeded on several fronts, namely: undisclosed business rivals, the Johnston's, Claude, and Daisy, but not necessarily in that order. Tony wanted to start with the Johnston's. It wasn't that he was ruling the other options out, but if he discovered that Daisy was involved, the only person he would be able to tell, if anyone at all, was her mother, and she was not up to a shock like that.

He asked Teresa for permission to have his friend, colleague and head gardener, Salvador, drive him around in one of the house vehicles. He would not have taken the Mercedes even it was available, which it wasn't because the insurance company was still deciding whether it should be repaired or replaced.

Tony arrived unexpectedly one morning at the Johnston's' halfway to Ronda, north west of Marbella. He could see a gardener washing their car as he pushed the buzzer on the gate, so there was a good chance that they were at home. He heard the maid pause and ask for permission to admit him, and he could imagine the Johnston's' reaction to his surprise visit. They didn't want to see him, but couldn't think of an excuse quickly enough to refuse him. A button was pushed and the gate slid back.

Mr. Johnston met him at the front door. He had been in the property business, buy-to-let in London, and had sold out when sixty-five years old, just before the Nineties' crash. When he had retired to Spain, it wasn't his loyal wife of long-standing that he had taken with him, it was his secretary, forty years his junior. He had left his wife at home. They insisted on being called Mr and Mrs. Johnston, but in reality they had never married, because his first wife would not grant him a divorce. He was thin, mean and selfish, and didn't have a friend in the world. He and John had understood one another, but John had been a much more decent sort of a man.

"Mandy and I were terribly shocked to hear about the attack on your car and John's death". He held out his hand, shook it and then led him through the villa to the pool at the back. "Can I get you something to drink, a beer or iced tea?"

"Thank you, a cold beer would go down well, since I don't have to drive today".

"You have a chauffeur outside? I'll have one of the girls take him some iced tea". Richard Johnston spoke into a walkie-talkie type communicator and sat back. "Now, Tony, how can I help you?"

"Well, first, when Mrs. Baltimore heard that I was coming up here, she asked me to thank you for the card".

Johnston looked nonplussed, but said, "I'm afraid Mandy would have sent that. She's an absolute gem at administration".

He was cool, and quick on the uptake, thought Tony. "I'm here to find out if there's anything you can tell me about the ambush".

"Joined the police force now, have you?"

"No, but I need to get to the bottom of this for my own peace of mind. I think it would help Mr Baltimore's family too, if they knew why it had happened?"

"Yes, well, I can only repeat to you what I have already told the police. Our anniversary was coming up, and Mandy wanted to celebrate it. We don't have many friends living up here, but I thought of John and Teresa. They are always good company, so I rang them and they accepted. It was as simple as that".

"How many times have just the four of you been out for a meal together?"

"I don't know exactly..."

"Mrs. Baltimore says never".

"Just what are you getting at?"

"What is bothering me is, how can assassins plan a murder, if they don't know where the target is going to be? Mrs. Baltimore said that she had only told the housekeeper. Who did you tell?"

They waited for the maid who had brought the refreshments to leave before continuing.

"I don't much care for your insinuations".

"And I don't much care whether you do or not. My boss and friend died as a result of that attack, and his wife and I were seriously injured. Now who did you tell, or who put you up to inviting them out?

"You called it your 'anniversary', but the woman you live with here is not your wife..."

"If you must know, we celebrate the first time that we had sex as our anniversary".

That was clever, thought Tony, because it meant that he could not disprove it. "Tell me, Johnston, who put you up to that charade?"

"I am not prepared to be interrogated by some hoodlum in my own house, please leave before I call the police".

"Call the police... that suits me fine, it'll save me a journey, because that is where I will be going with my suspicions as soon as I leave here, unless I feel that you are being straight with me".

Tony could see him weighing up the pros and cons, and that told him that he was hiding something. In all likelihood, someone had put him up to it.

"Has someone put the bite on you, Johnston? If you tell me, I will be able to help".

"I am sorry that I have not been able to help you, but I am a very busy man, and have to ask you to leave now".

"I'll go, Johnston, but I know that you're hiding something, and I will find out what it is. You can count on that, and I'll even tell you how I am going to do it. I'm going on a pub crawl this afternoon, and I will let everyone know that you have been most hospitable and informative. It will be interesting to see what happens after that, won't it?

"I'll see myself out".

∞

As Sal drove Tony to the waterfront in Los Boliches to begin his threatened pub crawl, he phoned DI Rodriguez.

"I've just left the Johnston's", he said, "the old man is pretty spooked about something. I reckon that someone forced him to set up the meeting with my boss, and I would not be surprised if he now finds an urgent need to leave the country. He's a weak link, so we don't want him to go anywhere. Could you take his passport off him and warn customs at all the airports and borders?"

"I can, but with Schengen, it is not as easy as it used to be… still, I'll see what we can do".

"I took his car's registration number too. I'll text it to you in a minute. Oh, one more thing, when word gets out that I was up there this afternoon, he might need some protection".

"But how will anyone know that you visited him today?"

"Easy. I'm on my way to tell everyone now". He hung up, and started to plan how he was going to play the next act.

His first three ports of call were their own busiest bars. He had the managers pour him pints of alcohol-free beer under the counter and told them to listen to the story he would tell and to pass it on to whomever they thought might help spread it.

He told each of them in the loud way that drunken people talk, that he had been up to see the Johnston's, because he was sure that they had been the willing bait in the trap that had gotten his boss killed and him shot. He suggested that Johnston had almost admitted it, but had had him thrown off the property before he did. "When I find out who put them up to it", he had said, "there will be mayhem, and sooner or later the Johnston's will crack!"

Most of the ex-pat residents knew who he was and what he was talking about and he could see them lapping it up. Many of the sillier, younger ones looked forward to the excitement of turf wars between the factions, as long as they weren't actually caught up in themselves.

Having sown those seeds in a few bars, he moved on to busy bars run by other families. He had to change his tactics slightly, could not take the managers into his confidence and had to drink real beer, but the story was basically the same. By the next day, the people who were most concerned about the Johnston's spilling the beans would know that Tony was onto something, if not them yet, and the obvious solution would be to plug the leak, otherwise known as the Johnston's.

Tony didn't want them dead before he knew who had been behind them, so he called DI Rodriguez again to make sure that he had arranged some protection for them, and when he arrived home, he flew a drone to watch the Johnston's villa. It was going to be a long night, so he called for a case of cold beer to be put in his office fridge and guided the sophisticated drone quadcopter.

Tony passed the registration number of every car that entered the vicinity of the Johnston's' villa onto DI Rodriguez, who had already finished work for the day. However, when he realized that he was not going to get any rest, he went back to his shared office.

"I'll want to know if any vehicle that I give you belongs to a known criminal gang or has been stolen", he said.

"Yes, thank you", he had replied huffily, "I do understand... I do know my job".

"Good, as long as we understand each other. Do you have an unmarked car near the house?"

"Yes. Jesus, you're worse than my boss! He treats everyone like an idiot as well".

"I have put a couple in danger, just as they did to us that day, if I am right. I don't like them, but I don't want to be responsible for getting them killed either. Is that a good enough reason for being extra cautious?"

"Yes", he said drawing out the word into a sigh. "I was taught to be cautious too".

"Good, I'll speak to you later". He flipped the top off another bottle and continued his vigil. However, he knew that he could not keep this up, even though he was officially 'on the sick', although he still regarded the Baltimore's safety as his job. He needed help. Nobody in the household knew how to handle one of his babies, and the only one who would be capable of learning quickly was Daisy. He thought about asking her. He hadn't completely ruled out the possibility that she had had some kind of rôle in the attack, but he was sure that she would want the Johnston's to be kept alive long enough to bear witness against her father's murderers.

At six a.m. he phoned DI Rodriguez to tell him that he had to go to bed.

"It's getting light now, Dan. I thought they would hit the villa between three and five. Anyway, I can't stay awake any longer, so it's completely up to you now. Good night". He resolved to recruit Daisy and begin her education in flying drones after breakfast.

∞

Meanwhile, the police had been making some progress of their own. An anonymous caller had alerted them to the fact that there was a video of The Samurai Sword Dojo being bombed. DI Rodriguez checked it out and clearly saw a pick-up stop opposite the club, a man stand up in the back and fire a bazooka or RPG at its entrance doors, which collapsed inwards milliseconds before a fireball erupted back out through them. At that point the vehicle had sped off, but the licence plate was plainly visible. It had proved to be stolen, as they had expected, and hadn't been recovered. *'Crushed already'*, thought DI Rodriguez.

They had also traced Claude's NIE, his foreigner's identity number, through the business, and through that his passport number and had asked France for assistance in tracing him in connection with at least one homicide. He was now on Europol's wanted list. Rumours that there had also been a François had not been substantiated, and it was presumed to be a false name if he did, because he was not in Spain's administrative system.

The telephone companies had been contacted and Daisy's old SIMM had been traced. However, the police could not disprove her story from the evidence that her phone records provided. Claude had indeed made many calls to that number on the night his Dojo had been fire-bombed, but Daisy had only answered two of them. DI Rodriguez had to admit that she might have destroyed her phone card so that her ardent admirer would stop pestering her, even though the calls might have been about something else, but that could not be proved. The police had to conclude that the fact that she had disposed of her SIMM was a dead end.

However, DI Rodriguez did not feel obliged to share this knowledge with his new partner.

Daisy also did a little surveillance work, but she didn't tell anyone. She peeped around the corner from the Alhambra to see if her former prisoner was back at work, which he was, and looked none the worse for his ordeal. In fact, he looked as if he had just returned from holiday. She was neither happy nor sad about his mental state of health, she just wished that none of this had ever happened. She stole away quickly out of guilt, because she was quite sure that he wouldn't recognize her or even know who she was.

∞

Daisy relished the idea of helping Tony with his two drones from two perspectives. She liked new technology and learning how to use it, and she wanted to deflect suspicion from herself by helping in the investigation as much possible, even though sometimes that was more in appearance than in reality.

Tony launched a drone, controlled it with his laptop and a joystick and had the image that it relayed back to them transferred to a seventy-two-inch screen. He demonstrated how to control the plane and after a while allowed her to try for herself. She found it remarkably easy, but he handed her the manual and told her to study it that afternoon. He judged that it would take two or three days before she could handle a plane solo, and another day or so before he would allow her to send one up or land it. Still, it was the surveillance that was important, not her ability to take off and land.

Tony's plan had not seemed to have the desired effect of flushing out the assailants, so he tried again, using a different tactic. He decided to approach the bosses personally and put his case for a cessation of hostilities at least against the Baltimore's. He knew that, although not many people would call the gangsters honourable, they did have certain codes, and that killing innocent women, when the head of their snake had already been cut off, was one of them.

∞

The one thing that became obvious from watching the Johnston's' villa was that they were not leaving it, and that told Tony that they were too frightened to. He knew that he was onto something there, but he still didn't know which way it would break.

Buying time by offering an unconditional ceasefire, at least for the moment, freed him up from having to protect the Baltimore's, giving him more time to concentrate on finding John's killers.

He needed a way of scaring the Johnston's into showing their hand and in the early hours of the morning, an idea occurred to him, but it was going to take some puzzling out.

At eleven am, he arranged a lift to the villa of an old acquaintance of his in Fuengirola. Tony had to hammer on Ronnie's door for several minutes before the middle-aged ex-serviceman would answer it.

Eventually the door opened, and a thin, ill-looking man opened the door. He had obviously just been woken up. The sun hurt his eyes and he rubbed and then shielded them.

"Tony? Is that you?"

"Yes, how are you doing you old reprobate? Still drinking and shagging all night?"

"Come on in. The living room was a mess; a naked girl got up off the couch when she saw Tony and left but at her own pace.

"Maria, get us a couple of coffees, a scotch and two beers, love! There's a darling… To what do I owe the pleasure, my friend?"

They hugged and then sat down.

"I need your advice, Ronnie".

The girl brought the alcohol with only a sarong around her waist. She put the tray down and smiled at Tony, but Ronnie slapped her behind and told her to close the door behind her.

"Word has it that you have been in the wars, my friend. I'm sorry to hear it".

Tony explained the situation.

"So, I need to force that bastard Johnston to come running to me for protection, and here's how I hope to do it".

Ronnie listened attentively, but that did not stop him drinking his beer. He shouted out loud, "Maria! Where's that frigging coffee? And another couple of beers, please".

She appeared minutes later in a bikini with the refreshments and left again without being asked to.

"OK, I know what you're after, Tony", his Scots accent still discernible, "and I'm sure I can help. Do you have any of the bits and pieces yourself?"

"Not at the moment… or perhaps we do. I first need to know what you want".

"Sure, and before I can know that, I will need to come out to yours to see what you've got".

"No, problem", he replied, your carriage awaits you outside, kind sir. Bring a bag, if you like and stay a few days".

"That's no way to talk about my future intended, er, girlfriend!" he replied jokingly. "OK, I'll do that. It'll be a pleasure to try my hand again".

"You know the score, Ronnie. Hush, hush". He was embarrassed about saying it to an old pro like Ronnie, but he felt that he had to, as in the instance with DI Rodriguez. Ronnie simply ignored him and called for Maria again.

17 JOHN'S PAPERS

Ronnie stayed in Tony's spare room, and Daisy found that she had to do more hours flying while he was there, but loved having him around and didn't mind. She found him funny and cheerful despite the obviously serious injuries that he had suffered to his back. She didn't know about his previous occupation, didn't ask and wasn't told.

The fact was that Ronnie had been the explosives expert in a crack SAS advance reconnaissance unit in Syria until an IED had put him out of active service for good, or 'hors de combat', as he liked to say, ten years previously They're unit had also flown drones, which were new to the British Army back then, and it was Ronnie who had suggested to his friend Tony to get the Baltimore's to buy a couple, since he had known what his job with them had entailed.

Daisy and Tony took up the surveillance work during the day time, but Ronnie did his bit during the night. Daisy enjoyed sitting with him as he told her anecdotes and stories from his past without once alluding to his special rôle. It did Tony a lot of good as well to have someone with him who could lighten the atmosphere.

Two days later they were ready for trials, but then Tony didn't want Daisy to know anything about it. At least not at the time. He spoke to Teresa one morning in the garden.

"Teri, I am working on a way of making the Johnston's reveal their hand, if they have anything to hide, but I don't want Daisy to see what I'm going to do".

"Why ever not? She's a big girl now?"

"Yes, but still impressionable, I think, and what I am about to do is not entirely legal. I don't want her to think that what I am about to do is acceptable. She will be in charge of your family businesses soon and you cannot afford to have her thinking that. She simply does not have the background or the experience".

"Ah, yes, I see. Well, in that case, I don't want to know about it either. However, I think I have a way of distracting her. What times of the day would you like her not to be around?"

"Let's say tomorrow afternoon to start with, and then possibly the following afternoon… and there will be a couple of late evenings too, but let's just start with tomorrow".

"Very well. I will tell her that I need her help at lunch tomorrow. All you will have to do is tell her that you can do without her for a few hours".

"Thanks, Teri. There will not be any comeback on the family, I promise".

"I trust you on that score, Tony, as John always did. Good luck in whatever it is that you have up your sleeve".

∞

After a few hours' sleep and breakfast, Daisy trotted over to Tony's bungalow as had become her habit to take her shift flying the surveillance drone. She was enjoying it and becoming more proficient every day. At lunchtime, when a trolley was brought in for Tony and Ronnie, she went back to the house to eat with her mother.

"I have been thinking, darling, that it is time we went through your father's papers. My English is all right for reading newspapers and novels, but I'm afraid that I will be hopelessly lost when it comes to legal stuff and financial things. Will you be able to give me a hand?"

"Sure, when, Mum?"

"After lunch, I thought".

"But Tony and I are working on a project…"

"Yes, I know about all that, my dear, but I have asked him whether he can miss you for a few hours and he said OK".

She didn't want to give up the excitement of remote flying, but it seemed to her that both jobs needed doing. "All right, Mum, if Tony has said that he can cover for me. I have been wondering about Dad's stuff myself too. I'd be happy to help".

Neither of them knew much about what papers John had kept or where he had stored them, but they decided to start with the safe, so they cleared everything off his desk including his in and out trays, telephone, computer and lamp, phoned for a large jug of coffee and two mugs, emptied the safe onto one end of the desk and sat opposite each other in the middle. They looked at one another as if they were about to go over the top, clinked coffee mugs, and then each took a paper or book from the top of the pile.

"I hope we find a list of Dad's passwords, Mum, so be on the lookout for one will you? I'm going to need to know how to get into Dad's computer records too. He didn't give you the passwords, did he?"

"No, dear".

"Not in his letter to you?"

"No, didn't he give them to you? That would have made more sense. He knew that I know nothing about computers, and care even less".

"No, he didn't, but I'm sure that we'll find them in this lot somewhere. Just be on the lookout for some random words or/and numbers that don't make sense in the context. Like 'iloveteri' all as one word, or 'teri54daisy95'. I'm not saying they will be those words, they're just examples.

"When you have read something, pass it to me and I'll put a sticker on it and mark it in this book, so we can find it again later".

∞

As soon as Daisy was out of the way, the two men inspected Tony's drones. They were both of the same type, modified DJI Inspire 1's with an independently-operated camera slung underneath.

Ronnie was on his haunches inspecting the cradle, but shaking his head.

"What do you think, mate?" asked Tony.

"Well, this cradle wasn't designed for the purpose we need, but then that was to be expected. I reckon we are going to need both cameras, so that means designing our own cradle and attaching it here under the fuselage. That won't be difficult… our problem will be getting the thing to do what we want it to. We will also need to enhance the batteries and the solar recharging units.

"Have you got the three mill stainless steel wire and MIG welder I asked for?"

"Sure, I had Salvador buy a dozen one-metre lengths of wire yesterday, and there's a welder and any tool you'll ever need in the workshop".

"OK, let's take a look". He withdrew a small tape from his pocket and started measuring up. "Take these measurements down for me", he said handing him a pocket notebook and pencil. "Have you got the manual for the drone too?"

"Sure", he said tapping his pocket.

"OK, let's have a look at this repair shop of yours".

∞

The women were finding it hard going. Teri frequently had to brush tears from her eyes. At first, it was just at the sight of John's handwriting in the ledgers and then at certain phrases he used.

"It's no good me looking at all these figures, darling, they don't mean anything to me. Why don't we put all the ledgers together and you can take them away to study at your leisure?"

"Yes, all right, Mum, but the problem I've got is that I don't know whether these are the real figures or made-up ones to show the accountant and the tax office. What do you think?"

"I wouldn't have a clue. I suppose I could ask the accountant for a set of last year's books and this year's up-to-date, and then you could compare them".

"Yes, good idea. They would probably only release them to you anyway. See, I don't know how much Dad trusted me. Did he give me the real figures or fantasy ones to work with?"

"I don't know, dear, but I do know that he did trust you and had complete confidence in you. Perhaps, he didn't give you the real figures though until you had had a bit more practice, eh?"

Daisy started to cry at her mother's kind words and then laugh at her misunderstanding of what she had meant by 'fantasy figures'. She rushed around the table and gave her a hug. "Oh, Mum. I love you very much. I had no idea that this would be so difficult. Look, here's the accountant's number. You give him a ring and order copies of the books, then I can mark that job as done and I'll open one of Dad's special bottles of wine. We can finish the coffee with a brandy later".

"All right, dear. We aren't going to finish all this lot today anyway and there's another safe in our room".

"So, there is, I had forgotten about that one... and I wouldn't be surprised if there is another one that neither of us knows about. You'll have to have a think about that". Daisy passed her mother the phone and went for the wine. As she did so, she saw the two men inside the workshop at the bottom of the garden and wondered what they were up to.

∞

Ronnie looked at his measurements as they sat at the bench in the workshop and made some mental calculations.

"Do you think it will work, Ron?"

"I don't see why not… Of course, the equipment we had to work with in the army was not home-made, but we did have to repair it in the field sometimes. We'll make it work, don't you worry".

"I know you will. Ron, I'm only thinking about time. I don't mean for you to make it; I mean for me to learn how to use it".

"Yes, well, don't worry about that either; it'll be simple enough. Right, I'll get started then. Where are the wire cutters, or a hacksaw? We'll also need some tin snips". Ronnie plugged in the MIG and put on the goggles while Tony removed the tools from their holders on the wall. "Great, now while I get on with this, perhaps you could find something to make a flat-bed… a bit of tin or thin lead, or even a piece of ply".

Ronnie cut several of the wires to size and bent most of them into a flat-bottomed 'U' shape and welded them together to form a wire basket six-inches long and the width of the fuselage. Then he tacked the piece of tin to the bottom of the inside and wrapped it up the front to seal the basket from one end and tacked it there too".

"That should be all right", he said standing back to admire and judge his work. "Now we bend the tops of these wires over ninety degrees to hang onto the top of the fuselage and we can go try it for fit". He hung it under the drone. "Perfect. Now we need a gate for the back. A servo-assisted plunger would push the gate open, but then we need to find one and insert a subroutine into the plane's coding to operate it. That can be done, and it tells you how to add commands to the operating system, but I always prefer simple mechanical methods, if possible, so we could do with a bit of spring wire… like on an old-fashioned wooden clothes peg, but not so heavy duty".

"Would a hobby store stock that?" asked Tony.

"A good one might… or a professional garage".

"I'll see if Sal can rustle us up something. In the meantime, I think that you've earned a beer".

"I didn't like to say anything, but I've been thinking that all day. Lead me to it".

"In the fridge in my place. I'll get you some spring wire".

"We need some sheet lead too, like they use for guttering – any gauge, but as light as you can find to save on fuel", he added as they headed back to Tony's.

∞

"Cheers, Mum, down the hatch!"

"You may as well move into this office, Daisy. I'm not going to use it, and you may find things that neither of us knew about".

She looked about the room that she had spent thousands of hours in since she was a child.

"It's a beautiful room. Yes, all right, I'd like that, Mum. Thanks".

They slowly worked their way through the pile, but the more she read, the more Daisy suspected that these were her father's official records – the ones he would take out with an innocent smile on his face, should officialdom ever come around with a search warrant. She heard a drone take off in the back garden and went to the French windows to watch.

"I wish I knew what they were up to", she said. "One thing's for sure, they haven't been watching the Johnston's' house this afternoon".

"Come on, love. Let's get through this pile and we'll call it a day. We can do the bedroom safe tomorrow. I've had enough for now anyway".

Daisy re-joined her mother, but her thoughts were in the garden, as the plane circled the house, landed and took off again and again. Thirty minutes later, Daisy could bear her curiosity no longer. "I'm sorry, Mum, but I've had enough for today. Let's stop now and I'll finish it tonight. I have to go and see what they're up to. Not knowing is driving me crazy!"

"Yes, all right, dear", she said resigned to the fact, and then in a lower voice meant only for herself, "at least I tried". Daisy heard her and shot her a quizzical look, but wanted to get out into the garden, so ignored it.

"What are you two up to?" she shouted as the plane approached from her right.

"Stay there, no closer!" shouted Tony holding up a hand in a policeman's stop sign as the drone flashed between them at head-height and climbed steeply. She continued to approach them.

"What are you playing at?" she asked smiling broadly. "Is this some sort of game?" She looked to her left where two sheets of newspaper, stapled together had been Sellotaped between two bamboo poles at ground level.

Ronnie thought it better to say nothing, but Tony eventually said, "Yes, sort of. The plane came in for another pass.

"It's still not right", said Ronnie, "I'm going to bring her down". Tony nodded assent.

The tree of them inspected the aircraft when it had come to a halt.

"What is that wire basket for?"

"That is a bay", said Tony reluctantly, "a bomb bay and that thing inside is our bomb".

"It looks like a lump of lead to me", she said getting down on her hands and knees.

"That's because it is a lump of lead", he replied. "We're trying to bomb that paper over there with it".

"Great! Can I have a go?"

"It's not functioning correctly yet", explained Ronnie, "we need to make some alterations". Then he turned to Tony and gave his opinion.

"The spring is too strong. It's holding the rear gate closed".

"It's all we've got…"

"Increase the weight of the bomb", suggested Daisy.

"We can't do that, because it is the exact weight of… We simply can't do it anyway, because it wouldn't fit in the bay", he said to Tony, but we could try lengthening the bay so that the bomb has more momentum to crash through the gate. The 'bomb' weights fourteen to sixteen ounces, so if I double the length of the bay, that should produce enough force to open the gate!"

He unstrapped the bay and headed back to the workshop. "Organise a few more beers, will you, please, Tony?"

Daisy looked at the forlorn Tony, shrugged, and said, "I'll have one too, please" and ran after Ronnie.

∞

It took Ronnie just over forty-five minutes to extend the bay and strap it back under the plane.

"OK, take her away, captain!" he said. Tony taxied the plane into the breeze and took off, but the 'bomb' fell out of its cage when the drone was no more than ten feet in the air. "Bring her down again!" he shouted exasperation audible in his voice. "You will have to be careful with the angle of ascent", he said, but he hadn't foreseen the potential problem either. They tried a few more times without success and then Ronnie had an idea.

"We need chocks to stop the bomb rolling out before we want it to".

"Like a sleeping policeman!" said Daisy.

"Precisely!" he said pointing at her and smiling. He unstrapped the cage and took it inside for modification. However, he did more than add a ridge of solder to prevent the bomb from rolling around, he added side panels too so that it would not snag on the wires.

"OK, take her away, Scotty!" Tony taxied and took off not climbing as steeply as he would normally have done and the bomb remained in place. Daisy applauded them both smiling.

"OK, Tony, now bring her in on a smooth decent path to about ten or twelve feet and about fifteen feet from the target", he said pointing at the newspapers, "throw her into the steepest, sharpest climb she can take without fear of stalling. Do you see what we are trying to do?" His audience looked puzzled. "Remember the Dam Busters' bouncing bombs in the film? Well, that is the effect we want but not on water obviously". Tony nodded, but Daisy was none the wiser and it showed on her face. "Well, you should know, Daisy, every Brit should know. Look it up on the Internet and prepare thyself to be amazed, for amazing it truly was".

Daisy smiled and Tony brought the drone around onto its flight path.

"OK, Biggles, go for it!" Tony guided the plane in and sheered up as instructed. They could clearly see the roll of lead hop over the ridge of weld and break through the gate as the plane ascended steeply, then the lead hit the grass and stayed there.

"Down again!" ordered Ronnie. "Well, that wasn't your fault, it was the gardeners". They didn't catch on, so he explained. "A fifteen-ounce object hitting the ground at that speed and angle would normally be expected to roll, but not on this lawn because your gardener looks after it too well.

"Load the bomb back in, Tony, and take her back up. Daisy, you take the second bamboo pole and come with me. We're going to put it across the drive, where it should have been in the first place for realistic trials".

The next time the bomb hit the drive ten feet from the target bounced a few inches high twice and broke through the paper. Daisy and Ronnie jumped for joy clapping, but all three of them had big grins on their faces.

"I told you not to worry because I'd make it easy for you, didn't I?"

"You did, and you were right, maestro... Thank you very much".

"Thank you, thank you, but that is not the finished product". He looked at Tony and pointed at Daisy behind her back with his chin, "We will need a detonation system to make it more realistic". Tony understood, but as far as they knew, Daisy still thought that it was some elaborate big boys' game.

"Do you have any ideas?" asked Daisy.

"Is the Pope a Catholic?" he asked. "Of course, I have ideas! The only thing is, I don't know if they'll work. As Sherlock Holmes used to say, this is a two-beer problem".

"Did he?" asked Daisy.

"Well, you've already had more than two", said Tony smiling.

"I mean two more. Those beers fixed our previous problems. This is a new one".

"Fair enough. Would you get them to send out a cooler box, Daisy? I imagine that my fridge is empty by now?"

Ronnie had been thinking about the problem for a while, since it had been obvious to him when Tony had told him what he had in mind.

His suggestion was typically simple for him. "We can tie a piece of string around each end of the bomb with a slip knot. If the strings are, say, three feet long, the bomb won't actually be released until much closer to the ground which will increase its propensity to roll. When the strings run out, the knots will slip and the bomb will bounce and roll onto its target. I have timed each drop and the bomb is in place two to three seconds after it hits the ground". Tony understood, but Daisy thought that the system had worked well without bits of string, though she didn't say anything, because they were the experts and it was their game. They made the alteration and the bomb did indeed roll further allowing it to be dropped further from the target, which made the rate of ascent slightly less critical.

After four completely successful bombing runs, he let the others have a go, and neither of them failed either.

When Daisy went to the loo, Ronnie said, "I take it that Daisy is not in on your real intention, so what do we do now, chief? We have to press on. We need to test the strings with the real McCoy. Do you have any?"

"Yes, about a dozen from the bad old days, but I expect they will still work".

"They should do, but we could put two in the bay, if you like. I would just have to add another sleeping policeman, but the results might be more than you want".

"No, I don't want that. If the first pass fails, we can try again".

"Sure, and that brings me to the next point. You did a great job when you have sight of the drone, but it will be different judging the height and distance on a screen, especially at night".

Tony was aware of that too.

That night, Daisy and Ronnie took turns at surveillance and Tony practised with the drone. It was Tony's apparent uncharacteristic dereliction of duty that made her suspect that she wasn't in possession of all the facts regarding their new game.

While Daisy grabbed a few hours' sleep in the early hours of the morning, and the drone that was already in the air confirmed that the coast was clear, they attempted their objective. They replaced the roll of lead with a live, primed hand grenade and tied the strings to the pin and the base, but the knot on the pin was fast.

"I'll try to give you a better perspective with the second drone", said Ronnie moving the laptop so that Tony could see both screens. "Good luck, skipper!" They shook on it, took a swig from their bottles and launched the second drone. It wasn't long before it rendezvoused with the first one and then began its long gradual descent. It passed over the villa's gates by a matter of feet, approached its target and rose sharply. The grenade rolled down the cage, crashed through the gate at the end, and was released into the air. Seconds later, the slip knot came undone and the weight of the grenade yanked the pin out on the other.

Free from the strings, it then bounced and rolled down the drive and exploded under the Johnston's' Mercedes, which they habitually left on the drive. They had images of the sheets of flame as the car jumped into the air, but no audio. The two remote pilots high-fived each other, and then saw Daisy standing behind them.

"You weren't going to tell me, were you?"

"No", admitted Tony. "I didn't want you to get the impression that what we have done is a valid way of sorting out problems".

"Why would I think that, do you have such small regard for my common sense?"

He looked at her long and hard. "You are young; I was frightened that you would pick up bad habits".

She wanted to shout at him that she wasn't a child, but her anger subsided as she remembered how all these problems had begun.

"You could have told me that and still kept me in the loop", she said huffily. Tony again got the impression that she hadn't told him everything either.

"What is done is done, let's see what happens next".

In fact, nothing happened until the car's fuel tank exploded and the emergency services arrived. Twelve minutes after that, DI Rodriguez rang him. He feigned that the call had woken him up and that he knew nothing about it.

"Are the Johnston's all right?" he asked sounding concerned, as the others brought the drones home.

18 THE SCREW TIGHTENS

"So, you did that last night, not to injure them, but to frighten them into coming forward?" asked Daisy after breakfast.

"Yes, exactly. Daisy, I don't know what weird and fantastic theories you have about me, but I am not a murderer and I don't enjoy seeing other people suffer either… and nor did your father for that matter. I am going to try to see them later and put into their minds that the explosion was caused by a car bomb that went off prematurely for some reason. I want them to think that their lives are in danger unless they tell us everything they know. Hell, I don't even care whether they get amnesty from conspiracy to murder!

"In fact, I need to have a little word with someone about that. I have to go out now and see a man about a dog. How about you, Ronnie? Do you want a lift back into Fuengirola? Or do you want to stay here for a couple more nights, if that's all right with you, Daisy?"

"Sure, never a dull moment since Ronnie's been here".

"Ron?"

"I'm happy here too. I'll stay until tomorrow and then see how it goes".

"Fine, I'll be back in a few hours". Tony eased himself up onto a stick and limped off to the waiting pick-up.

"He won't use that wheelchair or even the walking frame", said Daisy.

"He doesn't need to. He's old school. You have to give your body a chance to heal itself. If you mollycoddle it, it might just sit back and let you do it. He won't need that stick in a few days either, you mark my words. In fact, he might not even need it now, he could be acting".

Daisy gave him a harsh look. "He was badly injured in that ambush!"

"I know, but I've seen worse, and Tony is a strong and determined man. Shall we follow him, and make sure the old git doesn't get into trouble?"

"With the drones?" Ronnie nodded. "OK!"

As the truck pulled out of the gates, Tony phoned DI Rodriguez. "Can you meet me in Pablo's Coffee Bar in thirty minutes? I have an idea".

"So, you were up there last night, what did you make of it?" asked Tony when they were alone.

DI Rodriguez hesitated and took a sip of his coffee. "I'm not sure. It wasn't someone placing a car bomb, because there was no body… It probably wasn't a car bomb at all, because they haven't used the thing for at least a week, and their CCTV footage doesn't show any ninjas scaling the walls or parachuting in. That leaves the cook, the cleaner and the part-time gardener, all of whom have been with them for years, and don't seem to have any grudges against them. It's a mystery, wouldn't you say?"

"Yes, a real puzzler – a two beer problem…"

"A what?"

"Oh, it's just something a friend says. Well, look, I have a suggestion as to how we can turn that explosion to our advantage".

"Really? I thought someone would sooner or later… and my money was on you".

"Well, we could", he replied, calmly ignoring the insinuation, "quite separately, of course, suggest to Johnston that the bomb was probably a failed attempt on his life by the people who put him up to inviting the Baltimore's out to lunch that day. We could suggest that they might not be so lucky next time, and that it would be in their best interests to give up the names of those villains.

"You could even suggest that the courts would go easy on them if they turn state's evidence… or you could give them their passports back so that they could do a runner, as long as they never came back".

"Yes, we could do that. It's not strictly ethical though from my point of view".

"Perhaps not. OK, you could go as far as you feel comfortable, and I could be a little more forceful. I could even offer to get them out of the country myself without passports for a little holiday, of course, to help them settle their nerves…

"And if they didn't show up for the return journey, well… what could you do about that?"

"Oh, it wouldn't be me taking them out of the country DI, it would be someone they contacted off their own bats".

"Yes, that might work… nothing to do with either of us".

"Nothing at all – perish the thought!"

"Well, let's leave it at that then. When are you thinking of seeing them?"

"Within the hour, and you?"

"I thought I'd go up after lunch".

"Perfect. Do you have anybody up there right now?"

"Scenes of Crimes – forensics – are probably still there, but they won't bother you. Well, I'll be off then. Keep me informed".

Tony signalled to the waiter for the bill. "Two gateaux and two coffees, that'll be ten Euros, sir". Tony looked at the DI's smiling face as he closed the door.

"I was never here". Tony smiled, paid the bill and walked to the truck.

"Ronda now, Sal, but first I want to go past the gun club".

∞

The pick-up stopped outside the gate, and Tony hobbled up to the police guard and handed over his ID. "I've come to give Mr. and Mrs. Johnston my support", he said allowing himself to be frisked. The officer waved him through. Four people in white, paper overalls were poking about in the wreckage that used to be the Johnston's' Mercedes.

He nodded to them, and one pointed around the back. Tony walked around the side of the villa and saw a 'what does he want now' look form on Johnston's face.

"Hi, I heard about your spot of bother, I hope no-one was hurt". Mrs. Johnston burst into tears and ran inside.

"What do you want now? Can't you see that we've got enough problems without you too? Or come to gloat, have you?"

"May I sit down a moment? The old wounds, you know. You were lucky not to have any this morning, weren't you? Anyway, no I haven't come to gloat or add to your misery. In fact, I have come to see if I can help".

"How can you help me?"

"I'm coming to that", he said taking a seat across the table from the older man, "but first, have you any idea who did this to you last night?"

"No, and if I did, I would be telling the police – not you!"

"I don't think that that is quite true, Mr. Johnston. I think that you do have an idea who it was and the police are the last people you would want to tell".

Johnston looked down at his coffee and brandy and had a sip of both. "Could you get to the point, please?"

"Certainly, but could I have a cold beer first, I'm parched?" Johnston ordered two beers, more coffee and another brandy over his phone and a woman brought them out.

"Thank you", he said after a long sip. "I want to know who shot me and killed my boss and I think that you know who it was. I am not interested in you. My guess is that they forced you to take part either by blackmail or threats of some kind. I have studied you Mr. Johnston. I didn't like what I discovered, but I am sure that what you did to us is not your normal M.O. – it is just not your style… and anyway, you had nothing to gain from it… unless it was the promise not to bother you any more.

"But, Mr Johnston, as they say, 'When you sleep with dogs you catch fleas'. You made some pact with crooks and you expected them to honour their promise. I think that that was rather naïve, don't you?

"To them you are what they might call 'a loose end'. Loose ends are untidy and can be dangerous, so the best thing to do with them is cut them off. I think that that is what someone was trying to do to you last night, Mr Johnston, cut you off… at the throat. Does that make any sense to you, Mr. Johnston?" He downed his brandy and took a sip of beer. Tony could see that he had been worried before, but now he was really putting the wind up him by confirming his own worst fears.

"So, what would you suggest I do about, er, my predicament, if I were to be in the position that you describe, Mr. Walters?"

"Well, having been in personal security all my working life, I would say strike back if you have a chance of winning, otherwise scarper".

"How could one old man and his fashion-conscious wife beat a Mafia gang?"

"I don't think that they could…"

"And we can't scarper, as you so eloquently put it without…"

"Passports?"

"How did you know that?"

"It's quite normal for key witnesses and suspects to have their passports confiscated. It was just a guess based on experience".

Johnston finished his beer and called for more drinks. "So, given that both of your suggestions are quite useless, what are the alternatives, if an old man and his dotty wife were to find themselves in such a nasty situation?"

"Well, generals don't fight battles, they recruit soldiers to do that for them, and Europe only introduced passports about a hundred years ago. People got on quite well without them before that… and some people still do".

"Which soldiers, could this man hire, if he doesn't know any?"

"He could start with me".

"And why would you want to help?"

"As I said, I want to know who did this to us…"

"And take revenge?"

"Possibly, but not on all of them. The old man may have been a victim as well".

"What about reprisals? They would know that the old man had grassed".

"Then you scarper".

"And you could help with that too, I suppose?"

"As it happens, I could". Tony finished his beer giving Johnston time to think. "A lovely drop of stuff that". Johnston reached into the cooler for two more beers, opened them and passed one to Tony. He refilled his glass and held it up to the sun above his head. "The Aussies are right, it's the amber nectar". He took a gulp and put it back on the table. He pushed his chair back, stretched his legs out towards the pool and sighed.

Without warning, the glass exploded and the table jumped. A report sounded in the hills behind the rear of the property. Tony leaped on Johnston and dragged him indoors.

"What the Hell was that?" asked Johnston quivering.

"A gunshot, probably a rifle…"

"What! They're shooting at me now?"

"It could have been a stray bullet from someone hunting in the hills".

"Do you think that's likely?"

"No, not given what happened last night".

"Jesus, the place is swarming with police, there's an armed guard on my gate and I'm still not safe in my own house".

"Being safe at home in one's castle is a common misconception. If they want you, pros can get you any time, anywhere".

"OK, so what do we do now?" he asked hiding behind the sofa with Tony at his side.

"We? OK. Well, the first thing is to phone the police and report the incident. That lot outside are no good to you... except the one on the gate, but I wouldn't recommend walking out there yet. You ought to warn your wife to stay inside too, but first, tell me who put you up to it and why?"

"It was the Croats, or the Russians, I'm not really sure. No-one gave me his business card. I'm only going by the accents. Three men came here one day and threatened us... People think I'm rich... Mandy does. But the truth is that I ran up gambling debts last year and then my ex-wife took me to the cleaners. I've only got this place, the car, my pension and a few grand stashed in Gibraltar. The truth is that you've probably got a lot more than I have. They promised to wipe out my debts... it never crossed my mind that their way of doing that would be by wiping out me!"

Tony raised his eyebrows. The fact that he could joke about it raised his opinion of the man. "What is the name of the casino?"

"The Golden Dream, do you know it? In Benalmadena..."

Tony nodded – he knew everywhere. "All right, Mr. Johnston, go and find your wife, stay inside with her and phone the police. I'll mention it to the guard on the gate too on my way out. Keep your head down and do what the police tell you to, I'll be in touch very soon". With that he went to the front door bent over, and half hobbled and half ran to the gate.

"Mr. Johnston thinks there's a sniper shooting at him from the hills. He's all right, he's inside, but he's very shaken up". The officer ran to the house and Tony got into the pick-up".

"Where to now, boss?"

"I think we can go home now, Sal. That was a good day's work".

∞

"Before I tell you that, Ronnie", said Tony to his friend over a beer in the small back garden of his bungalow, "I want you to know that this could get very heavy. You know... do you really want to risk your lovely, soft life for a heap of hassle?"

"No, I don't, but if you come up with the right plan, you might not get any hassle, and you might need me to help you formulate that. Anyway, what sort of a life would I have if I let an old friend with a gammy leg and a bullet hole in him go into a righteous battle on his own?"

"You've got a gammy leg as well, and a dodgy back!"

"Yes, but I've had mine a lot longer than you. I know what I can and cannot do. You're likely to go charging in there as if you were still a twenty year-old and have to take a puff on your inhaler to get your breath back!"

Tony had to laugh. "That's true", he conceded. "Thanks, Ron. Welcome aboard! Have another beer, mate".

"So, what's the plan? Cheers!"

"Cheers! There isn't one yet". He told him about his conversations with DI Rodriguez and Johnston. "The sniper shot clinched it for me. Carlos, the manager of Daisy's gun club, told me when he visited me in hospital that his cousin's boy was the sniper who drove off the bushwhackers. He's just been demobbed and was with his father nearby when the ambush occurred. Most of the old farmers around here are crack shots, but this boy, well, he's about twenty-eight now, has always been remarkable. They say that he can take the third pea out of a pod at a hundred metres, so I asked Carlos to ask him to give Johnston and me a demonstration. He was instructed to smash my glass exactly three minutes after I gave him the signal by holding the glass up and letting the sun glint off it. I don't mind telling you that I got as far away from that glass as I could without making it obvious, but I needn't have worried. It was a perfect shot. I knew it was coming and it shocked me, but old man Johnston nearly had a heart attack. I would have felt quite sorry for him, if he hadn't been the one who got me shot".

"Yes, you did jump, I saw you".

"You saw me? How?"

"Daisy and I followed you with the drones".

"Aw, no! So she knows about it too?"

"Yes, well, we weren't to know that you were up to no good, were we? We went to keep an eye on you. You have to expect this kind of thing, if you don't tell your partner what your plans are".

"OK, OK, no hard feelings, but Daisy doesn't know that I staged the shot".

"No, but she isn't stupid and she knows that you're capable of doing it. It probably won't take long for the penny to drop".

"Where is she now, anyway?"

"Going through her Dad's papers"

"Right. Well, I'll tell her the truth if she asks.

"Getting back to The Golden Dream. It's owned by neither of the 'official' Croatian or Russian gangs. It belongs to an independent, although I'm sure that he is Eastern European. People call him Jan the Man. Someone told me he was Czech".

"I've heard of Jan the Man, but I don't know exactly where he comes from".

"No, he's a bit of a mystery. How do you fancy a night on the town with that lovely lady of yours? Put your glad rags on and take her for a meal and a game of roulette. A grand ought to cover it".

"What? The meal...?"

"Don't tear the arse out of it! When can you go?"

"Er, I'll give her a bell and see about tomorrow night".

"Perfect. Thanks, mate. I know I don't need to tell you what we need to know, but I will ask you to be careful. Don't put yourself in danger by being too obvious".

"Yeah, yeah, yeah... telling your granny how to suck eggs again!"

"It still doesn't make sense though. Why would a one-man band like Jan want to take on John? Sure, John has casinos and gambling dens, but nothing in Benalmadena. There is no competition, and certainly no conflict".

"Perhaps he's planning something?"

"But he is still small fry compared to John. No, we are still missing a few pieces of the jigsaw, my friend. I'll tell you one thing though, I feel relieved that we aren't going up against the Croats or the Russians. Those guys play serious". At that moment Tony's mobile rang.

"Good afternoon, DI Rodriguez, how did you get on?"

"Oh, I left a completely distraught Mr and Mrs. Johnston about an hour ago. I gather you were there when the sniper struck?"

"Yes, we were having a chat and a few beers like old pals. We were having such great fun, until someone spoiled it". Tony grinned at Ronnie.

"Yes, I can imagine. Forensics are checking the hole in the table and looking for the bullet as we speak. I don't suppose the bullet and the hole will bear any resemblance to the holes in the ambush vehicle, will they?"

"They might do, but that round and calibre are commonly used for hunting in these parts, and if you are suggesting that the shooter might be the same person, this guy missed a sitting duck, the other one hit someone on the move".

"Yes, I have been thinking about that... Of course, he might have been aiming at the glass... a sort of demonstration, if you like".

"I wouldn't know, Inspector. It could have been a stray bullet too..."

"Yes, possibly, but at least neither of you was hurt. That's the main thing. Do you have anything to tell me?"

"Yes, the coffee and cakes are on you next time, and our man may decide to cooperate soon, I shouldn't wonder".

"Well, that's something for you to look forward to, and for me... Keep in touch". They both hung up.

"He's all right, that one. I can't help stringing him along sometimes, but there's a Hell of a lot worse in the force than DI Rodriguez"

"I've been thinking...

"What?"

"Couldn't you make it two grand?"

"I suppose so".

∞

When the taxi arrived for Ronnie and Maria they looked a million dollars. He was wearing a white dinner jacket, red bow tie with white spots and black trousers and Maria, a shimmering, low-cut, backless evening gown with her hair piled on top of her head. Despite Ronnie's obvious limp and lop-sidedness, they both looked the picture of elegance. They decided, or at least Ronnie did, to dine first, so that the management had the chance to notice them. They had caviare, prawns and Chablis to start, followed by a main course of mixed game and Châteaux Neuf du Pape.

Then they sat at the bar and had a couple of cocktails. No-one appeared to know them, but then he did not frequent that village. Under those circumstances, they had decided beforehand to play the part of well-off holidaymakers. Maria was not completely au fait with what was going on, but she liked the idea of rôle-playing for the evening.

They tried complimenting the club for its ambiance, the staff for their competence and the owner for his good taste, but no tactic could get anyone to reveal anything about the management. Maria had a lucky win on zero, which at the time, Ronnie thought was a mug's bet, and collected six hundred Euros, deciding that the night was not going to be any more fruitful in the club, they left, but called into the small, posh wine bar next door. There the staff were happy to show how much they knew about the 'lovely man', who owned next door.

"He comes in here regularly when he wants a break from his own place. It's always nice to see him and his wife", said the joint owner. "Not that the same can be said for all of his staff! But if there's ever a problem, we only have to tell Jan, and he sorts it out for us".

"It was such a shame what happened to Hanna's brother, wasn't it, David?"

"Pardon, I was thinking about something. What was that, dear?"

"I was just saying to Mr and Mrs… er?"

"Grayling, Steve and Joyce."

"I was just saying to Steve and Joyce about Hanna's brother. They just came out of there four hundred Euros up!"

"Sorry?"

"Steve and Joyce had a gorgeous meal next door and won six hundred on roulette! But I was telling them about Hanna's brother's ordeal. Please, do try to pay attention, dear!

"Anyway, he was kidnapped and tortured for a few days the other week. They even threatened to cut his whatsits off! The poor boy. He's bearing up well though, isn't he, David? David! I said that Hanna's nephew is bearing up well despite his ordeal".

"Yes, love, very well, considering…"

"He's such a nice boy. He's a bouncer down at the Stardust Club in Marbella. Do you know it?"

"No, we only arrived a few nights ago, but we like it here very much, don't we, dear?" said Ronnie.

"Oh, yes, I think we could live around here quite easily", agreed Maria

They included the owners of the bar in the next round for being so sociable and 'to share their winnings', and then left suggesting that they would return the following evening, if their busy schedule allowed it and took a taxi back to Fuengirola and more than a few nightcaps.

∞

The following lunchtime, Ronnie arrived at the Baltimore's.

"Here's your two grand back. We had a great evening and won a few bob".

"Keep it, Ron. They can afford it. Did you find anything out?"

"Yes, but it doesn't fit in with anything we know, or at least that I know. It seems that Jan the Man's wife's nephew, who is a 'lovely boy' that works at the Stardust as a doorman, was abducted and tortured a few weeks ago. Apparently, they even threatened to cut his goolies off. He's all right now. It seems that his family was more upset about the experience than he was, but that is difficult to believe".

"Right, I see, but who did this, why and where?"

"I don't know. They didn't say, and I didn't like to get too personal".

"No, but it's bloody intriguing, isn't it?"

"It certainly is".

"We… John, did not sanction this. I can guarantee that one hundred percent... It's not only not John's hallmark, but he's not gotten involved for ages. It has to have been an impersonator, no, an impostor... no not even that... Someone who could have been reasonably thought to be acting on his behalf... That could only be me... or Mrs. Baltimore, but you can rule her out straight away... and that only leaves..."

"Daisy!" they said together

"But why would Daisy do a thing like that? I've known her all her life... it just doesn't fit her character. I just don't get it... but she is the logical suspect".

"To quote my mentor, Sherlock, again, 'When all reasonable alternatives...' You know the family and its business better than I do,

Tony. This is not my call, but tell me what you need doing and I'll do it".

However, Tony just sat there, staring into space and shaking his head. "If that is true, then Daisy is responsible for her father's death... and she must realise that as well".

Ronnie just looked at his friend's face, but was non-committal, allowing him to come to his own conclusions.

"That must be weighing on her conscience..." said Tony after a while. "Pass me another beer, mate. I can't believe it".

"Well, it looks as if it's the only answer at the moment, but there are checks you can make..."

"Yes, I could ask her..."

"...and you could walk into the lion's den".

19 THE MISSING LINK

Tony awoke with a hangover, but also a resolve to get to the bottom of what had happened. He was still deeply shocked to think that Daisy had been responsible, although whichever way he turned the facts around in his head, she seemed the logical culprit. Not only that, but as a logical man, he knew that he had always thought that she had known more than she had let on.

He knew that he had tried to deny his gut feelings because of his friendship with and respect for her father, but if he was going to guarantee the cessation of violence, he knew that he had to allow for every possibility.

When he saw Daisy after breakfast, it was hard for him.

"Hiya, guys, what are we going to do today?" she asked. He said nothing, allowing Ron to take the lead, but he couldn't help thinking that she was a hard-nosed bitch. He tried to overcome this new feeling for her, but even reminding himself that she was his beloved ex-boss's daughter did not make it any easier.

He excused himself and went out into the garden. He found it difficult to look at her, and she sensed the hostility.

"What's the matter with him this morning? Did you both tie one on last night?"

"Yes, we did, but Tony's rather upset. He learned last night that someone he trusted, someone he would have given up his life for, was probably not worth it. And that's tough, because it means that not only is your judgement in error, but you have lost a good friend as well".

Daisy did not acknowledge that she understood or even say anything, she just turned down her lips and looked sad. Ronnie watched her and tried to work out how much of it was play-acting. He came down on the side of play-acting, and admired her for her skill at such a young age on one level.

"I'm just going to chill out today", he said in answer to her original question, but I should imagine that Tony has more to do".

Daisy felt a wall of ice that she had never experienced at any time in her life before.

∞

Tony looked up the Golden Dream Casino, and rang them. A young woman's voice answered.

"Hello, good afternoon. I have some information that Jan Skalovo will find interesting. I am not a rep or a salesman, let's make that very clear. Please put me on to one of your superiors".

He could feel the hesitation of one who is a gatekeeper.

"Please hold, sir", she said and musak played. Suddenly, there was a click.

"Hello, how can I help you? Mr Skalovo is very busy at the moment, Mr....?"

"Walters. I work for the Baltimore's. I think that Mr. Skalovo will speak to me about a mutual interest if you ask him. Any time today will suit me".

Another click, and, "Skalovo speaking. Four o'clock in our club this afternoon. Come alone" and another click followed by a dead tone.

Tony arrived punctually dressed in baggy, shorts, a loose fitting shirt and sandals. He was expecting a strip search and wanted to make it easy on himself. He got his search and was embarrassed by his stiff joints. He was also scanned for concealed weapons.

"Thank you, Mr Walters, now what have you come to say?"

"First, Mr Skalovo, I would like to say that I would like this to be a sociable occasion from which both your party and mine benefit equally.

So, please allow me to buy the first round. A San Mig for me and whatever you're having".

Skalovo nodded and two bottles with a glass for Tony appeared almost instantly. Tony ignored the glass. 'Cheers, Jan! And please call me Tony. Here's to the health of our families". He held out his bottle and Jan touched it with his.

"Second, I would like to say, that I don't think that you're a stupid man, and would not have taken such action against us, a far larger firm, unless you had felt that your honour, or that of your family, had been besmirched, er, tarnished by someone in our team.

"So, in order to sort this misunderstanding, for that is what I am convinced that it is, I need you to tell me exactly what happened".

"I admire your logic and frankness, Tony. It is really quite simple. My wife's nephew is the bouncer at the Stardust...", he paused to look at Tony and he nodded. "He went missing a month or so ago, and was treated appallingly. Anyway, to cut a long story short, one of the abductors was out bragging to his friends one night, and the information that one of our friends overheard, and relayed back to us, lead us to believe that your outfit was responsible".

"That... that is what I need to hear... what was that 'information' exactly. Please, think carefully, Jan, this is vital".

Jan marshalled his memories, spoke to an employee in a language that Tony couldn't follow, and then said, "This man, his name was Charlie, said that the thing they used to tie around Stefan's balls and stretch them was called a tawse. Then he said 'but we call it Daisy's Chain'. We picked this prick Charlie up, and, after some persuasion, he told us that he worked for that Frenchie with the martial arts centre. After that it was easy, because everyone knows that he was shagging your boss' daughter whose name happens to be Daisy.

"I am not boasting about our intelligence, Tony, but really, the relationship is not rocket science!"

"I can easily see how someone could come to that conclusion, Jan, I really can, but it is still the wrong one. I don't know the real answer at this moment, but we haven't employed a Charlie for years; John would never have lifted a finger to help Claude, the 'Frenchie', because he thought he was a gold digger and Daisy has never had any power within John's organisation. Not only that, but if John had wanted to hurt your wife's nephew, he would have got me to do it. No, I'm sorry, but none of this makes sense... and I really want you to understand that we are not looking for revenge, we just want to know what really happened.

"Can I get you another beer?" Jan nodded and two more appeared.

"Tony, I can see your predicament, but I am at a loss to see what to do about it".

"Yes, Jan, so am I… for the moment, but I will take your words away with me and mull them over. In the meantime, it would be a great comfort to both of our families, if we can agree here and now, that there will be no more violence between us, until we properly understand what happened to your wife's nephew and why.

"Let's keep in touch".

"One question, Tony. What, or who, led you to me?"

Tony hesitated.

"That's all right, that says it all. The Brits on the hill".

Tony said nothing then the two men stood up, shook hands, and Tony left, after leaving twenty Euros on the bar for his round.

As soon as he was in the pick-up, he phoned Ronnie.

"The Johnston's are in serious danger. Tell Daisy to get up to *The Finca* - that bar at the beginning of the road to their place right now; wait for them, and then take them to somewhere quiet in Mijas Costa. Then launch a drone with at least one bomb on board to protect her. Time is of the essence, Ron. I reckon you've got twenty minutes, certainly not thirty".

He rang off and phoned the Johnston's.

"Johnston, no questions now, please. Fill one bag with your most valuable possessions and get your gardener to take you to *The Finca*, the pub near you. Sit outside and look out for a young blonde woman called Daisy in a Porche. She will take you to a rendezvous. This is not a joke, OK? You have fifteen minutes. Jan, the boss of the Golden Dream thinks that you bubbled him.

"No, no, shut up, you don't have time to ask how now".

Tony told Salvador to speed up to hook up with the Johnston's.

∞

"But I don't understand how he found out, unless you told him?" said Johnston angrily in the safe house in La Linea, near the border with Gibraltar, a little while after leaving Mijas Costa.

"To be honest, Johnston, I don't care what you think. I saved your life. If you want to go back to your villa, that's up to you. I don't care any more. A high-speed launch will be here at three fifteen in the morning, and I don't give a rat's arse whether you get on it or not. It will take you as far away as you pay it to. I suggest Morocco, near Saidia, and tell the police that your wife's bag with your passports in it was stolen last night while you were out drinking. When they ask which your country of departure was, say anything you like except Spain.

"Bye-bye, Mr. Johnston, I hope you survive and also that I never see you again".

∞

The morning after the drama with the Johnston's, Tony was sitting with Ronnie in his back garden.

"So, how did it go at the Golden Dream yesterday? You haven't had a chance to tell me yet", asked Ronnie.

"Well, I think. He's going to have to go away and think about what I told him, just as I have to mull over what he told me... and to tell the truth, I would rather be him finding out the truth, than me, because I don't like what I heard... I didn't like any of it or its implications".

"Do you want to talk it through, boss?"

"Yes, but I need to get it straight in my own head first".

"A two-beer problem?"

"Perhaps a two-case one..."

"I like those, they're the most interesting... and the most enjoyable to solve".

∞

The upshot of Tony's deliberations was unpalatable, and he confessed them to Ronnie the next morning. "I know I told you the way my thoughts were heading last night, but even after sleeping on it, I can't come up with any other conclusion. Daisy's actions were the cause of her father's death and her mother's and my injuries".

"OK, Tony, you are going to have to put that to her, aren't you?"

"Yes... but it is not something that I relish".

"No, me ol' mate, I shouldn't think it is. You have a soft spot for her, but she must already know what you have just found out..."

"Yes, and in a way, that makes me despise her... if I'm capable of that, because she obviously thought the world of her father, and hasn't shown any signs of remorse whatsoever.... That's the bit that I can't understand. If she made a mistake, even a colossal one, why didn't she either go to her father or come to me?"

"God knows, mate. Young people, women, young women, who understands 'em?"

"No, there has to be more to it than that".

"In that case, you're going to have to ask her. Do you want me to be there?"

"No, I've known her all her life, this is between me and her".

"Fair enough, good luck, buddy".

∞

Tony got the first chance to have a chat with her, when he was ready for one, after lunch.

"Daisy, can I have a word, please?"

"Sure, what's it about?"

"It concerns the ambush and the Johnston's".

"All right, but I don't know anything about it or them".

"Perhaps you don't realize that you do, we'll see. Let's go somewhere quiet. Where would suit you?"

"Outside by the pool? Want a beer?"

"Sure, why not to both?" When they were comfortable, he told her about how he had thought it odd that the Johnston's should invite her parents out for their anniversary, when they weren't even good friends, and he had later found out that they weren't even married. He admitted that he had put the frighteners on them to encourage them to seek his help, and that that had led him to Jan, and told her the story that he had had to tell.

"So", he concluded, "a French guy called Claude who uses something he calls Daisy's Chain to torture a prisoner, sort of implicates you, doesn't it, Daisy? And if you don't think that it does, that was Jan's conclusion and that was what led to the ambush: your mother being injured, me getting shot and your father getting killed. And if I had been Jan, I would have thought the same, and your Dad would have agreed.

"So, over to you. The ball is in your court..."

Her first reaction was to horrified at what Tony must be thinking about her, then her mind froze.

"Daisy, if you are wondering how to wriggle out of this one, I suggest that you don't bother. Do yourself a favour. Every single moment that you spend thinking, the less likely it is that I will believe what you say, so just spit it out!

"I'm waiting, or I could just go straight to your mother. After all, I am officially on the sick... this is not my case".

"All right, all right, this is difficult for me..."

"My heart bleeds... your mother and I spent weeks lying in hospital and your Dad is lying in his grave..." He watched tears appear in her eyes and wondered whether it was an act or whether he had turned the thumbscrews too tight".

She related honestly about the original incident at the Stardust, and how she had baited the bouncer the second time and told Claude about it, but left out that she had hoped that he would avenge her. She said that Claude had told her several days afterwards, because her father had told her to reduce her contact with the Frenchman who the press was assuming to be her boyfriend. She said that she knew that the bouncer had been kept in his garage, and said that that was probably 'The Cave'. She made no hint that she had used the back of the rifle range or that she had ever been in his presence.

"Then Claude said that he was bored with the kidnapping, but wanted to end it 'cleanly". When he told me that that meant killing him, I asked him not to, for my sake. Honest, Uncle Tony.

"Then I read one morning that a naked man had been found on a roundabout near the Miramar in Fuengirola, and Claude said that that was him. I was so relieved, until Claude said that one of his team, a Charlie, I think, had been killed, and the nightmare started all over again, culminating in the ambush and Dad's death.

"I wish I'd never met Claude, really I do. He was like obsessed with me... it was scary. The night that they bombed his club, he rang from somewhere 'far away', or so he said and told me he was never coming back. He even begged me to go with him, but I flushed my SIMM down the toilet so he couldn't ring me again and blocked his email and Facebook accounts. I haven't heard from him since, and that's the honest truth as well.

"I know that he did that terrible thing for me... to impress me, but I had no hand in it at all. You've got to believe me Uncle Tony... you've got to. I've got no-one else to turn to... and if Mum knew, I think it would kill her".

Tony recognised his own tactics being used against him, but hadn't yet made up his mind how much of her story was true.

"You do believe me, don't you, Uncle Tony?"

"Let's just say that there are parts to and aspects of your story that I cannot corroborate yet, but I will get to work on it and let you know.

"Now, Daisy, if you will excuse me, I want to get started".

"Of course, of course! Just one thing, how much does my mother know?"

He looked at her and saw a little girl who didn't want a neighbour to tell her parents that she had been naughty.

"I have never talked to her on this subject, and have no intention of doing so until I am happy that I know the whole truth and not just most of it".

Tony returned to his own back garden, and opened another beer. He had been drinking more since he had come out of hospital than he had done for decades, but he hadn't had so many 'two-beer problems' for decades either.

Ronnie had gone home to collect more clothes, but he was expected back late in the afternoon. Tony hoped that he would have a solid scenario to present to him by then.

∞

He didn't, but he told Ronnie everything that Daisy had told him and sat back for his considered opinion.

"Do you know what I would think? I think that you should accept her story, whether it is completely true or not and run with it. I doubt that Claude will ever come back here and argue with it... not only would his life not be worth a Three-Euro note, but even if he proves her story to be wrong, it doesn't make his involvement any the more excusable. Then you have the fact that your loyalties lie to the Baltimore's. Sending their one and only child to the clink would not be a good career move, would it? And Jan's party feels that honour has been satisfied

"Therefore, just let sleeping dogs lie... why make work for yourself and risk sending old mother Baltimore around the twist? Nah, I would leave things as they are, mate.

"It's not your job anyway, and if the police uncover fresh evidence, that is not your fault, is it? And Daisy's punishment will be to know that her father died for her stupidity, if she is lying, and that she will be looking over her shoulder every minute for the rest of her life".

Tony nodded in agreement at each point that Ronnie made.

"I think you're right, Ron, thanks. Cheers... It still doesn't sit right with me, but everyone else seems satisfied with the status quo, so who am I to rock the boat?"

"That's the spirit, look at the bigger picture... the greater good. No-one would gain anything by having Daisy sent to gaol".

"No, you are totally correct in what you are saying. Thanks again, mate. I owe you big time for all your help. What do you say to having a little celebratory firework display of our own to get rid of one of our own loose ends?"

"I'm all for celebrations, fireworks and cleaning up loose ends, but how do you mean?"

"We need to dump the drone we did all the work with..."

"Gotcha! Let's load her up now!"

They pushed the plane out of its small hanger and fitted a fully-charged battery pack. "A two-bomb solution?" asked Ronnie.

"Sure, why not?" Ronnie cut the four lengths of string, tied them to the grenades and placed them in the bay. This time however, the strings to the pins were shorted than the other two, and they were all tied fast. They put a crate of beer in the back of the pick-up, which Ronnie sat on, and Tony drove them to a hilltop overlooking a secluded beach with the drone following them at a hundred feet. While Tony parked up and joined him in the back, Ronnie kept the drone circling overhead.

"Here're the controls, skip, she's all yours".

"You do the honours, Ron..."

"I wouldn't dream of it, she's your bird and it was your mission, and now you conclude it".

"OK, thanks". He brought the plane down gradually until it passed six feet over their heads and headed out over the Mediterranean, then they shook hands, and he put her into a steep climb. They could clearly see the grenades drop out with field glasses and dangle there for the length of the fuse, which had been set at maximum. There followed a huge fireball and the bangs of the two exploding the grenades. Small pieces of plane floated down to the sea on fire, but there was very little chance of anything traceable ever being recovered.

They cheered and high-fived, had a couple more beers enjoying the view and drove back to the Baltimore's.

224

20 THE WASH

If it hadn't been for the beer, Tony knew that he would not have been able to sleep that night.

Ronnie had been right, he could not bring the real culprit to justice or his accomplice, Daisy, without bitterly hurting her mother, whom he judged to have suffered enough. He accepted Daisy's story that she had not taken part in Stefan's abduction, but he still thought that there was a hole in her story. The problem for him was what to do next, and he decided that waiting to see how things panned out was the best option.

Daisy called in to see him after breakfast.

"Have you decided what your next move will be?" she asked a little too nervously.

"Yes, Daisy", he told her, although he hadn't until that moment.

"What is it?"

"I'm afraid I can't tell you that yet". She had dropped so far in his estimation that he no longer cared for her feelings.

"So, when will you tell me? I thought that we were a team…" but the words rang hollow even in her own ears the moment they had left her lips.

Tony looked at her sternly and it said everything that she didn't want to hear, but he added to her distress on purpose, "Yes, I thought we were as well, but team mates don't lie and team mates work for the team and team mates do not do what you did…" He turned his back on her and she walked away seconds later.

He had frequently broken the law in his professional life, he was not whiter than white and he knew that, but he had never punished anyone for his own personal pride and he couldn't understand it. On the one hand, he could not make her pay for her mistakes in court, yet on the other, he wanted her to suffer as well.

Feeling that he was no longer needed in the Baltimore's, Ronnie hugged his friend and went back to his life, but not before saying, "If you ever have any more two-beer problems, just come and get me, Ton. I haven't had so much fun for years".

"I couldn't have done it without you, Ron. I will always be grateful".

They hugged, Maria drove him home and Tony returned to the waterfall in his garden to have another beer, do some more serious thinking and draw up a plan.

∞

Tony knocked on the door of the Golden Dream in his tourist gear and was admitted without a search. Jan was waiting for him at the bar with a large young man with a kindly, docile almost bovine face.

"Good afternoon, Tony. This is my wife's nephew, Stefan".

"Nice to meet you, Stefan. Thanks for agreeing to meet me, and thank you, Jan, for arranging it". They all shook hands but the 'boy' didn't speak. "Do you speak English, Stefan?"

"Yes", came the low rumble of a voice. "I learned it in school for ten years, and in the army".

"You speak it very well. Can we have a chat in the corner, just you and me?" He looked first briefly at Stefan and then at Jan, who pointed at a table some ten yards away. "Do you drink beer, Stefan?"

"I like the draught Estrella. It is very good beer".

Tony asked for two pints and they retired to the table.

"Cheers", said Tony holding forward his glass. The young man clinked glasses. "I'm sure you know what I want to talk to you about, so we might as well get on with it, but it very important, so if I say anything that you do not understand, please stop me and say so. Understood?" He nodded and took a huge gulp of beer.

"I am very sorry about what happened to you, but I want you to understand that the family I represent did not sanction it. Why would they? They had nothing to gain from it. However, having said that, after a lot of research, I can see why some people might come to that conclusion. Do you have any idea why someone would have wanted to do that to you? Do you have any enemies?"

He looked at his beer and shook his head, then looked up. "I have spent many hours thinking about this, but I cannot find a reason for it".

"Can you remember any details that you think I ought to know?"

"It was humiliating".

"Yes, I'm sure it was, but do you remember any voices or accents or any of your surroundings? Any little thing that might help me get a fix on who did it and where?"

"I was blindfolded and had earphones on and was in a sack most of the time, but the first part of the time, I was on a smooth floor, and the second part, the longest time, on small rocks. It was uncomfortable, more uncomfortable. I definitely heard a French voice, at least one, and maybe a woman's. The one who fondled my, er, bollocks was either a woman or gay. I know because she was having fun".

Tony smiled at the simple logic, but didn't point out that the person might just have been deriving pleasure from sadism and being in control. In any case, the man's simple explanation already fitted what he had feared to admit might be possible – that Daisy had been lying again and was far more involved than she had admitted.

"OK, thanks, Stefan. How do you feel about the situation now?"

"How do you mean?"

"Well, are you still angry, do you still want revenge?"

Stefan held up his glass to the barman and two fingers. He nodded and brought them over.

"Angry? Yes, it was not right, but I have had my revenge. Bad things happen in battles… some things happen and you don't know why… If you think too much, you go crazy… and get killed. No-one can win every time… Ha, ha, ha, that is why Jan makes big money here!"

Tony had to laugh, he liked the man's way of thinking.

"So, you are happy with the status quo, er, the way things are at the moment? I guarantee you that our family bears neither you nor your family any ill will… any bad feelings".

"Yes. Never take life for granted…Live each day to the full for who knows what tomorrow brings?"

"Have you told the police any of this?"

"No, I do not talk to the police".

"Great! I like your attitude. Let's go and tell Jan what we were just saying". They walked over to the waiting owner of the club and Tony told him of their conversation.

"Are you happy with that, Stefan?"

"Yes, Uncle Jan, it is over for me".

"Good, then it is over for me too". The three men cemented the accord With a Slivovitch and a handshake and Tony left a happy man.

"Where to, boss?" asked Salvador.

"Let's just sit here a moment, while I have a little think".

The most obvious patch of stony ground that a Frenchman and a girl would have access to was the mine.

"The gun club, please, Sal", he said.

∞

"So, you haven't noticed any unusual comings or goings here, Carlos? Especially a month or so ago?"

"No, Señor Tony, not that I saw. Why? Is there a problem?"

"I don't know. It was just something someone said to me that made me think of here. Oh, well, it was just a thought".

"How is señorita Daisy, Tony?"

"Oh, she's well. She hasn't been up here as much as she used to because she is trying to sort out her father's estate… You know go through all his papers with her mother".

"Si, it is a big job. I remember when my poor father died… it was very sad and very difficult, but for Don John? Oh, my, he has so much business!"

"Yes…"

"Please, give her my best wishes, and say that she need not worry about the club. Everything is going tickety-boo here. It is good, no, 'tickety-boo'?"

"Yes, tickety-boo is a good word", he smiled.

"I heard it on an old film last night and I liked it, so I looked it up in the dictionary".

"It's a fine old word, Carlos. I'd better be off now, but I'll be back to see you tomorrow or the day after. See you".

"Yes, see you, señor Tony… Oh, Tony, you can tell the señorita that those workmen never came back, if she gives me their number, I can chase them up for her, she doesn't have to do it herself".

"I'll tell her. Which workmen were they, Carlos?

"I don't know the name of the firm, maybe they were French, the boss was definitely from north of the border. They were going to give Daisy a quote for some work in the rifle range".

"Really? Could you show me where?"

"I wasn't actually there, but I got the gist of the plan. Come with me".

He showed Tony how the current system of moving random targets onto the firing range involved people standing in the service doorways pulling wires on pulleys.

"See, like this", he said moving a paper tiger out onto the range and bringing it back. "Daisy wanted to automate it to make it cheaper in the long run. There are eight service doors going right to the back, so at the moment we need eight people. It is very expensive".

"Yes, I see. Do you mind if I have a look around? You can go back to your work; I'll be all right alone".

"Sure, but be careful on the range. There is no-one there at the moment, but you never know. Do you want me to keep it clear for thirty minutes?"

"Yes, all right, that's a good idea?"

"I'll stop by before I go to give you the all clear", and with that Carlos left satisfied.

Tony walked the length of the service passage looking in at every doorway until he reached the end and the door in the wall that sealed off the tunnel. He opened it and looked inside. It was pitch black, but he operated the torch facility on his mobile and stepped inside. The first thing he noticed was the stony ground, and larger rocks that could be sat on. Closer inspection revealed Galois cigarette stubs – dozens of them. Many people smoked Galois, but they did suggest a French person, although workmen could have left them there before, when the mine was being converted. It was only circumstantial evidence, but that word, 'French' kept cropping up and when it did, Daisy was never far away.

He closed the door, said 'Goodbye' to Carlos, and had Salvador take him home.

∞

Tony pushed a trolley with a cooler box of beer on it to his favourite seat in the garden by his small fountain, phoned Daisy and asked her to meet him in his back garden.

"I went to see Stefan today?"

"Really? Who is that?"

"The bouncer at the Stardust".

"Oh, is he all right?"

"Yes, in fact he seems a nice kid. I liked him. I can see why nobody can understand why anyone would want to hurt him. He acts like a big lummox, but he has a good outlook on life".

"So why, Daisy?"

"I'm sorry, why what?"

"Why would somebody do that to him?"

"How should I know? He must make enemies being on the door like that. Perhaps, he stopped someone going in, or a boy got jealous because he was chatting up his girlfriend. I don't know, there could be many reasons!"

"Yes, there could be grievances, but most people, the vast majority, would get angry and let it go. In any case, not many people would have the resources to imprison someone… and especially not somewhere secluded, somewhere with a stony floor where no-one ever goes like a disused mine shaft". He was staring hard at the hairline on Daisy's head, until she lifted her gaze at the word 'mine' and he was looking into her eyes.

He saw fear.

"I was up at the gun club today by the way, and Carlos asked for the number of the French firm you asked to price some work for you. He wants to liaise with them to save you the bother 'during these difficult times'. Who were they, Daisy?"

"Er, just a firm I asked to give us a price for automating the target pulleys".

"Claude was up there, wasn't he?"

"He introduced me to the firm which was to quote for us, yes".

"Smoke Galois cigarettes, does he?"

"No, he's into fitness, he doesn't smoke at all".

"His friends do then, don't they?"

"I never met any of his friends – only a few clients at the club".

"Carlos said that two men called to see you, and I found dozens of Galois stubs behind the back wall… and guess what? It matches the description that Stefan gave me of the place he was imprisoned. 'The Cave', wasn't it?"

She shook her head. "I don't know. How should I know?"

"Oh, I think you know all right, you just don't want to say so. How many of you were involved?" She shook her head slowly, looking down again. "Let me help you. There was Claude; another Frenchman, who smoked Galois; there was the man who was killed, Charlie; and there was a woman", she looked up quickly at that, "and Stefan".

"Why do I say there was a woman? Because Stefan said that he could tell when she played with his balls and his dick". Daisy's mouth opened as if she was going to deny deriving any pleasure from the act and Tony divined it accurately. "It was you, wasn't it, Daisy?"

"It could have been a jealous boyfriend and his girlfriend who fancied the bouncer?"

"A Frenchman and his girlfriend hiding out in your gun club?"

She sighed deeply and then nodded slowly.

"But it was not my idea, and I did not take part in the kidnapping. I swear it!" Tony was inclined to believe her, but said nothing.

"Go on then, tell me the whole story, and don't leave anything out. I know a lot more than I have told you that I know, so I will know if you are lying to me again, and I will promise you this, that if I catch you lying, I will tell your mother everything, and if she tells me to, I will go to the police.

"Now, pass me another beer out of the cooler, please, take one yourself and begin from the beginning".

He listened to the whole of Daisy's story, which he judged to be accurate, and it was indeed so, without saying a word, although he did make notes. She broke down into tears at some points, but never lost control and Tony realised for the first time what a hard person this woman could be. Somehow, he had missed the part in her life when she had transformed from being a sweet little girl into a hard-nosed woman who was capable of torture.

He was sure that he wouldn't have missed such a massive change in anyone else, so he put it down to love, the love of his friends' daughter, whom he had always treated like family. It was something to store in the back of his brain for future reference, he thought, not that he was ever likely to be in the same position again at his stage of his life. Retirement seemed like a good option to him, when Teresa didn't need him any longer, because he didn't think that he wanted to work for someone like Daisy, someone who got pleasure from someone else's pain.

Quite a few minutes of silence passed between them with him looking into the sky over the top of Daisy's head, and her studying the ground around her feet.

"What are you going to do now, Uncle Tony?" she asked when she could bear the silence no longer. He wished he had never allowed her to call him 'uncle' now.

"I'm working on that. Obviously, I will have to make a report to your mother, and I will need to say something to DI Rodriguez".

"What will you tell them?"

"I'm not sure yet, what do you think I ought to tell them?"

"I think you ought to blame Claude and his accomplices and leave me and the gun club out of it".

"Yes, I bet you would. Poor little rich girl gets away with being a spiteful fool, who got two people killed, one shot and her mother put in hospital… but should any blame be attached to her? Oh, no, Heaven forbid!

"Whatever happened to you, Daisy?

"I think you'd better leave now, I've got some thinking to do, and I need to phone a man about a dog".

She got up and slunk away trying to look remorseful, but pretty certain that her dear old Uncle Tony would not throw her to the wolves.

∞

"Hello, DI Rodriguez, how are you? Can we meet for that coffee you promised me? Good, thirty minutes? OK, see you there then".

When they had shaken hands and sat down, Tony began as he meant to go on - with a lie. "I'm sorry I haven't been in touch recently, Dan, but the nurse said there was a risk of the wound going sceptic because I have been moving about too much. I've been sitting in the garden for nearly three whole days as bored as a cabbage".

"How's it now?" he asked indicating Tony's shoulder with his chin.

"Oh, a lot better thanks. She was right. A few days' complete rest and I'm OK again. Anyway, my Intel tells me that the Johnston's have done a runner, is that true?"

"Yes, a few days ago! I didn't tell you because I thought you knew".

"No. I'm out of touch, completely out of touch, sorry. Is there anything else I should know?"

"I don't think so, have you got anything for me?"

"I think so, but it depends how much credence you want to put in it. It's only hearsay, but I believe that it's true. One of our men was talking to someone in Fuengirola last night and he was told that the people who ambushed us now realise that they made a mistake. They now know that it was that French gigolo who was sniffing around Daisy.

"Apparently, he had a couple of birds on the go and one of them fancied that bouncer, so he kidnapped him to teach him a lesson. Unfortunately for him, things went pear-shaped and he lost his bottle so they dumped the man. The guy they killed never worked for us, I told you that, but he did associate with that Frenchman. I don't know whether he was involved or not… he could have been an innocent bystander for all I know".

"So, you think that that's it then, the end of the story?"

"Yes, I do. I have done a bit of phoning around myself and think it definitely is".

"How about the Johnston's?"

"They really did have gambling debts and he was brassic after his wife divorced him, and he did set us up – that part is true. It's just that we weren't actually to blame for the kidnapping, they got that bit wrong. They added two and two and made five.

"I have talked to Mrs. Baltimore and Daisy, and they are both of the opinion that nothing will bring John back and they don't have the stomach for a war, so just let things be…"

"That is all very neat and very surprising, Tony, but since I don't have anything to add to it, I will put it in my report and pass it up to my boss and let him decide what he wants to do next.

"No war? You're sure about that?"

"Positive. We're just not up to one without John, and even with him, it has been such a long time since the last one… No, no war, you can count on that. I even talked to Stefan, you know, the bouncer, about it and he said he is happy as things are".

"Fair enough. It's been nice doing business with you. See you around, Tony", and he left.

"Would sir like anything else?" said a voice over his right shoulder.

"No, er, no thanks".

"That will be ten Euros then, please, sir".

Tony sighed, shook his head, paid the waiter and left.

∞

Having practised his story on a professional, he went to see Mrs. Baltimore. "Could I speak to you alone, Teresa? It is about recent events".

"Am I going to get the full picture now of why John was murdered and why we have been subjected to all this?"

"Yes. The police have been working on the case since the day it all started and I have been working with them to find out what really happened and why".

"Good. Let's go into the drawing room. Would you join me in a glass of wine, I think that I am going to need one? Please, take a seat". She phoned for a bottle of red Rioja and two glasses. "How is your shoulder?" she asked as the maid poured the wine. "You may leave the bottle there. We can help ourselves. Oh, and we are not to be disturbed.

"Tony, salud, over to you".

He told her basically the same story that he had told the police, but he added that they had been wrongly targeted because of Daisy's association with Claude.

"That was not her fault of course, but…"

"…but if she had not been hanging around with him, none of this would ever have happened to us, and John would still be alive".

Tony made no reply, but looked sympathetically into her eyes. He saw no bitterness, no reproach, just sadness and loneliness.

Daisy appeared in the doorway. "Hello, both, may I join you?"

"Would you like me to leave now, Teresa?"

"No, you stay there, we haven't finished our wine yet. No, Daisy, not this time. Please leave us alone". It was the first time in her adult life that she had been refused and was visibly taken aback.

"Oh, all right then", she said imploring Tony for leniency with her eyes, before closing the door behind her.

"Are you sure about all that?"

"Yes, as sure as I'll ever be without talking to Claude".

"And Daisy took no part in it?"

"She has told me many times that she didn't take part in the kidnapping". The answer was true if warped.

"And the police are happy?"

"Yes, I just had coffee with DI Rodriguez and I spoke to the kidnap victim too and he is satisfied. There will definitely be no more trouble unless we start it".

"What do you recommend I do, Tony? You are my most trusted friend and advisor".

"You don't actually have to do anything, Teresa. There is no reason why you can't just carry on the way things are, but if you do want to make some changes, think long and hard about them before you make them, and if you want my help, I will always be there for you. Whatever you decide".

"Thank you, dear Tony", she said reaching forward to touch his hand, tears in her eyes. "I think I will go and lie down now, do you mind? You stay here and finish the wine, or take it with you, if you'd rather go home.

"I'll see you later. Thank you for everything".

Once she had left the room, he slipped out through the French windows and returned home. He didn't want to risk being waylaid by Daisy. He wasn't in the mood to talk to her again that day.

21 JUSTICE, ROUGHLY

Tony kept himself to himself in his house and garden, sometimes flying the second drone just for the enjoyment. He was avoiding contact with Daisy, and would have liked to have gone away for a few days, but he was expecting Teresa to call for him at any time. It had been two days since he had told her and he hadn't seen her during that time.

He could sense the end of an era approaching quickly, and wondered what he would do with himself if he didn't have the Baltimore's to take care of. It was all he had known for thirty years, more than half of his life, although he was still only fifty-five, and when he was in shape he could pass for ten years younger than that.

When he was a boy, he had wanted to join the army. He had done that but hadn't taken to being bossed about, so he had left after his three-year term was up. He was too old to go back in there now, he joked with himself. He came to the conclusion that he would probably be with the Baltimore's until he was no good for anything else except helping out in the garden.

Third under-gardener didn't sound very inspiring, he chuckled, not when he had been Chief of Security for twenty-five years.

He let out a long, audible breath as he opened another bottle. His nurse would be bringing him his diet lunch soon, but he didn't feel like it.

Things were just not the same without John. They had been friends and colleagues as much as employer and employee and he missed their special relationship – their friendship. He liked Teresa, he liked her a lot, and felt that she felt the same way towards him, but it wasn't the same; never would be and probably never could be. He had never had a female best friend – not that he had many male ones either after he had left the Regiment.

His phone rang and it took him by surprise. A sign of the times, only a month or more before, it would have been ringing all day long, now it hardly ever did.

"Hello, Teresa. How are you? Good… Yes, I'm well too. Sure, I'll come over at two o'clock. See you then". It was the call he had been waiting for; the meeting that would probably decide his future would begin in two hours' time and he couldn't wait for it to start.

∞

At five to two, he walked around the back of the house and waited for someone to invite him in. It was what Teresa had expected and she was looking out for him. "Come on in, Tony, no need to stand on ceremony!" but she knew that he always did. "Take a seat at the table. Rioja red?" but knowing that he wouldn't refuse, she had already started to pour it.

"I have spent some time thinking about one thing and another over the last couple of days, and I would value your opinion", she said passing him his wine and sitting opposite him.

"I have two versions to suggest, but first, salud by the way, but first I want to point out that I would not have proposed either if John were still alive, because the businesses were very much his babies, not mine. I don't have a head for figures and wouldn't know whether I was being cheated or not".

"You have, Daisy, she is very good at that sort of thing".

"Yes, that is true, but I will come to her later". It was then that Tony noticed that she had written down everything that she wanted to say like a script, so it was better not to break her flow.

"Sorry for interrupting", he said.

"Don't worry. Anyway, one thing is for certain, and that is that I do not want to own any business that the police or society might disapprove of. I think I heard John refer to them once as 'the illegals'. Well, I never said anything in those days, because it was none of my business. If anything went wrong, John and you sorted it out. I am not prepared to sort out illegal problems, and I don't want Daisy or you to have to do it on my behalf, because, as I am sure you know, John left everything to me". She looked up and Tony nodded.

"That brings us to the legitimate businesses. Basically, we can either sell the lot, keep some or keep them all". She paused and looked at him. He wasn't sure whether he was being asked his opinion or not, so he just nodded that he understood and held her gaze.

"I want you to help me decide whether to sell all, part or none of the legals". He just nodded again, seeing that she had not turned the page yet.

"You will need time to give a valuable judgement, I understand that, but I want you to bear this in mind too, I don't want Daisy to have the opportunity of hurting anyone again". He saw the pain in her eyes, nodded and felt that he had to say something.

"That will be difficult, Teresa, she is wealthy, and people will work for her".

"Yes, I understand that, but if her access to money is restricted, then so is the amount of damage that she can do?"

Tony was beginning to catch her drift and to see a side of Teresa that he had not been shown before.

They talked about Teresa's proposals for an hour or more before she came to a conclusion.

"So, Tony, will you be able to help me put this plan into operation?"

"Yes, of course, Teresa. I will be here ready to do your bidding for as long as I am able or as long as you need me".

"You are so sweet, and so loyal. Will you stay and help me tell Daisy my decision. Just for moral support, I'll do all the talking, you just watch and enjoy the wine. I have read between the lines, and I know my daughter, and I know that you have tried to cover up for her to save me embarrassment, but you Brits forget that this is Spain. I don't mean that nastily, but you live here as if it is a part of the UK, you forget that we talk to each other too, and many Spaniards tell me things that they would never tell you. You have your networks, but we also have ours". She picked up her mobile and called her daughter. A minute later, Daisy entered, obviously expecting to be summoned.

"Hi, are you done?"

"Yes, dear, come and sit with us, bring a glass. Have a drop of wine. I have been running my proposals for the firm past Tony for his professional opinion. However, I want you to know that what I am about to say comes only from me, but I want Tony to bear witness to my intentions.

"First and foremost, I don't want any more illegal activity in this family, and I know that there has been quite a lot of it. But no more. I have therefore instructed Tony to sell all the illegals".

"Good idea, Mum!" she looked at Tony and nodded, but he did not react.

"That brings us to the legitimate side of the firm. If I were a younger woman, I might have wanted to keep some or all of them, but at sixty-three, I can't really be bothered. I don't want the hassle..."

"That's OK, I understand that, Tony and I can look after those for you, can't we, Tony?" Again she looked at him and again he didn't react.

"So, I have decided to sell those as well. The sales of all that should bring in a million or a million and a half, but we don't even need that money; we have enough in the bank to live several lifetimes over".

"So, you are selling everything?"

"Yes..."

"Who to?"

"Whoever can afford them. I offered them to Tony, but he wasn't interested".

"Oh, charming! You offered them to him, before your own daughter!"

"I don't want you to have them, Daisy. I would never sell any of them to you..."

"But why?"

"You are not responsible enough, and I don't want any more hassle, as I just said".

"But I wouldn't cause you any!"

"Maybe, but I cannot be certain of that, in light of the kidnapping and subsequent ambush, which caused the death of your father, I might add".

Daisy shot Tony a vicious glance, and Teresa saw it, confirming her suspicions that her daughter had been more involved that anyone had told her, and that Tony had tried to spare her feelings.

"My decision has nothing to do with Tony, he has been here only to advise me whether my ideas were feasible... and they are".

"But that makes me redundant..."

"You can help Tony with the sales..."

"And after that?"

"Oh, I have plans for after that, you won't be short of things to do, don't you worry about that".

"But you are depriving me of my inheritance!"

"No, darling, your father left everything to me, as you already know..."

"All right, my destiny then!"

"You are not destined to run John's empire, I can tell you that much, but perhaps another one. Just sell off the businesses, let's get the money in the bank, and then we'll set you up". Daisy relaxed visibly.

"All right, I can go with that, as long as you have included me in your grand plan".

"Yes, there is room for you as well. Trust me, I'm your mother, I know what is best for you".

∞

The businesses were offered to their managers on very favourable terms, but if they didn't want them, they were offered to rivals with a recommendation that they keep the present staff. It took a little over three months to sell them off and complete the paperwork.

When it was done, Teresa gave a house party for her staff and Ronnie and his girlfriend. They had a wonderful afternoon, especially Teresa and Tony, who were relieved that so much pressure had been lifted from their shoulders. However, work was still going on, although of a different nature. Teresa, through Tony, bought a church in Fuengirola that had fallen into disuse and had it converted into a smaller place of worship with a dozen small rooms upstairs. An extension was put on the back for a kitchen and laundry facilities. Tony oversaw the conversion and when it was ready, Teresa took him and Daisy down to inspect it.

"What is it?" grinned Daisy. "A church with a hotel on top?"

"Yes, sort of", answered her mother. This is the first of your new empire".

"But what is it?"

"It's a hospice for women in need, and you will be running it".

"What? You want me to live in here?" she asked as they were walking around inside it.

"No, you have a home with me and always will have, but it will be your job to run this facility, and I will pay you a wage for doing so. When you have learned how to run this one well enough, I will build another one in a different town, and your wages will be increased, and then another and so on. What do you think?"

"I don't know, Mum, what if I don't want to?"

"Er, in that case, I will stop your allowance, well, I have already done that as from today anyway, to be honest, so if you don't fancy this job, you could buy the local paper and see what's available... I don't know, what do other young girls of your age do when they need a job?

"Daisy, this is an opportunity for you to make your mark on the world, don't you see that? There are literally millions of young women roaming Europe with little kids and no hope. You could give them hope. They could come to you for help and you could give it to them!"

"With a dozen rooms?"

"You couldn't even run a three-bedroomed guest-house at the moment, young lady! Learn to get the most out of this one first, and I promise that there will be more. We will register it as a charity, say, Daisy's Chain of Hospices for Women, and collect money for charity, and charge a small rent, and I will make up the difference. We can do it together, but I cannot do it without you. What do you say now?"

"I don't know... Oh, all right, Mum, I'll give it a shot! When do we begin?"

"We can start tomorrow, if you like. We'll drive around the outskirts of town and bring a dozen of the most needy women with children here. It is as easy as that! You, not only you, one just has to want to help, and I will be standing alongside you. I will tell you two stories when we get home, that I don't think you know".

Tony drove them back in their new Mercedes, which had arrived the day before.

Teresa took Daisy into the drawing room and sat her down. "You may find this shocking, or at least surprising.

"My history is one of persecution and homelessness, until I met your father, or perhaps just before that, and he saw me working in a market in Fuengirola and offered me a job as his cook. Yes, I used to do the same job as Maria. You didn't know that, did you?"

"You did mention it once…"

"Anyway, my family was socialist in its political views, and Franco persecuted socialists. My parents were killed and I wandered the countryside for days until a kind family of strangers took me in. I was thirteen or so and not unattractive… think about the dangers I faced and the sleepless nights I had. I slept behind boulders in the mountains and shivered at night. I was constantly terrified that I would be abused or even killed. It happened… and there was no-one to stop it or complain to.

"This is now happening all over again but with the Arab women fleeing war in their countries to protect their children… Their situation is not much different to what mine was, except that there was far much less money about in my day. Europe is rich now, but the plight of these homeless women is the same. The next time you see a poor girl, think of her as me fifty years ago, and the next time you see one with a scruffy little kid, think that that could have been you.

"We were lucky, you and I, and never forget it. John saved us from a future that I thought was guaranteed for me and the child that I was sure I would have one day". There were tears in her eyes.

"John's story was different, but not much, in the scheme of things. His mother was a child refugee from war-torn Europe a hundred years ago. She was raped by John's father's brother and John was born… so, the man he called father was really his uncle. His mother shot his father, her rapist, dead, and his children shot her dead in retaliation right in front of his eyes.

"That is not much different to what happened to me, is it?"

Daisy could only shake her head.

"You give yourself airs and graces because you are from a wealthy family, but now you know… not that any of this is your fault. You didn't cause our situation, but you didn't make your own money either.

You are reaping the benefit of other people's hard work, and don't ever forget that… Not that any of us begrudge you your good fortune… We love you and are happy for you. I would never have told you all this unless you had asked, or unless it was important for you to know… and that is why I am telling you now.

"All rich people owe a debt to society, and especially people like us do, because we know where we come from. We remember, because it wasn't all that long ago. Now, are you in or are you out?"

"I'm up for it, Mum, I guess, but what you just told me will take a while to sink in. Dad did tell me a bit about his life before and so did you, but I guess I wasn't ready to hear it".

"It happens. 'A man hears what he wants to hear and disregards the rest'. So, we begin tomorrow… Oh, I almost forgot, although I don't know how I could have – age, I suppose. I was going through some of your Dad's stuff one night - I had been trying to get a little more done every day, and I found references to Women's Hostels in London. It was what gave me the idea for our scheme. John never stopped donating to Women's Refuges… not from the time he was about twenty-one.

"I should imagine that that was when his adopted father John told him about his real parents. He changed which hostels he supported quite often – it doesn't say why – but he didn't miss one month's payment in sixty years. He started paying £1 a month and last month, after sixty years, the direct debit was for £500. If we make a success of this project, we will be continuing John's work. He would be so proud of you, and so will I be… and so will you be.

"You will gain more respect for yourself by helping people than by hurting them, or ignoring suffering when you could have helped. And you can help, Daisy, that is the privilege that you were born with – it was not really the money; that just makes it easier.

"So, I have given some thought to this. Neither of us knows how to run a guest house let alone a hospice, so I have asked a group of local nuns to train you up, and you can recruit a few people to help you, and be trained at the same time. When you are ready to go it alone with your own team, the nuns will go back to their normal work. I don't know how long that will take… three months, six months, a year? It depends how quickly you and your team learn and in the meantime, I will help out where I can and look around for our next property.

"Does that sound good to you?"

"Er, yes, Mum… it's just all happening so quickly".

"John was working towards this for sixty years and Tony and I have been converting that old church for the last three months. It is only that you have just been let in on the secret. This is not a flash in the pan".

"No, all right, I don't suppose it is when you put it like that… You know what? Actually, I can't wait to start tomorrow morning!"

"I'm glad to hear it, I'll phone the Abbess and tell her we're on for tomorrow. If we ask them to be there at nine, we can go out at eight, pick up our first couple of families and take them to the hospice, let the nuns take care of them while we go out and get some more".

"OK, but let's not fill it up straight away ourselves, let's allow some people to find us as well".

"All right, my dear, we'll half fill it".

"See you at dinner, Mum. I love you".

"I love you too, darling".

Teresa walked out into the garden hoping to have a word with Tony. When she didn't see him, she did something that she had never done before, she walked around to his bungalow and called his name. He appeared at the side of his house from the back garden.

"Hello, Teresa. Is anything the matter? Would you like to come in?"

"Nothing is the matter, Tony. If you are in the garden, I will join you for a few minutes, if I am not intruding".

"Of course, my pleasure, it's through here. Please, sit down".

"It is lovely here, Tony, so tranquil. I see you're drinking a beer. May I have one? I don't remember the last time I drank a cold beer… ten, twenty years ago?"

"I can get you some wine, if you prefer it, Teresa…"

"No, beer will be fine; it will bring back old memories. Cheers, Tony. How are your wounds?"

"All but healed now, thanks, and your bruises?"

"They went long ago. I wanted to thank you for all your help with Daisy. I was expecting more resistance, but she has accepted her Fate. At first, her Ego saw what was on offer as a demotion, but I think that we have helped her see that it will do her more good to run the hospices than run girls, bars and casinos".

"She is not a stupid girl".

"No, and she had no real alternative unless she wanted to work for someone else!" Teresa laughed softly and held her bottle forward. Tony chuckled too and clinked bottles with her.

"She will enjoy it once she gets stuck in. Did she choose to work with the nuns or hired help?"

"The nuns. I have to phone the Abbess and tell her that we begin at nine tomorrow. Will you be able to drive us?"

"I would have been affronted if you hadn't asked me to. What time?".

"Eight, is that all right with you?"

"Certainly".

"Good. Come over to the house when you're ready. I'd better go and make that phone call. thanks for the beer, we'll have to do it again one day".

"You are always welcome, Teresa. See you tomorrow".

22 THE FIRST LINK

They left their wealthy neighbourhood in their large, brand-new Mercedes and headed for the outskirts of Marbella, but they were surprised not to find any young women with children. There were plenty of men sleeping rough, but most of them were older Spaniards, so they set off for Fuengirola. They had more luck there, where they found two women with head scarves and their two children sitting under a large tree eating fruit.

Tony stopped a hundred yards past them so as not to frighten them, and Daisy and Teresa walked back to talk to them. Tony watched them sit with the women and offer them food that they had brought with them.

The women accepted the food gratefully, but could not speak either Spanish or English. It was an obvious problem that neither Teresa nor Daisy had not foreseen. They had expected that all the long-distance travellers would have been able to speak at least a few words of English. They tried to persuade the Muslim women to go with them, but something was holding them back.

Daisy had an idea and asked the women where they had come from by mentioning the names of various countries. They nodded and smiled at the word 'Syria', so she typed into her phone's translator: 'Please come with us, we have a room for you' and had it translated. The women read the message, talked between themselves in their own language and then one of them took Daisy's phone, switched the languages around, typed something and returned it to Daisy. 'Thank you', it read.

Daisy and Teresa helped them up, took their bundles and led them to their car. Once inside, they realised that there would be no room for another family, so they drove to a coffee shop not far from the hospice, bought them breakfast and waited for nine o'clock when the nuns would arrive.

When they all met up at the hospice, they were glad that the Abbess had had the foresight to send them a nun who spoke Arabic. It worked out that the two adults in the two families were related, so one woman, Alicia, left her child with her cousin, and went with the Baltimore's to act as translator and ambassador. By lunchtime, they had filled six of the twelve rooms and they joined the nuns in processing the women and their children, which involved administrative affairs, bathing, medical check-ups, and eating. They were also offered new clothes, but some of the women wouldn't exchange their traditional Muslim garb for Western clothing.

Daisy and Teresa were quickly learning that they had a lot to learn.

∞

Word soon got around about the hospice, so it was full within two more days. From then on, they were turning away young families, and not only Muslim ones, every day. Daisy and Teresa found that the hardest part, but many of the nuns had worked as missionaries in the poorest areas of the world and had hardened themselves to it a little. What they had expected to be able to treat as a day job, soon turned into two twelve-hour shifts.

"Something is going to have to change down at the hospice", said Daisy to her mother, exhausted one evening. We have applied to be registered as a charity, so we will soon be able to collect money, and the adult residents have taken over the cooking and cleaning, but we cannot have them live there indefinitely. I think that the hospice should be a halfway house. We are doing this to help the young and their families, not to relieve the government of some of its responsibilities".

"What do you suggest?" asked Teresa, "We can't just turf them out after a month or two".

"No, but, if we could recruit some undergraduate lawyers from the local universities to help the women fill in their application forms for

253

residency or social security, whatever it is that they need, that would move them onto community housing more quickly, which would free our rooms up more quickly as well.

"And I think that if we sell the idea to the students properly, they will do it free of charge".

"Why would they do that, er, pro bono publico?"

"Because it is work experience, and charity work always looks good on a CV and, many people do want to help, they just don't know how to get involved".

"It might work, dear, no harm in trying. Is there anything you want me to do?"

No, I'll draw up some ideas and show them to you tomorrow to see what you think".

"OK... I have been having a few ideas of my own too. How about if we get the women to cultivate the land at the back of the church? I'm sure that most of them will have had vegetable plots and a few chickens before... and I was in Mercadona's the other day and noticed that they have a box for shoppers to donate food. Why don't we register the hospice with all the supermarkets, so that we are eligible for a share of that?"

"Yeah, yes, I like it, and could you ask Tony to look out for another site for us, please? I know that we don't know everything about running a hospice yet, but we are getting there, and making the second link in our chain of hospices might take a while".

"We know more about what we want in the design too now, and perhaps the current residents could help in the construction or decoration of the place. It is common enough to see women working on building sites in some countries".

"We could look into that. Health and safety might be an issue, but if we could help train at least some of the women and older children to gain skills, it would help them fit into society better here... We ought to find out what skills they have and see if we could organise them into making some money for themselves... We could open a stall in the market..."

"Strange, that would be taking me back full circle to before I met your Dad..."

"Would you like that, Mum?"

"Yes, I think that I would..."

"Then let's do it!" she grinned.

∞

Daisy was enjoying working at and running the hospice. She had never engaged in physical work before, but soon found that being tired at the end of a productive day was most satisfying. She had never helped anyone except her parents and Tony before either and found that equally gratifying. She did four things the next day.

First, she set a date for the initial "integration class', the aim of which was to teach the families Spanish and English, and how to fit into European society. She intended to take her turn teaching and to make an effort to learn Arabic.

Second, she took the women into the grounds and, with their input, sketched out the proposed vegetable garden and chicken coup. The women liked that idea, because they were invariably worn out when they arrived, but after a few days they wanted something to do, and wanted to earn their keep. They all had some level of experience in the garden, and all had cooked almost every day of their lives.

Third, she bought an impressive executive desk and put it near the front window in the lobby, so that any student lawyers who helped would feel that their dignity had not been undermined.

And fourth, she asked the nun who spoke Arabic to draw up a questionnaire for the assessment of the residents' skills, requiring them to be handed back to her by lunchtime the following morning.

She was pleased with her day's work again, and was confident that the hospice would soon be running itself, at least internally. There was still quite a lot of paperwork that needed to be done on a regular basis, but she was hoping that a few of the student lawyers or a volunteer would help with that one day soon.

That evening over dinner, Daisy gave an account of the day's progress, and said, "Mum, I want to build the hospice a website, but for that I need a name for it".

"I don't understand, dear, a name for what? The website?"

"Well, yes, but that will be the same as the name for the hospices".

"I thought that we had settled that months ago. We said, 'Daisy's Chain of Hospices for Women', didn't we?"

"Yes, I do remember something about that, but don't you want to be included as well? Or Dad?"

"No, not me... I won't be involved for more than a few more years. It'll be all yours then. As for your father, well, that's sweet of you, but he'll be proud to see your name up there. John never was much of one for standing in the limelight. He hated it and didn't trust people who did enjoy it. Don't worry, I can see that you're uncomfortable with it too. You take after him, but it does need a figurehead, and that has to be you".

"All right, well, how about: 'Daisy's Chain - Hospices for Women (inspired by John and Teresa Baltimore)".

"Yes, all right, if you insist. That would be nice, though it's a bit of a mouthful to put on the board above the door, isn't it? Perhaps you could just put 'Daisy's Chain' above the door, and use the rest on your letterheads and website?"

"All right, Mum, I'll settle for that. I'm going to the uni tomorrow morning to ask for volunteer solicitors, do you want to come?"

"No, a pretty girl will have more chance alone than with her old mother".

"You look more like my sister than my mother..." smiled Daisy.

"Thank you, darling, but I doubt that. No, you go alone and I'll see how the search for a new property is coming along".

They left it at that and went to bed tired again.

∞

After breakfast, Daisy drove to the university at Malaga. She had forgotten to make an appointment, but asked to speak to the head of the law department anyway.

"He is very busy, Miss, er?"

"Baltimore, Daisy Baltimore".

"Miss Baltimore, may I ask what it is concerning?"

"You can tell him that I have an idea, which will make it easier for his graduates to find employment".

"May I ask how you will be doing that?"

"No, I will only talk to him, but if he's not interested, I'll go elsewhere". She made a phone call, and asked Daisy to follow her.

"I can only give you five minutes, Miss Baltimore", he said shaking her hand. "How may I be of assistance?"

Daisy explained her scheme and how she proposed to promote anyone who helped in the media, and on their new website, which was being designed 'as we speak'.

"It is an interesting proposition, and I will certainly mention it in some ears, but that is all I can do... except suggest that you pin a notice on the student noticeboard in this department. I'm sure that someone will be pleased to help".

Daisy left disappointed, but not defeated. She called into the stationery shop in the foyer of the department, bought some speech reminder cards, wrote her message and looked for an appropriate place on the noticeboard to pin it. Most of the other adverts were by typists, or by solicitors offering to coach students for exams, but some were from websites designers. She pinned up her card and looked at some of the example websites on her phone. One caught her eye in particular, so she phoned the number and arranged to meet a Luis in the hospice that afternoon. She had lunch in the student canteen, and then returned to the hospice.

Luis, a young man of about her own age, arrived punctually at two with a winning smile on his face. Daisy sat him at the solicitor's desk and explained what the hospice was all about, then she took him into the kitchen to make coffee and see what cake or biscuits were available to go with it. Two Muslim women and a Spanish girl were preparing the evening meal. They waved at Daisy and she did the same back, then carried the tray back to the table and they sat down again.

"So, you work here, do you, Daisy?" he asked watching a nun walking past.

She thought for a split second before replying simply 'Yes, but I'm not a nun. They are here temporarily to teach us newbies how to run a hospice. There were six of them in the beginning, but we are down to two now, because we have a few volunteers and the residents do a lot of the work themselves'.

"I'm impressed. I had no idea that anyone around here gave a second thought to the plight of the homeless, wherever they come from".

"Well, this place hasn't been open long, but it is a start", she replied, holding out a saucer of plain biscuits.

"I think it's wonderful... Are you a volunteer or an employee?"

"Er, an employee, I suppose".

"I bet it's long hours for not much pay".

"It is long hours, yes, but I'm not complaining about the pay. I'm very happy here... In fact, it's the best job I've ever had".

"Some people are born to help others... It's in their heart and in their soul", he said looking deep into her eyes.

"Yes, well, my mother got me the job. It probably wouldn't have occurred to me if she hadn't", she replied not wanting to deceive him.

"Oh, I'm sure that it would have eventually... you have a kind face".

"Thank you, Luis; would you like to see the rest of the facility now?" He smiled. "Good, this way. You've seen the communal kitchen", she said putting the tray on a counter just inside the door. "Then the rooms are on the gallery up there. Up these stairs.

"They are all occupied, so I can't show you one, but they are pretty basic. Twelve rooms, fours toilets and showers. Then back downstairs and out into the garden. We are going to develop this into a vegetable garden with chickens, starting tomorrow, I guess, and then back inside at the rear of the building, is a place for worship. Interdenominational, of course, although all the residents at the moment are Muslims.

"Well, what do you think, Luis, will you be able to make a decent website or blog for us that reflects what you have seen here?"

"Yes, I'll put a few ideas together and then bring them to you the day after tomorrow, if you like. One thing, do you already have a domain name?"

"Er, no, but I know what management wants, I will secure it tonight".

"Good", he said taking a pen from his shirt pocket and holding it over his notebook. Daisy hadn't foreseen this and so walked away. "Er, Daisy, what is it? I need to know in order to put it in the design".

She turned and walked back to him. "Daisy's Chain Hospices for Women (inspired by John and Teresa Baltimore)", she said.

"Daisy, as in your name, Daisy?"

"Yes".

"Cool, and you still work here?"

"I wouldn't want to work anywhere else".

"That's great, Daisy, I admire you for that. It's been great meeting you and seeing what you're about. I'll be in touch soon. Here's my card... for if the domain name is already taken". He gave her a big smile and she returned it.

"OK, thanks, Luis. See you". She walked him to his car and waved him off.

She liked him.

∞

Daisy went home at seven, and secured the domain name she wanted, daisyschain.com, then on impulse, she took out Luis' card and phoned him.

"Luis", came the reply.

"Er, hi, it's Daisy. I hope I'm not disturbing you".

"No, not at all, I'm relaxing in my bath".

"That's where I want to be..." she replied.

"In my bath? Be my guest come on over", he joked easily.

Daisy blushed. "No, er, sorry, I'm just tired, I mean in my bath..."

"I know. I'm only joking with you".

"Er, I phoned to say that I have just bought the domain name, daisyschain.com. I thought you might want to know. I'll be off now then..."

"Yes, thanks for that, Daisy, it'll save me possibly having to do things twice".

"Yes, that's what I was thinking. Good night then".

"Good night, are you going to have a bath too?"

"Dinner first, then a bath, and bed".

"You sound as if you need it. Take care, Daisy. Good night".

Daisy lay in bed later that night considering how her life had changed. It seemed incredible to her that she was the same woman who had not been sickened by the imprisonment of an innocent man by her friend, and that she had attempted to inflict mental and physical torture on him while he was completely helpless and unable to either flee or defend himself. She believed in life after death, but she still consoled herself that at least her father had never come to hear about it, although she wasn't at all sure how much her mother knew.

Not much, she hoped.

Otherwise, she was certain that she would never be able to look her in the eyes again... especially after what the victim had said, that she had enjoyed fondling him. She thought that that was a lie. She liked to think that he was mistaken, but she couldn't be certain. It was as if it had been another woman doing that, and in the corridor afterwards with the man listening to them behind the door. That couldn't have been her. It was completely uncharacteristic, she thought, and yet, it had happened, she could not escape that fact no matter how she tried or dressed it up.

She slept easily, but dreamed that she was talking to Luis, who was tied up in a sack in his bath with only his smiling face visible.

∞

At breakfast, Daisy was distant, but there was nothing wrong, she was just trying to remember what she and Luis had been taking about in her dream.

"Daisy... Daisy! Do you want me to come in today?"

"Er, no, sorry, Mum. I'm giving a class in Spanish at ten, and English this afternoon. Er, I need to enter the results from the questionnaire and collate them... er, then, no, I don't remember any more, but it's in my diary. Why?"

"I think that we have found a second property, and I want to check it out?"

"Yes, sure. You carry on. Drop by in the afternoon, if you like and we can have a coffee.

"OK, I'll try, but I'll let you know".

∞

Luis turned up unexpectedly at eleven thirty. "I was so inspired by what you have going on here, that, after I got out of the bath, I just had to start on your site immediately. I worked on it all night. Can I show you? I know that I should have rung first, but... impulse, eh?"

Daisy smiled broadly and took him into the tiny office used by whoever was in charge at the time. Luis sat down opposite Daisy.

"You look exhausted. Let me get you some coffee and a bite to eat".

"Coffee, OK, but no food... unless you have a few biscuits or some cake". She crossed the small foyer and asked in the kitchen, then returned.

"Ten minutes", she said.

Luis showed her three draft websites as he topped up his calories.

"I'm impressed", she said. "I don't know which I prefer. We need to get my mother involved. She said that she might call in today, because... well, just because. Anyway, I'll see if she can make it earlier, because you look as if you need to go to bed". He looked at her and smiled, tilting his head. "You know very well what I mean".

"Sure", he agreed and waited while Daisy phoned her mother.

"We can meet her for lunch nearby", she said, "in an hour's time".

"OK, I'd like to meet your mother. To be honest with you, I'd never heard of the Baltimore family, before I met you, but I asked my Dad last night, and he said that I must have been walking around half asleep all my life. I mean, when he mentioned what you own, I have heard of some of that, but I never heard the name behind them".

"Don't worry, that's how we, my Dad and my Mum, preferred it. They didn't want to be famous..."

"Just rich... sorry, that was uncalled for".

"Don't worry about it, I used to get that all the time. It used to make me really angry. I would probably have thumped you for saying that five years ago..."

"... and I would have deserved it. I can't imagine you getting angry".

"... but it's water off a duck's back now. On yes. I'm a black belt in full-contact Karate, but I've studied Aikido and boxing too, so watch out! Anyway, my family was rich before they came to Spain, and that was fifty-odd years ago. Dad was just an active person, he needed to have something to do".

"Has he passed away then?"

"Yes, he died as a result of injuries suffered in a car crash not so long ago..."

"I'm sorry..."

"The car was ambushed and the driver shot... he lost control of the car, but it wasn't his fault..."

"I wasn't thinking it was, if he had a bullet in him. Did he die too?".

"No, exactly. No, he didn't die, but he spent a long time recuperating. It's not all fun and games being well-off. Anyway, that's all behind us now. We sold everything my mother owned except the house and the car, and Mum's using the money to do this", she said looking around her. She went out to finalise another one today".

"She sounds like a nice lady. I'm looking forward to meeting her".

"Thank you, she is".

"Like mother, like daughter..."

Daisy blushed, and thought, 'If only he knew', but said, "Come on, we might as well get going. Shall we take your car, mine, or both?"

"Well, mine is just a pokey CV, I don't know what you've got, but it has to be better than that!" She was hoping that it wouldn't put him off her, but she knew that he would find out one day anyway.

"I keep it around the side", she said leading the way out of the front doors. When he saw it, he whistled.

"A Porche 911 Carrera cabriolet!"

"It was a gift from my parents for passing my finals", she said apologetically and instantly regretted taking the defensive.

"So was mine..." he replied.

Whenever Daisy and Luis had spoken together, it had always been in English, and it had not occurred to either of them that there was an alternative. However, when he was introduced to Teresa, he knew instantly that she was Andalusian and spoke to her in Spanish. It came as a surprise to him when Daisy joined in.

"I am sorry, Señora Baltimore, to hear of the recent passing of your husband. It must have been a terrible blow for one still so young". Teresa could not help smiling at the compliment. "Daisy didn't tell me that her mother was a flower of this land, so I had assumed that you were British. I can see now where she derives her beauty from".

"Flatterer! But don't stop, it doesn't happen so often when one is older, especially when most of one's acquaintances are British".

"No, they miss the beauty of the mature woman", he replied.

"It takes an exceptional, perceptive young man to notice". Daisy just sat and watched the pair of them enjoying themselves with a wide grin on her face. "Daisy, you didn't tell me that you were bringing such a polite and handsome young man to lunch!

"So, young man, Luis, Daisy tells me that you have designed a few websites for us. I look forward to seeing those after lunch. What are you going to have?"

They decided to share a large seafood stew and salad, and a bottle of local white wine. After it, they had coffee, and Teresa asked for the table to be cleared so that Luis could show them his ideas on his laptop.

"I recommend that you choose the design that most matches the image that you want to project, and then we can fine-tweak it later to suit that image perfectly. These are the three themes", he said displaying them slowly. Daisy and her mother discussed them and chose the third one.

"All right, a blog or a website?"

Daisy explained the difference to her mother, but it didn't really register. "A hybrid, I think, Luis", she said. "The main site will be a blog with pages and interactive posts, but instead of archiving old content to where no-one will ever see it again, I want to post it to the website section. Naturally, there will be large, very obvious links on both sections so that visitors can easily jump between them.

"What do you think, Mum?"

"I don't know what you just said, my dear. You know me and computers, but it sounded good. What do you think, Luis?"

"It is an unusual approach, but not unheard of. I can do that easily enough. Is there anything else?"

"I would like a picture of my Mum and Dad in the header on every page... it doesn't have to be prominent, but I'd like them there, just the same".

"Sort of in the background, standing close together, looking out over yonder?" he said.

"Yes, that's it... overlooking this great project of theirs".

"Ours, Daisy, my dear". She just smiled and reached for her mother's hand. Luis found the scene very touching.

"Would you want me to load the site onto the domain you bought last night, Daisy, and then hand the management of the site over to you, or would you want me to make any updates for you?"

Daisy looked at her mother, but she didn't voice an opinion.

"What do you think, mother, shall we run the website updates ourselves, or retain Luis to do it for us?"

"Oh, we need an expert website that is maintained by an expert, such as Luis. I cannot do it, and you certainly won't have the time when you have a few more hospices to manage. Luis is a good man, so keep him onside, before someone else snaffles him up. Mark my words, never let a good man get away" Daisy knew what she was trying to do and blushed.

To escape her embarrassment, Daisy declared that she had to go back to work, and called for the bill. When Teresa saw Luis put his hand in his pocket, she said, "No, young man. I invited you to show me your ideas, so I will foot the bill. Tell him, Daisy!" She looked at him, shrugged and grinned.

"Are you sure?"

"She's sure, don't worry".

"In that case, thank you. I enjoyed lunch, it was excellent - a superb choice of food and excellently matched by the selection of wine. Does anyone mind if I go to the Gents?"

"Nobody minds", said Daisy and watched him walk away.

"You have a good one there, Daisy. You hang on to him".

"Mum, we only met yesterday! Give over, will you?"

"Good men are hard to find, especially for women with money. He's a good one, and he's besotted with you". Daisy blushed. "And I can see that you like him too! Come on admit it! You can't lie to your old Mum, I've known you too long, and I have never seen you look like this before".

"He's very nice, yes..."

"He's gorgeous! Polite, intelligent, talented and handsome! What are you talking about?"

"Yes, well, he is, yes. Shush, he's coming back. Please don't embarrass me..."

Teresa handed her card over to the waiter and signed the chit.

"Well, young man, it has been very nice to meet you. I hope you will make a habit of coming to lunch with us... or dinner at the house! What do you say, Daisy?"

"Yes, good idea, we can talk about the new hospice..."

"Yes, for a little while, but we can socialise and get to know each other as well. Daisy, you be sure to arrange a date with Luis, and Luis, don't let her forget. I'll go on ahead, you two can take your time. Bye-bye for now, but see you again soon".

"I'm sorry about that, Luis. Mother can be a little overpowering..."

"No need to apologise. I think she's great and I'd love to have lunch, dinner or any other meal with you any time you can". He took her hand and held it, "Thanks for lunch, Daisy..." he said looking into her eyes, and they both forgot to shake hands.

∞

That evening at home, over dinner, Teresa had some news for Daisy.

"We have secured another disused church near Estepono, so not so far away. Tony says that the solicitors say that we should be in possession of it within six to eight weeks. I'll take you to see it tomorrow, if you like. It's bigger than the one we have already... the architect says that we might get thirty rooms in it".

"That's fantastic, Mum! Yes, I'd love to come and see it with you tomorrow. Estepono – not far away at all. I think it is important to keep the hospices close together in the beginning, don't you?

"You're the boss, dear, but I think you're right. That young man you had with you today, seemed very nice..."

"Luis? Yes, he's busy building our website today".

"I would say he's building more than that... He couldn't take his eyes off you".

"Aw, Mum, we're just working together..."

"Right, so why are you blushing?"

"I'm not!"

"OK, but why not invite him to come to Estepono with us tomorrow? Just so that he can incorporate the new church into the website? You know, a sort of before and after... This is what it used to look like, and then, when it's occupied and now... Or, even better: this is what we have, now we need sponsors to do it up?"

"Yes, OK, Mum... that sounds like a sound tactic. I'll ring him from my room later".

"Good. I like him".

23 EPILOGUE

The second link in Daisy's Chain was completed four months later tripling the charity's capacity. It was also accepted as a registered charity and started to collect donations from the government, other charities and the public via its website and public fund-raising events. The local supermarkets also added the hospices to their list of worthy charities and donated and collected food for them.

A small team of student solicitors helped them out on a regular basis and Daisy and Luis made sure that they received plenty of publicity and praise on their website for their assistance.

Many local dignitaries wanted to become associated with Daisy's Chain, because it not only took homeless young women and their children off the roadsides, but it helped them to integrate into Spanish society, by teaching the basics of Spanish and English, the two most common languages used locally, and helped settle the children in schools or apprenticeships.

Daisy, with the increasing support of Luis, was soon running five hospices and that figure would continue to grow, as did their relationship. They got married eighteen months later, and Teresa used the occasion to retire. She kept her 'hand in' from time to time, but she had always intended that the chain of hospices should train Daisy to walk the straight and narrow, that she might gain the self-respect that she needed from helping others rather than being just a tycoon.

Teresa asked Tony what he would like to do, and he said that he had always thought that he would like to own a restaurant, although he was by no means a cook let alone a chef.

Teresa bought him a restaurant and had it completely refurbished for him. Out of gratitude for her help and because of his deep attachment and affection for the Baltimore family, he chose his staff from the hospices and donated his surplus food to them too. Residents and staff at the hospices were entitled to a permanent discount which varied with the season. Out of respect for Andalucía, which he loved so much, and the Arabic background of most of the staff, he called the restaurant 'Cooking That's Moorish' and it swiftly gained an excellent reputation for its cuisine and ambiance among the residents of the Spanish and ex-pat community on the Costa del Sol.

The End.

ANDROPOV'S CUCKOO

A Story of Love, Intrigue and The KGB

by

Owen Jones

1 WILLIAM DAVIES

"He's coming back, Peter!"

"Hang on to him!" ordered the cardiovascular surgeon as he quickly scanned the machines and monitors on the racks above the opposite side of the bed with a well-practiced eye. "Don't let him lose consciousness again, it might be the last time if we do."

All the flashing, spiking and streaming lights on all the monitors were normalising, as were the beeps and buzzing sounds.

"Come on, William, don't go to sleep on us now," he urged his patient.

"I'm trying not to," I heard myself saying in my head, but I couldn't get my lips to voice my thoughts. In fact, for a while, I thought that I had died ten minutes before I heard the first voice speak. The only reason I had for doubting my demise was that I'm a Spiritualist, and I have always believed that friends and relatives waited on the Other Side to welcome the dying over. There had been no-one waiting for me…

Not that I have many friends or relatives dead or alive, although there was one I knew I could count on.

I had to put myself into the doctors' hands and trust in their ability. I wanted to give them a sign that I could hear them, so I tried to drum my fingers and wiggle my toes, but had no idea whether they were moving or not. I guessed not by the lack of reaction from the doctors and nurses who were obviously surrounding the bed trying to help me.

"His eyes are twitching, I think he's trying to open them," observed a female voice emotionally. Emboldened by such encouragement I tried harder, and, after a minute or so, I could see a kindly male face smiling down at me through a crack in my eyelids.

"Welcome back, William", he said seeming to mean it, "we thought we'd lost you that time. Welcome back to the land of the living. I'm terribly sorry about this, Old Man, but I have to rush off now that you're going to be all right, but these ladies and gentlemen are supremely competent and will take care of you just as well as I could. I'll see you later".

He whispered his instructions to the others and left.

It is strange, but when you have very little strength left, you can feel it ebbing or returning remarkably easily. In my case, I was getting stronger by the second. I don't know what drugs they've given me, but they and the will to live are working wonders.

"We'll keep you in tonight, William, but if the signs are good tomorrow, you can go back to your own bed. That'll be nice, won't it?"

I tried to nod and smile, but instead, I felt a tear run out of my left eye down over my temple and into my ear. I haven't slept in my own bed for nearly three years, but I knew what she meant of course. She was just trying to be kind… upbeat, and I did appreciate it. It's just that it's funny what you think about when you realise that you might be drawing your last breaths.

I don't consider myself religious, although I suppose others might. I believe simply in life after death, reincarnation and Karma. Therefore, death has never held any terrors for me, and life is only slightly preferable because it allows a wider range of experiences and more of them.

My last thoughts had not been about life or death or even meeting my Maker, they had been about the people I have loved, and especially the females, because I had always preferred theirs to male company. You could argue that that was my life flashing before my eyes, but it was a niche, edited version and it didn't flash. It lingered in a languid, lavish, seductive fashion.

In fact, I don't believe that that film of my life would have finished if I had died from the heart attack when I thought I might have. It would have carried on and I would have been without a body – the only change.

I have been a big, strong man all my adult life: over six feet and over sixteen stones, but fit and healthy with it. I have been ill and broken bones, but nothing has floored me for long. However, I fear that those days are at an end, because that was the second heart attack you just saw me recover from, and I am realistic enough to know, that I will probably not be able to ignore the third call to leave this Mortal Coil.

To be honest, I'm not all that sure that I would want to anyway. I am now seventy-one, living in an old people's home in southern Spain and my wife and friends have all gone on before me. Don't get me wrong, it is a very comfortable hospice, operated especially for English-speaking oldies like myself. It really is very nice, but it's not home, as I am sure you can appreciate and the bed they referred to as my 'own', is not the one I shared with my wife until she died two years, three months and seventeen days ago.

Actually, she was rushed from our bed into hospital and died there without recovering consciousness. She didn't survive her first heart attack. It's a shame, I thought she would have… when the time came. I slept in a hotel after that for a while and then I moved into the hospice – God's Waiting Room, we residents call it!

Anyway, I digress, but I'm afraid you will have to forgive me, dear reader, for it is true, an old man's mind does wander. However, if you have the tenacity to stick with me to the end, I will tell you the story of a woman that I want the whole world to know.

Trying to tell the story of someone else is difficult, and in this case it is obscured by the mists of time and an old man's power of recollection, but I will get there, I promise you that most sincerely

I am the eldest child in my family, of my generation in our family, I should say, three years older than my next sibling, so for a long time, I was like an only child. I was lucky though, because there were lots of children in the nearest five houses to ours and as luck would have it, eight of those nine children were girls. I loved them all in my preschool days as I had no sisters of my own… I have fond memories of playing Daddy to their Mummy at make-believe tea parties.

Most of them were years older than myself, so when they started school they found new friends and eventually, so did I. It was there that at the age of six I fell in love with a girl called Debbie. One day, after school, at the age of seven, we were sitting on the swings in the thunder, lightening and rain and hoped that a bolt of lightening would send us to a romantic death together. It didn't, of course, all it got us was a telling-off from our parents.

Then there was Sally when we were nine. I used to stalk her and when she said that I was the third most handsome boy she knew, I was in Seventh Heaven. At fifteen there was Lesley, whom I loved from afar, but never ever spoke to, and so it went on until I was seventeen.

I will never forget those wonderful girls, our innocence and the great times we had, or I wanted to have, together.

Some things you cannot tell, even at seventy-one and fresh off your death bed, and other things you don't want to tell because they are memories best savoured in private. I often wonder whether those early loves, for lovers they were not, remember me fondly too, but I will never know now and that is probably for the best. I can pretend that they do.

You see, I cannot ask them, because I have always moved around and never kept in touch. It is a reason for the lack of friends and close family. First, I went to university a hundred and fifty miles from home and then I joined the Diplomatic Service, which also involved travelling... but I am starting to get ahead of myself.

Between the ages of eighteen and twenty-three, the girls I was going out with started to become women, and that was even more exciting. I remember Janine, Glenys and Andrea... so many more friends and lovers alike. I dream about them all often, and in a way which is not disrespectful to my wife.

The nurse has come to put me to sleep... not like an old dog, you understand, more in the manner of a sick child, which I am frightened I am in danger of becoming. It is a reason for wanting to tell you my story soon. I will do my best to get on with it tomorrow.

∞

Muesli and fresh pineapple crowned with plain yoghurt for breakfast accompanied by a cup of weak herbal tea. I can't tell which one from the flavour, but it is all very nice, if predictable. I am not going to be in a fit state for jogging for a while, so I need plenty of roughage. The tea is probably a mild laxative as well.

Anyway, I have become aware over night, that, if my story is going to be published one day, it needs to be written down or recorded. A Dictaphone would be the least strenuous on me, so I asked the nurse who brought my breakfast to arrange for the hospice staff to buy me one. She tried to get out of doing it by reminding me that I would be 'going home' within eight hours, so I could ask them myself.

I wasn't having any of that though. 'I haven't forgotten I'm going back to the hospice today if I'm well enough!' I told her. 'Phone them to get me a Dictaphone as I asked, please!' She went off in a huff, but at my age we are allowed to be a bit crotchety from time to time, it's expected of us and one of the compensations for old age. You could call it a prize for surpassing the allotted three score years and ten.

When my plates are being cleared away by a different nurse, I ask about my Dictaphone again. Ten minutes later she phoned me back on my bedside phone to say that it was being taken care of. They are pretty obliging here, on the whole, and where I live too.

While we are waiting for them to take me 'home', where my Dictaphone should be waiting so that I can recount the story I have been promising you, I will fill in the time by telling you a little more about myself, but don't worry, I will keep it brief. I do not want to bore you and the real story is not about me anyway. This is not an ego trip, as the dear old Hippies used to say.

I loved the Seventies, but was too young to enjoy the Sixties.

I was born the eldest child in Cardiff, South Wales, the UK to an industrious working-class family. My father was a carpenter when he finished his National Service, but soon had his own construction firm and he and my mother soon had a family of five boys too. We all grew up fit, strong and happy. Our parents were Spiritualists, and Dad took us to Church with him every Friday night when he did his healing to give my mother a well-deserved 'night off'.

However, religion was never forced upon us. In fact, our schools were Church of Wales, cubs and scouts were Methodist and our closest aunty was Catholic. Religion was just not an issue in our family or neighbourhood. The first two things I can remember my mother saying are that she would die before she was forty-two and that I should become a diplomat. Both of which came true.

English was my mother language, but I learned Welsh from the age of six and then French, German, Latin, Dutch and Russian to fluency and a little Chinese and Spanish. The Diplomatic Service pays a bonus for every language you can speak, which was a big attraction for me. So was the promise of foreign travel, as I had travelled and studied abroad by the time I was fifteen. I was a confident traveller by eighteen.

I particularly liked to hitch-hike, but then all the young people did it back in those days and it was safer than it is now for some reason.

As a person, I tend to be a loner and a thinker, although I wouldn't claim to come to more sensible conclusions than anyone else. However, I do try to, and that was one of the reasons they employed me in the Diplomatic Service. I had a great life in the Service, and lots of fun… but there I go again hijacking this story, bending it towards me and my life... Oh, yes, I forgot… we're waiting for the Dictaphone before we can get onto the nitty-gritty, aren't we?

I apologise for that, but I am as impatient as you must be. Honestly!

The journey from the hospital to the hospice was only a few kilometres, so didn't take long in the large comfortable ambulance they provided. In fact, we left the hospital without warning at eleven a.m. and I was sitting in a large comfortable chair in the hospice grounds overlooking the beautiful marina in Marbella waiting for my lunch by noon.

Now, I realise that you have been waiting quite a while for me to get to the point of this book, I haven't forgotten, although I can't quite remember how long it's been exactly, so when the nurse brought me my lunch, I asked about the machine again. She used her mobile to ring the desk, and assured me that it would be delivered within the hour. I smiled, thanked her and tucked into my boiled fish and salad, followed by yoghurt and tea again.

I like that sort of food, but I have always been easy to please in culinary matters as long as I'm not asked to eat junk food. In earlier days, I favoured Indian and then Thai food, but that is all but denied me now, as is cheese, my clear all-time favourite. I have always had a passion for cheese, fresh, crispy bread and red wine or beer, which are also very rare treats these days.

The food and the hour have both disappeared now, but the only change to my circumstances is that I feel sleepy. It's the sea air probably. If they don't bring me my new toy soon, I'll be asleep again… dreaming about people from my youth, people perhaps long dead… Maybe, I should be as well, what useful purpose am I serving here? Eating and drinking and spending money, but to what end? Just to keep myself alive? No-one cares except the owners of the hospice, and that would soon stop if my money ran out, which it won't… The dear old British government will see to that until I pop my clogs.

In a way though, I am being held back from my inevitable journey through yet another death and rebirth. I just can't help thinking that my money would be better spent elsewhere. I'm drifting again, I sense it. I need to stay alive to tell you my story, which is not really my story because it is not about me, I know, I've told you that before, but I have known this story for most of my life. That's why I'm keeping myself alive, not just for the sake of it.

If the truth be known, I am anxious to continue on to the next leg of my journey and have been for two years, seven months and fourteen days. I miss her so much, I could cry every time I think of her, tough old bastard that I think that I am… pretend that I am. Eventually, everyone believes the image and lets you get on with it… not realising that that's the last thing you want them to do really. I'm just too scared to show my feelings, that's the truth… but then most men are.

Well, it's too late to change now… Maybe in the next life or the one after that. It's a good job that infinity is so long, it gives you plenty of time to correct your failings and weaknesses and, Lord knows, I need it.

I'm getting a sudden, unexpected memory of Ricky, a boy from university. He was from Battersea and affected a Cockney accent. He tried to act like the cock of the walk, but asked me to take him for an Indian curry one night because he'd never had one and wanted to impress a girl who said it was her favourite food. He got so drunk on red wine and beer that he fell face down in his Chicken Madras blowing bubbles! Ha, ha, ha… Good old days. A waiter and I cleaned him up and I took him home to his girlfriend, who had a houseful of nude photos of herself taken by her female flatmate.

I can't remember the flatmate's name, but she was Jewish and took me to bed that night with more red wine. I feel bad that I can't remember her name, but Maria or Marsha seems to fit the face I see in my head. Strange, I haven't thought about those three people for almost fifty years.

Excuse me, I must have drifted off. There is a note protruding from under my saucer: 'Your Dictaphone is at reception. Please ring and it will be brought out to you'. I am as happy for you as for myself, dear reader, because now I will be able to fulfil my promise and you will be able to assess whether what I have been saying is true or not. Just a moment, please, while I make a call.

"Here you are, William. I took the liberty of putting it on charge while you were asleep. Have fun with it", said the girl who delivered it.

"Yes, thank you, I will," I replied cheerily, but thought 'What a saucy mare!' Some of the younger ones treat us all as if we're senile. It drives me mad. It is true that some of us are totally doolally tap, but not all… not yet.

I played with the Nokia, turning it over in my hands looking for familiar features. It was a simple one, just what I wanted… could be voice-activated too. I was no stranger to modern technology, but another sudden thought came into my mind. I have written thousands of reports, but never written a biography. Read many, yes, but not written one. I can't think how to start. Really! This is most annoying. I, we, have been waiting for the recorder for twenty-four hours and now I still can't start!

I picked up my saucer to finish my tea, and a warm breeze blew the note down the lawn. I realise that the story I want to tell, her story, could not have taken place unless other events had happened first... Well, in that case, since you have indulged me thus far, I will push you a little further and take you back to the very beginning, as far as I am humanly able. The real beginning of this story is in yet another country, which found itself in very trying circumstances almost a decade before even I was born.

The woman I really want to tell you about went by many names, but she was born Natalya in Soviet Kazakhstan, although we will have to start in Japan with the Mizuki family. I have pieced their story together over the decades from various case notes which I was able to uncover in my professional life as a diplomat, and from things that I was told and overheard. So, with my fully-functioning, brand-new Dictaphone, I will now tell you about the first performers in our drama, Yui Mizuki and her family and hope that I don't receive that third curtain call before we get to the end.

ABOUT THE AUTHOR

Owen Jones was born in Barry, South Wales, where he lived until going to Portsmouth to study Russian at 18. After finishing his degree, he moved to s'Hertogenbosch in the Netherlands where he lived for ten years.

At 32, Owen moved back to Barry to work with in his family's construction company, first as a painter and then as a director, or, as the bank once corrected him, a painter and decorator. He was also office manager for ten years.

At the age of 50 Owen moved to Thailand to live with a Thai girl that he had met while there on holiday. He married the woman and now lives in her village of birth in remote northern Thailand.

As Owen puts it:

<u>'Born in the Land of Song,</u>

<u>Living in the Land of Smiles'.</u>

282

CONTACT DETAILS

Would you, please, leave a review of this book at the address where you bought it right now, please, before you forget

It will help the author and the readers, who come after you... it really will. Your opinion counts more than you may think it does.

Thank you,

Owen

PS: Please be my friend and keep in touch using the following contact details:

BlueSky: owen-author.bsky.social
Facebook: AngunJones
TikTok: @owen_author
X: @owen_author
Blog: Megan Publishing Services

BOOKS BY THE SAME AUTHOR

Behind The Smile
The Story of Lek, a Bar Girl in Pattaya
Volume I: Daddy's Hobby
Volume II: An Exciting Future
Volume III: Maya – Illusion
Volume IV: The Lady in the Tree
Volume V: Stepping Stones
Volume VI: The Dream
Volume VII: The Beginning

-

Alien House
A Story of Love, Hope and Alien Intervention

-

Andropov's Cuckoo
A Story of Love Intrigue and The KGB

-

Annwn – Heaven - *series*
A Night in Annwn
The Strange Story of Old Willy Jones's NDE
Life in Annwn
Thhe Story of Willy Jones's Life in Heaven
Leaving Annwn
Returning to Earth on a Mission!

-

Asian Shorts
An Anthology of Short Stories Involving Asians or Asia

-

The Bull at the Gate
The Day the Sky Fell !

-

Tiger Lily of Bangkok — *Series*
Volume I: **Tiger Lily of Bangkok**
When the Seeds of Revenge Blossom!
Volume II: **Tiger Lily of Bangkok in London**
The Tiger Re-awakens!

-

The Disallowed
Chupacabras on Backpacker Blood Milkshake

-

Fate Twister
The Strange Story of Wayne Gamm

-

The Psychic Megan Series
A Spirit Guide, A Ghost Tiger, and One Scary Mother!
The Misconception
Megan's Thirteenth
Megan's School Trip
Megan's School Exams
Megan's Followers
Megan and the Lost Cat
Megan and the Mayoress
Megan Faces Derision
Megan's Grandparents' Visit
Megan's Father Falls Ill
Megan Goes on Holiday

Owen Jones

Megan and the Burglar
Megan and the Cyclist
Megan and the Old Lady
Megan's Garden
Megan Goes To the Zoo
Megan Goes Hiking
Megan and the W. I. Cookery Competition
Megan Goes Riding
Megan Goes Yachting
Megan at Carnival
Megan at Christmas
Megan Catches Covid-19

Non-Fiction:

How to Give Your Dog a Real Dog's Life
(and make him love you for it)

The Eternal Plan
– Revealed
(written by Colin Jones, compiled by Owen Jones)

Authorship
Publishing Your Book On You Own